THE COBRA'S SONG

ALSO BY SUPRIYA KELKAR

American as Paneer Pie
That Thing about Bollywood

THE COBRA'S SONG

SUPRIYA KELKAR

Simon & Schuster Books for Young Readers

NEW YORK   LONDON   TORONTO   SYDNEY   NEW DELHI

SIMON & SCHUSTER BOOKS FOR YOUNG READERS
An imprint of Simon & Schuster Children's Publishing Division
1230 Avenue of the Americas, New York, New York 10020

SIMON & SCHUSTER BOOKS FOR YOUNG READERS
and related marks are trademarks of Simon & Schuster, Inc.
For information about special discounts for bulk purchases, please contact
Simon & Schuster Special Sales at 1-866-506-1949 or business@simonandschuster.com.
The Simon & Schuster Speakers Bureau can bring authors to your live event.
For more information or to book an event, contact the Simon & Schuster Speakers Bureau at
1-866-248-3049 or visit our website at www.simonspeakers.com.
Interior design by Hilary Zarycky
The text for this book was set in Adobe Caslon Pro.
The illustrations for this book were made of cut-and-torn paper collage and mixed-media,
rendered digitally in Procreate
Manufactured in the United States of America
0423 FFG
First Edition
2 4 6 8 10 9 7 5 3 1
Library of Congress Cataloging-in-Publication Data
Names: Kelkar, Supriya, 1980- author.
Title: The cobra's song / Supriya Kelkar.
Description: First edition. | New York : Simon & Schuster Books for Young Readers, [2023]
| Audience: Ages 8 to 12. | Audience: Grades 7-9. | Summary: When ten-year-old Indian
American Geetanjali, part of a family of classical Hindustani music singers, believes her neighbor
has become an ichchaadari naagin, a cobra that can turn human, she must overcome her fears and
harness the power of her voice before the naagin changes the whole town into snakes.
Identifiers: LCCN 2022037720 (print) | LCCN 2022037721 (ebook)
ISBN 9781665911887 (hardcover) | ISBN 9781665911900 (ebook)
Subjects: CYAC: Singing—Fiction | Self-confidence—Fiction. | Cobras—Fiction. | Snakes—
Fiction. | Magic—Fiction. | Mythology, Indic—Fiction. | Family life—Fiction. | East Indian
Americans—Fiction. | LCGFT: Novels.
Classification: LCC PZ7.1.K417 Co 2023 (print) | LCC PZ7.1.K417 (ebook) | DDC [Fic]—dc23
LC record available at https://lccn.loc.gov/2022037720
LC ebook record available at https://lccn.loc.gov/2022037721

To Aai, for the stories.
To Dad and the real-life Geetanjali, for filling our world with music.
And in memory of Limca—thanks for being by my side through it all
and providing the soundtrack.

Deepak's house

The creek

Penn's house

Heena Mavshi's house

Geetanjali's house

DEADWOOD

The Commons

Good Doggy

Reptile Rescue Center

The park

CHAPTER 1

It all started with a song. That was pretty much the way things worked in our family. When my aaji was born, she claimed she sang so loudly, the whole neighborhood could hear her voice trickling out the bungalow window in India.

I'm pretty sure my grandmother was exaggerating and that she was born crying, like most newborns. But she swore that the babies in our family came into this world singing. Including me. Besides, Aaji and Aai, my grandmother and mom, were two really famous classical singers in India. We came from a long line of Hindustani classical singers, going back centuries, so maybe there was a teeny-tiny chance Aaji's story *was* real.

And maybe, in just a few weeks, my baby brother will arrive singing, I thought as my best friend, Penn, and I galloped in place, him on a big bad wolf and me on a pig spring rider, at Deadwood Commons, the park in the middle of our neighborhood.

Just ahead, under the wooden shelter with picnic benches that families could eat lunches on, three middle school kids were huddled around a cell phone, staring intently at it and laughing. I recognized the tallest one, Rohan, who had ridden the bus with us in elementary school, back when we were in third grade and he was in fifth.

"Did I tell you our Bark in the Park song got approved?" Penn asked, bunching his knees up on the wolf so he fit a little better. We had been playing on these old springy toys since we were in first grade, so I guess one of us was bound to outgrow them at some point. "I finally get to sing onstage and not for school. My mom even said she'd take time off work to be there for it."

"That's amazing," I said.

"Guess I should get used to singing in public, huh?" Penn brushed one of his blond ringlets out of his eyes and cleared his throat. "Happy bark day to you," Penn began to sing, a little shakily, and a lot off-key.

"Bark is for trees. Trees line the park," I continued, controlling my voice despite the literal spring in the pig's step. I beamed at Penn, proud of the lyrics I had written for this song full of words that had multiple meanings. Since kindergarten, figuring out the different meanings one word can have was kind of my thing. I already had filled two neon-yellow notebooks and was working on a third.

"Dogs like to bark at Bark in the Park!" we both sang loudly, together.

From under the shelter, Rohan laughed even louder, rolling back on the concrete until his shoulder-length black hair grazed the ground.

"What are you two singing?" he called out to us.

I looked at Penn, my palms starting to sweat. Rohan wasn't asking in a nice way. He was asking it like he was ready to say something mean as soon as we answered.

"Geetanjali wrote it," Penn replied, slowing down on his wolf. "We're singing it at Bark in the Park."

Rohan looked at his friends. "That makes sense. Because it sounds like this when you sing it . . ." He threw his head back and howled, "A-wooooo!"

His friends sneered; their laughs seemed to echo in the hollow shelter.

"Ignore them," I muttered as Penn's cheeks started to burn pink; I wished they'd stop laughing or that I had the guts to tell them they were being mean. "You were good," I added, feeling my belly bounce around even more than it did when I was rocking on the pig.

Rohan and his friends finally went back to staring at Rohan's phone and I breathed a little easier, trying not to think about how we would be going to school with them next fall when we were sixth graders. "You're going to do great singing onstage at Bark in the Park, just like at school," I said.

Penn forced a smile and nodded.

I wondered if he knew I had sort of lied about his singing. He wasn't hitting every note like me, but I had been doing this all my life. Aai taught Hindustani classical singing classes in our basement every week, and each class performed at various Indian cultural associations' events all the time. Unlike Penn, I practically grew up onstage. In fact, I'd be singing onstage with Aai at a celebration of the Marathi Hindu new year, Gudhi Padwa, tonight. So why was I suddenly feeling anxious about singing with Penn?

I looked at the middle schoolers. Rohan's back was to us now, and he had clearly moved on to talking about other things.

Penn turned to me. "I'm nervous, but I know it will be good for me to go up there and do it, and you'll be with me, so I won't be as scared." Penn seemed to be saying this more to himself than to me. "Plus, the winner gets a gift certificate to Good Doggy."

"Wait. You're getting a dog?" I asked with a quiver of jealousy. Penn had just gotten a creepy pet snake named Gertrude. She was Penn's reward for getting good grades on his tests last semester. (And his mom-guilt present, since Mrs. Witherspoon had to miss yet another of his Rubik's Cube competitions because of work.)

Penn adored Gertrude, but I didn't get the fuss about a pet snake. It didn't interact with you the way a dog would, which was my ideal pet, and one I'd been begging my parents to get me for ages. My parents decided to give me a little brother instead.

"No," Penn replied, running his fingers through his blond curls. "Good Doggy sells all sorts of pet stuff. I'm going to get Gertrude a bigger terrarium if we win." Penn groaned, turning his legs to the side. "Can we do something else now? I'm way too tall for the wolf and it's really hurting my knees."

I watched Penn turn his head to the Wall of Doom, a super-dangerous, not-up-to-code (in my expert opinion) rock-climbing wall that the homeowner's association had just installed in our playground last week. It made me nervous just to look at it.

"How about we go home and play soccer in your yard?" I suggested, not wanting to test my luck on risky playground equipment.

Penn groaned. "We just did that yesterday."

"Okay, then, how about we ride our bikes to the library?"

"We did that Thursday after school, when I wanted to visit

the snakes at Reptile Rescue Center," Penn countered.

I looked around us at the few clumps of snow left in the March grass. It was now my turn to sigh.

"So how about we climb the wall?" Penn asked, heading toward it.

"There's a reason it's called the Wall of Doom, you know," I said to Penn.

Penn shook his head. "Nobody calls it that except for you. You always think of the worst possible things that can happen when you don't like something."

I frowned. "Do not." Although, I kinda did. But it was sort of like Aaji's exaggerating-things trait. Except instead of making a story better, my habit just made me more scared.

"Besides," Penn continued, "Deepak told me he'd meet me here to climb the wall, so you might as well join us."

I scrunched my face up and swung my leg forcefully over the pig. I suddenly didn't want to be at the park anymore. Deepak, the new kid in our fifth-grade class, had just moved here last month and lived on the other side of the creek behind Penn's backyard. He was good at everything, from my mom's singing class to becoming friends with Penn to climbing the Wall of Doom, apparently. I didn't feel the need to be around that show-off, either.

"Please?" Penn asked, reaching his hand timidly toward a pink grip near the bottom of the wall.

Behind him, Rohan and his friends were running past the bulletin board with the neighborhood announcements and jumping up to tap the lowest wooden beam on the roof. A gust of wind caused a neon-green flyer from the bulletin board to zip near us.

I dug my tennis shoe into the bit of snow crumbling away on the grass. "Why don't you climb it while you're waiting for Deepak, and I'll time you?" I suggested.

Penn's smile faded, but he quickly nodded and threw me his watch.

My stomach dropped as I hit the timer. Penn scaled the wall, going higher and higher. The word "scale" has lots of different meanings. It could mean the bumps on the skin of a snake. It could mean a musical scale. It could mean climbing higher. The list went on and on. And so did Penn, climbing up and up, till he was almost to the top.

But what if his palms were sweaty and he fell? What if the wall was slick from some tiny remaining drops of the rain-snow mix we had last night, and he lost his footing and fell? What if he got dizzy at the top and fell? What if he got distracted and . . . yeah, fell?

I shook my head, doing my best to throw out the bad thoughts and stop my imagination from getting the best of me.

"Whoa," Penn squealed, just missing the grip and almost losing his footing along with it.

Or maybe I should let my imagination do its thing. Clearly, it was better to be prepared for the worst-case scenario than surprised by it.

"You should probably come down!" I rushed toward Penn.

Penn furrowed his eyebrows at me and sighed, slowly making his way down. "Thanks for cheering me on, Geetanjali," he grumbled sarcastically. "You can stop the timer; I didn't make it all the way up, so it doesn't count."

I cleared my watch and pulled the sleeves of my hoodie

down past my hands. What was he talking about? I always cheered Penn on. I was the one who agreed to sing onstage with him in June, despite how embarrassing it might be since he couldn't sing really well. "You should be thanking me for saving your life. This is why we should stick to doing things I suggest, like soccer. It's just safer," I retorted. Then a staticky announcement shouted at us.

"Attention, everyone!"

Startled, Penn slipped and fell a couple feet, landing hard on his bottom in a pile of mulch.

"You okay?" I asked, rushing to his side.

Penn nodded, brushing himself off as we turned toward the sound.

It was Lark Conovan. Her mom was mayor of Deadwood. They lived on the other side of the neighborhood, where the woods were the thickest, and where all the big, sprawling homes in Deadwood were, with their spaced-out yards and acres of privacy. She was a grade younger than us, but Penn and I saw her on the bus every morning, sitting alone in the first seat.

"Friends and fans, you're invited to the show of the century. Gather round for my latest hit song!" Lark announced into a blue portable microphone that amplified her voice and matched the navy-blue stegosaurus bike helmet she wore on her head.

Apparently, everyone had decided today was the day to sing in the park.

I bent down to pick up the neon-green flyer and watched as Lark threw her head back and began to belt out the latest Skye Suh-Oliviera hit into the microphone. Except, unlike super-famous pop star Skye, Lark couldn't hold a tune. Not like Penn, who missed a note here and there. Lark didn't hit any note. That didn't seem to stop her, though. She sang loudly, off-key, her voice cracking.

"What is she doing?" I whispered to Penn as we neared the impromptu show, my ears burning in embarrassment on her behalf.

Penn shrugged. "I've seen her sing into her microphone on her bike before. I think she just likes to sing."

Lark added some dance moves to her song, twisting and twirling, making it even harder on herself to sing. The kids in the shelter began laughing hysterically. Rohan was wiping tears from his face. Next to him, a girl was holding her ponytail in front of her eyes to cover them and was cringing as she laughed. The other kid took out his phone and began to record her.

This was even worse than when they laughed at me and Penn. What if they sent the video to the entire middle school and everyone teased Lark for the rest of the year? I barely knew Lark, but I didn't want her humiliated by these bullies.

Penn shook his head. "We have to stop this."

"Go tell her to stop singing so they'll stop laughing," I whispered.

"What?" Penn whispered back angrily as Rohan's high-pitched laughter almost drowned out Lark's song. Her lip was trembling in fear, but she kept going, looking at me and Penn for help. "No. One of us needs to tell Rohan and his friends to stop laughing so she can keep singing."

"Oh. Right," I replied as Penn gave me a small frown, like he was disappointed in me. He was right. I hadn't stopped them from laughing at Penn earlier, either. Obviously, I was the wrong candidate for the job: I wasn't brave enough to speak up.

Lark's face was flushed and she was stumbling over her lyrics, but she kept going. I opened my mouth but froze. What if I told them to stop and then they started laughing at me, too? Or what if they had a comeback and I didn't have a comeback for *their* comeback? I was able to tell Penn he was good and try to undo the damage of Rohan and his friends a few minutes earlier, but this was different. This involved me *stopping* Rohan and his friends, and I couldn't find the words to do that. Even if I did find them, I wasn't sure I could get them out. I nudged Penn. "Do it."

"They're seventh graders. You do it," Penn whispered back as the humiliating laughter grew louder and louder.

"Stop it!" said a voice from behind us.

Lark abruptly stopped singing as Penn and I turned to see Deepak standing behind us, his black hair glistening in the sunlight rather heroically.

"Stop laughing at her," Deepak said to the older kids so forcefully, his lips almost got snagged in his braces. "Haven't you heard of being inclusive and empowering each other?"

"Oh. Well, can't we all just get along?" Rohan snorted, mocking Deepak.

The other kids snickered.

"Let's go. Let the little kids play at the park," Rohan added, walking away from us with his friends.

"How long was that going on?" Deepak asked Lark.

"Oh, just, like, half my song," she announced into the microphone so it echoed loudly in the shelter.

"Why didn't they listen when you told them to stop?" Deepak asked us.

"We didn't actually get to that. We were trying to figure out what to say," Penn answered, a trickle of sweat making its way down his cheek.

"And how to say it," I added.

"What's there to think about?" Deepak asked. "You just speak up."

Lark turned to me with a look that seemed to last forever. One that made my stomach churn with guilt and my throat feel kind of tight.

I broke her stare and quickly turned to pin the neon flyer for the Mayor's Community Grant that had landed next to my foot back to the bulletin board.

"We're climbing the wall," Deepak said to Lark. "Did you know static friction is formed when your hands or feet make contact with the grip? That helps rock climbers climb. And some scientists even climb to monitor bat populations," he added, like he didn't know how to make Lark feel better, so he just decided to throw a bunch of random facts her way. "Want to climb it with us?"

"No thanks," Lark said, her eyes gleaming like they were about to spill over with tears. "My voice teacher is coming by in a few minutes for my lesson. See you around." She gave Deepak a sad smile and took off on her bike, heading down the path and out of sight.

As Penn and Deepak started climbing the wall, I stared back at the shelter where Rohan's laughter from just minutes earlier still haunted the air. What did Lark expect from me and

Penn? We were just fifth graders. Rohan and his friends were older. It isn't easy to stand up to middle schoolers or we would have. *I think.* A queasy feeling was rising in my throat. Sure, we were fifth graders. But Lark was a fourth grader. She must have been even more scared than us.

I slid my hood over my head, wishing I could disappear into it. Was Lark going to cry when she got home? Was she going to tell her voice teacher what happened and quit singing?

Anytime something bad happened, I thought about the moment over and over. That time in January when my dad hurt his ankle trying to help me? I can't look at his feet anymore. Or that time when I was in first grade and tried to speak Marathi to my cousins in India and everyone laughed? There's a reason I don't speak Marathi now.

Had I just helped Lark form a memory like that, one that she would never forget? This wasn't doomsday thinking. I knew this feeling from experience. And the thought of having played a part in making someone else feel bad about themselves felt gross, like a thick, sludgy soup of guilt stuck in my throat.

CHAPTER 2

That evening, I kept thinking about Lark as I stood backstage at Novi High School, the school thirty minutes away from Deadwood, that our Maharashtra Mandal had rented out to celebrate Gudhi Padwa.

"You ready?" Aai asked in the wings, adjusting the midnight-blue and mango-orange paithani sari she was wearing over her belly. It was covered in woven gold paisleys, and the padar over her shoulder had purple, magenta, and green woven peacocks and parrots sitting on flowery vines. "My strong, powerful, Geetanjali. You're going to do so well. The baby is kicking in anticipation." She smiled.

I nodded, my bangs grazing the upside-down crescent-shaped, traditional Marathi tikli I wore on my forehead. Aai was eight months pregnant, and this was going to be our last performance onstage together before my baby brother was born. I was ready. We were showcasing songs I had been singing my whole life, and despite being afraid of lots of things, I didn't have stage fright.

As a bunch of younger kids did a bharatanatyam dance onstage, I peeked out at the audience. Baba was in the front row, his cell phone ready to record us when it was our turn onstage. Jatin Kaka, our family friend and next-door neighbor, with thick gray hair and his left foot wrapped in gauze, walked up to the empty seat next to Baba.

I felt an immediate pit in my belly, thinking about Baba's sprained ankle from earlier this year and my part in it. I saw Baba point to Jatin Kaka's foot, probably asking him what happened. Jatin Kaka replied, gesturing to Baba's ankle, and then they both started laughing.

"I bet they're talking about how my out-of-control imagination made Baba sprain his ankle," I said softly.

"Nonsense!" said a loud whisper behind me.

I turned to see Heena Mavshi, Jatin Kaka's wife, standing behind me, her shiny copper snake bangle visible from the little light backstage.

"Your aai had to use the bathroom," Heena Mavshi said, smiling at me.

I nodded. Aai had to do that a lot recently.

"They're not laughing at you or talking about that old story. Jatin Kaka's foot is the new talk of the mandal. He slipped on the last patch of ice left in all of Michigan last week. It's just a sprain. He'll be okay in a few days, the doctor said. And if they're laughing, it's because I'm sure Jatin is telling your dad one of his corny jokes again."

I gave Heena Mavshi a small smile. Jatin Kaka did make a lot of those. Like, what's a snake's favorite place in Ann Arbor? The Natural Hisstory Museum. And as someone who enjoyed words, I liked his jokes.

I exhaled, trying to think about our performance to avoid looking at Baba and Jatin Kaka.

"Anyway, don't get stuck in your head about the bad things

that could be, shona," Heena Mavshi continued, using the nickname she called every kid. "Focus on how much fun you're going to have onstage with your mom. That's the good thing that *will* be." She reached into her cloth bag covered in traditional mirrorwork and pulled out a small note card. "For you," she said, putting the small piece of cardstock in my hand.

Heena Mavshi gave me a small note card like this every couple of weeks. They weren't blank note cards. They didn't have science notes or drafts of a speech written on them either. They were her mini masterpieces. Heena Mavshi was a painter. And before she painted anything on a big canvas, she first used her finger to draw it out on her leg anytime she was sitting, and then she'd make a practice painting on a note card and give it to me.

I looked down at the art. It was swirls of pastels and neons, intertwining snakelike, and running loosely around the notecard.

"I call it, *Potential*," Heena Mavshi said softly.

Aai rushed toward us, back from the bathroom and slightly out of breath. She peeked over my shoulder and smiled. "It's beautiful."

"Better than my painting of the cobra and mongoose that disturbs you every time you enter my house, huh?" Heena Mavshi winked, talking about the gigantic, wall-size painting she had in her living room of the two enemies in nature, fighting each other.

"Your painting doesn't disturb me," Aai whispered, sweating a little. I couldn't tell if it was from feeling hot from her sprint from the bathroom to us, or if it was because she wasn't exactly telling the truth. Aai was creeped out by snakes and she hated looking at them, so I knew she didn't like it. "It just reminds me of the cobras that scared me growing up. But it's still a beautiful piece of art."

"And it isn't about snakes being bad, or about fighting your enemy," I chimed in as the bharatanatyam dancers wrapped up their performance. "It's about conquering whatever is in your way at the moment. Whatever's stopping you."

Heena Mavshi beamed. "You always get my art, shona. You and your aaji. Jatin Kaka and I leave this weekend for India and when we come back in a few months, we'll have her with us!"

I nodded as the audience applauded and the kid dancers headed offstage, rushing by us with excited giggles. Aaji normally flew by herself, but she had fallen in her bungalow in February and her hip was still healing, so Aai asked Aaji to fly back with Heena Mavshi, so she wouldn't be alone.

"Let's go," Aai said, just as a volunteer nodded to us and motioned toward the stage.

"Go conquer whatever's in your way and let the world hear your beautiful voice," Heena Mavshi called out, waving to me.

I wiped my palms on my purple-and-green salwar kurta, adjusted the sky-blue chiffon odhni around my neck, pressed my tikli, making sure it was firmly in place between my eyes, and walked onto the stage behind Aai.

Aai and I touched the stage and put our hands to our foreheads, doing namaskar as a sign of respect and gratitude, before we took our places on the stage to perform. Then Aai did a namaskar to the audience, her palms together as she did a slight bow, thanking them for listening. Aai sat behind her harmonium that one of the stage volunteers had already put down. And I sat next to her, behind one of the microphones.

I looked out at the audience full of family and friends, and gave my dad a small smile as Aai announced the song we were singing and what raag it was in.

Raags are groupings of notes in classical Hindustani music, kind of like a scale but not exactly. Each raag has set notes in it, and the songs that are in those raags only consist of those notes. There are, like, a million of them, and I'd been memorizing them since I was little.

Aai began to play the first few notes on the harmonium keyboard. I took a deep breath, pushing aside whatever was in my way, ready to sing as my cue neared. I counted the beats to my introduction. I opened my mouth to belt out the song I had been learning for as long as I could remember. I knew it so well, I didn't even have to think about the lyrics. It just came naturally.

And then I winced. Because every note that escaped my mouth was off. My high note was too high. My low note not low enough. A little boy in the front row near Baba covered his ears, and I watched his dad keep trying to pry his hands off them. But the kid refused.

Was this what Lark had gone through at the Commons when Rohan and his friends had laughed at her?

I tried to sing it right. I tried to find my sur, my pitch, but I ended up overcompensating and singing even higher than I was supposed to. It was so bad, I bet even my baby brother in Aai's belly was appalled. I exhaled, ready for the next stanza. And then I squeaked so loudly, the microphone squealed with feedback, and everyone in the audience, including Baba, winced, rushing to cover their ears just like the boy in the front row. It was an unnerving sight: an audience of hundreds of people with their hands over their ears.

Even if it was just for a second, it was mortifying. I felt tears sting my eyes. I looked at Aai, who smiled like nothing had happened and sang louder.

I let her perform our raag solo, and stared at my bare feet in silence, swallowing the rest of my song.

CHAPTER 3

It had been three months since Gudhi Padwa, and a lot had changed. My baby brother, Alaap, had been born, and was now two months old. I'm pretty sure he was born wailing off-key, but Aaji told me on the phone from Pune that it was a song, just a different type of song. Either way, he was a sweet, smiling, cuddly baby. (When he wasn't sobbing.) Aai had taken a break from teaching singing classes to take care of Alaap. School was over and I was officially a rising sixth grader on summer vacation.

But the most exciting change of all was about to happen. Aaji's flight had landed, and in about an hour she'd be by my side, for the rest of summer.

I grinned, happy butterflies fluttering inside me as I set one of my neon-yellow notebooks onto the silver trunk next to my bed and rushed down the stairs and out the door to the garage, which felt extra hot from baking in the sun. I bent down ever so briefly to check the clear purple plastic mouse house by the garage stairs. Baba had put it out there in May, ever since I spotted mouse poop by the electric lawnmower. The mouse house still had a cracker in it but no mouse.

Up ahead, just past a crow missing some feathers who was pecking the groundcover, Baba was in the car, waiting in the driveway. He rolled down the window. The sound of his radio voice announcing an ad for a new Indian grocery store filled my neighborhood, courtesy of his weekly Hindi movie music radio program, *Geetanjali*.

Yup. Same name as me. People always asked if the show was named after me. I wish. The truth was, I was born after Baba's show started. So, *I* was named after a radio program. It was like my parents couldn't be bothered to think of another name. They did for Alaap, though.

A thumping Bollywood song began to play next, startling the crow. It took flight hurriedly, dropping a shiny penny from its beak as it flew off.

I had read crows liked to collect shiny things and sometimes gave these objects to people, but I had never seen it in person. I grabbed the penny and glanced around to see if anyone else was bothered by the music Baba was blasting. I looked at the sunny yellow ranch house across the street, where Penn was sitting high up in the maple tree in his front yard, Gertrude coiled around his neck and hand. Penn turned in our direction. He was making a face, which I'm sure was from the music; then he caught my eye and gave me a huge smile.

"Is your grandma here yet?" Penn called out. He loved eating all the different lonchee, pickles, that Aaji made out of limes, or raw mangos, or watermelon rind, or onions, or basically any fruit or vegetable you could preserve.

"Almost." I smiled, nearing him as Aai rushed out of the garage and buckled Alaap into his car seat. I kept an eye on the snake through the foliage in case she decided to come flying down at me and I'd need to duck.

I swatted at some of the many mosquitoes that hung around our street, thanks to the tiny creek that ran through the woods behind Penn's house, surrounded by the deadwood our town was named after.

"Our therapist said Mom and I have to do thirty minutes of special time together, but surprise, surprise, she got a phone call from work just as I got a board game out," Penn said.

I spotted Mrs. Witherspoon through the front window, pacing in her study on her cell phone, her blond ponytail bouncing, as Penn continued.

"So I thought I'd spend my special time with Gertrude and take her for a climb since you're busy. Deepak's at a protest with his mom, but he's going to meet me later at the Commons to climb the wall. You can come too, if you're free."

My stomach dropped at the mention of the Wall of Doom. Not only did the thought of it remind me of what had happened with Lark a few months ago, but lately Penn had been on there every Saturday morning with Deepak before coming over to my house to play soccer or write stories. They'd invited me, of course, but it didn't always feel like they really wanted me there.

"I'll probably be busy with Aaji for a while," I said, bouncing on my toes while I thought of all the fun we were going to have eating pickles and playing cards as I impressed her with my knowledge of the many meanings of all different kinds of words, even simple words like "pickle" (which could mean something preserved in vinegar or brine, or mean a difficult situation), and "card" (which could be a noun, like a playing card, or a verb, like when someone checks another person's ID).

"But how about we skip the wall and just play a board game or watch a movie or play soccer next time? It's more fun," I added, picking activities that didn't involve possibly falling off a wall or falling off a tree and breaking a bone. Or playing with a snake.

"How about we practice for Bark in the Park? We have less than two weeks," Penn countered.

I chewed my lip. "Sure," I said, although I wasn't feeling even remotely *sure* about singing onstage again after what had happened during my last performance.

"Aaji will be through customs by the time we get there," Baba called out to me over the car radio.

"And I don't want to be stuck on the drive back when Alaap has to nurse again," Aai added from the front seat as Baba pulled the car out of our driveway and neared the curb beside me.

Lately, nursing Alaap and holding him over the baby toilet to go to the bathroom seemed to be all Aai talked about. She almost missed the fifth grade clap-out on the last day of school because she was nursing him and got to school a couple minutes late.

I waved to Penn, who had started to climb down the tree, and headed into the car.

"Not to mention Heena is going to have a bunch of bags with her that we'll need to help her with," Baba added, motioning toward the stormy gray house next door where Heena Mavshi lived.

Aai clicked her tongue. "Poor thing."

Baba sighed. "I still can't believe Jatin's gone. Nobody made me laugh like him."

I felt my face flush a little, thinking about the last time Baba and Jatin Kaka were laughing together.

"How did it happen?" asked Penn. He wasn't close family friends with the Karwandes like we were, using titles like "mavshi," maternal aunt, or "kaka," paternal uncle, for them. He just knew them as Mr. and Mrs. Karwande, but he had heard that Jatin Kaka passed away this spring.

Baba stuck his head farther out the window. "He had a heart attack at the airport in France, on a layover before their flight to India."

"That's sad," Penn said.

I nodded, looking at the shrubs around Heena Mavshi's house that Jatin Kaka used to spend hours trimming when the weather was warm. Aai had rushed over to their house yesterday, while Alaap napped, and landscaped their yard so it would look neat and tidy when Heena Mavshi got back from India. That was usually my favorite (small amount of) time in the day that Aai spent talking to me, but Heena Mavshi was always so nice to me, giving me her little paintings, so I didn't mind Aai using that time to help her. Maybe I could even offer to do that when Heena Mavshi was all settled in.

"Don't worry. We'll cheer her up when she gets here and she'll be all better," Baba said.

"You mean we'll give her the time she needs to mourn her loss and find closure?" Aai asked, reaching her arm past me to give Alaap's cheeks a little tickle.

"You're right," Baba said, turning the radio up a little. "Sorry. Geetu, hurry up before I stick my foot in my mouth again, please?"

I quickly buckled my seat belt and waved bye to my friend, whose head was cocked to the next song on the radio. I rolled up the window, grateful to drive away from Penn's weird looks about the music that I couldn't help but tap my feet to.

CHAPTER 4

As our car curved off the freeway, taking the exit for the airport, Alaap cooed in his car seat as he slept, looking adorable in his little pink onesie that matched the rosy color of his cheeks. I gently brushed his soft black curls with my index finger.

"His chin's not on his chest, right?" Aai asked, craning her neck to check on him.

I shook my head.

"Remind me to schedule his next two monthly check-ups," she continued. "Actually, I'll just put the reminders in my phone. And I was thinking, maybe we could take Aaji to the new baby store in Northville to get Alaap some wooden animal toys and then maybe the Canton Indian clothes store to let Aaji pick out some outfits for him?"

"What about the bookstore?" I asked, thinking about how normally once Aaji's jet lag wore off, she'd take me to a bookstore in Ann Arbor to pick out as many books as I wanted as a present from her.

"Oh, I'm not sure if we'll have time to go all the way to Ann Arbor this summer with everything going on with the new baby and Aaji's health. But you could pick out a wooden animal for yourself at the baby store. Doesn't that sound fun?"

I shrugged.

"Besides, you have Bark in the Park to prep for too, right? Unless . . . are you thinking of not singing with Penn?" Aai asked.

"What? I didn't say that," I replied, but it was kind of true. Although I loved going to the dog festival in our town, getting to pet all the rescues that my parents would never let us adopt, I wasn't sure I was ready to sing in front of a crowd again.

"I've seen the way you chew your lip whenever that poor boy talks about how excited he is to finally get to sing onstage. You can't let one mess-up at Gudhi Padwa affect your voice forever. And what about Accent Mark in the Park?" Aai said. "It might be your last time to sing onstage with Aaji."

"Wait, why would it be my last time to sing onstage with her?" I asked, biting my lip before realizing Aai knew that was something I did when I was feeling anxious.

"Nothing. I just meant she's getting older."

I stopped gnawing down. I knew Aaji was getting older. We all were. But Aaji was also getting weaker, having fallen a couple times before this latest fall that hurt her hip. Would this trip to Michigan be her last if no one could escort her here, the way Heena Mavshi had done? I didn't want to think of Aaji not being by my side when things got tough.

"It's just a month and a half away," Aai continued.

I guess I should have been grateful that my mother's lecture was a way to stop thinking about Aaji not being here one day.

"And Channel Twelve is going to be filming our performance. Don't you want to show Aaji and the world how much you've changed since Gudhi Padwa? How brave you are and how strong your voice is?"

Sure, a lot had changed since Gudhi Padwa, like Aai and Baba spending way more time taking care of Alaap than they did hanging out with me. But I wasn't sure *I* had changed since I froze onstage. Instead, I used the excuse of no singing classes after Alaap was born to focus on looking up words in dictionaries and reading books and watching TV. I didn't crack open my raag binder even once to practice. And I stopped singing Skye Suh-Oliviera songs and Bollywood hits in the shower.

I didn't want to sing at Bark in the Park, and I definitely didn't want to sing at Accent Mark in the Park a few weeks later. The poorly named town festival dedicated to diversity was just one of the many poorly named town festivals here in Deadwood, like they were trying too hard to make the town sound fun instead of creepy.

"I'm going to sing with Penn. I said I would, but it doesn't mean I'm going to like it," I muttered, a little irritated by how judgmental Aai was sounding. Hadn't she ever choked onstage before? And if she hadn't, didn't she at least have sympathy for people who did, especially when the person in question was her own daughter? Or was she too busy planning baby-store outings for Alaap to think of me anymore?

"I heard something on NPR about how kids can lose their confidence around your age and imagine the worst-case scenario and let their nerves get the best of them. Catastrophic thinking."

I looked at all the creases spreading across Aai's forehead as she craned her neck toward me. Her eyes were getting so shiny. I didn't want her to become any more upset than she already was. I liked singing. But right now I just felt bad about how embarrassing my last performance was. It made me think of Rohan and his friends bullying Lark and how I just stood to the side and watched. I had been afraid to use my voice. And then I messed up onstage with Aai when I used to feel so confident singing in front of people. It felt safer, better, to just blend in and be a part of the crowd than stand out like Penn or Lark. I didn't want to face people out in the audience at Bark in the Park, waiting for me to mess up; I already messed up badly enough at Gudhi Padwa. I needed to find my voice again, but I wasn't sure how.

"Your mom's right," Baba said, moving the sun visor to his left to block the rays from obstructing his view. "Don't ever let fear stifle your voice. Your voice is important. It can change the world. I'd be so sad if I never got to hear your song again."

"Song" had a bunch of meanings. It meant something you sing, of course, but it also could mean the noise an animal makes. Like a birdsong. Or a whale song. You know what else "song" meant? It meant a small amount of something. That's how I felt about singing. A lesser version of Aai and Aaji.

Aai groaned in the front seat. "I forgot to eat before we left. You know how hungry breastfeeding makes me. I'm craving dahi papdi. Doesn't that sound good, Geetanjali?"

I breathed easier, grateful for a change of subject thanks to Aai's racing mind, full of Alaap's needs and her own hanger.

"Why do you always pick the unhealthiest foods?" Dad replied before I could nod or drool in agreement; the fried rectangles of dough loaded with potatoes, chickpeas, yogurt, cilantro-mint chutney, and tamarind chutney did sound good. "You know what would fill you up better? A wholesome, complete meal. Waran-bhaat, bhaji-poli . . . ," he continued, mentioning one of our staple meals of lentil soup, rice, vegetables, and whole wheat flatbread.

"I crave fat after nursing. You wouldn't get it. But thanks for mansplaining," Aai muttered.

"Mansplaining?" Now it was Dad's turn to groan. "You sound like Maya," he said, talking about Deepak's mom, who was always organizing and speaking out against injustice when she wasn't treating patients in the hospital.

I folded and unfolded the bottom of my shirt, bracing for Aai to snap back.

"When you start lactating, you can tell me what's a good meal," Aai replied, a lot calmer than I expected, except for the part where she was loudly drumming her fingers on her window.

"You're right. Sorry. Looks like we'll have to distract Aai from her hunger pangs until we can get home," Dad said to me as he turned toward the airport parking structure. "So, Geetanjali, if the airport is twenty miles from our house, and we are going sixty miles per hour, how long will it take us to reach it?"

I blew my bangs out of my eyes. An impromptu math quiz? How was giving me a math problem going to solve Aai's problem?

"Geetanjali?" asked Baba.

"Twelve hundred," I replied, half trying, as I ran my finger down Alaap's soft little knuckles. I wasn't interested in math the way I was with other things. Baba didn't understand how much fun it was to look up different meanings of words in the dictionary. He didn't think word tricks or writing were as important as math.

"Twelve hundred?" he asked, sounding a little appalled.

A plane roared as it took off, casting a shadow over our car. Startled, I gasped.

"Geetu?" Baba said again, pulling into a spot.

"Twelve hundred minutes," I clarified, after double-checking that sixty times twenty was 1,200.

Dad sighed. "Twenty minutes. Sixty miles per hour means you are going one mile a minute."

There it was. I could hear his disappointment in me in every syllable.

Luckily, Aaji would be here this summer, reminding me of all the things I was good at, like picking out the strangest ice cream flavors to combine into the best-tasting split-scoop special from our favorite shop in downtown Deadwood, or stringing tiny jasmine flowers from our mogra plants into a gajra for our hair.

"You have to try harder," Baba said, getting out of the car to unbuckle Alaap. "I know you're good at math. But I want you to excel at it. Because it's a real-life skill. Your word tricks aren't going to save the day the way math can."

Baba and a lot of parents in our neighborhood were all engineers at Ford, so math was their thing. But words were mine. Baba always seemed to think that everything I knew about definitions wasn't as great as being amazing at math. I wanted to tell him he was wrong, but I didn't know how.

"But you just said all that stuff about how important it was to use my voice," I said softly.

"Right but . . ." Baba picked Alaap up. "I meant I don't want you to be shy and timid."

"Maybe her voice *will* save the day," Aai said. "If she can get over these new fears," she added before quickly softening. "Sorry. That was harsh," Aai said, giving me a small smile as she got out of the car. "I'm really hungry."

Aaji couldn't get here soon enough.

CHAPTER 5

Despite how I was feeling in the car, my heart began to dance as we neared the carousel at the far end of the baggage claim. Because there, right next to the rotating luggage, was someone that I was actually in sync with.

Aaji was dressed in a pistachio-colored cotton Marathi nauvari sari, made of nine yards of fabric instead of six, the skirt part tucked in a way that almost resembled pants. She looked like she had lost weight since last summer as she pushed the trolley with her bags on it.

Her wrinkly skin was loose on her forearms where her gold bangles made music as they clanged against one another. Her diamond nose ring on her left nostril twinkled. And her flower-shaped kudya, diamond earrings with seven petals, shimmered when they caught the lights. She held her favorite patchwork shawl, and her gray hand-knitted sweater was over her pink blouse. Her thinning, waist-long gray hair was braided and nestled into a bun at the back of her head.

I ran and threw myself into Aaji's frail arms, inhaling the smell of sandalwood and rose from her favorite Indian soap.

"Careful, Geetanjali! You'll hurt Aaji!" Aai said, reaching over me to give her mom a hug and a quick namaskar just above her feet. "How's your hip?"

"Oh, just fine," Aaji said as Baba also bowed down to her in a namaskar. She put her hand on his head to bless him and Aai. "Guess what I found?" Aaji asked, her right hand now shaking a little as she dug through her cotton embroidered tote bag with little circular mirrors all over it, and pulled out a long, skinny, dark-gray key.

"The key to the trunk?" I asked excitedly. Aaji had given me her mother's old silver trunk years ago, but it was locked and the key was missing. We always wondered what was inside and would take guesses when we spoke on the phone. I was certain it was full of ancient jewelry. Aaji thought it would have a comb or bobby pins or a piece of paper with the household hishob on it, the running tally of your income and expenses.

"Your mystery will finally be solved." Aai smiled before giving me a small nudge. "Do namaskar."

As Aaji put the key back in her bag, I put my hands together in a namaste and bowed above Aaji's feet to respectfully greet her.

"Khushal raha," Aaji said softly, blessing me with well-being; I'd missed her melodic voice so much.

"And there he is!" Aaji said, reaching for Alaap. "My naatu!" she added, using the Marathi word for "grandson." "I heard we're going to go buy you some nice toys and clothes!" she said, hugging my brother, who cooed in her arms.

Instead of taking me to the bookstore, I thought to myself. What if Aaji was going to be just like Aai and Baba, only thinking about Alaap this summer? What if Aaji barely had time for me on this trip and it really was the last time she came to America?

Before I could come up with any more worst-case scenarios, Heena Mavshi, dressed in a sleeveless magenta kurti and gray sweatpants, ran toward us with a trolley loaded with her bags. "Hi, shona!" she called out, and pinched my cheeks. I flinched. Her fingers felt like Freezie Pops, ice-cold, and all sharp corners. And her thick copper bangle shaped like a snake almost knocked my teeth out as it swung on her wrist.

"Hi, Heena Mavshi," I said in my high-pitched, talking-to-grown-ups voice as I backed away from the dental hazard.

"We'll help you," Baba said, taking the trolley from her and giving Heena Mavshi a small hug.

"Oh! And here's the little baby!" Heena Mavshi yelped, scooping Alaap up. He began to whimper a little, probably from how cold her touch was. "Oh no. Do you want your aai?" she asked, handing him back to my mother. "I'm so glad I can finally meet you, shona!"

"How are you?" Aai asked as Aaji helped her slide Alaap back into his wrap.

Heena shrugged, her bubbliness momentarily gone. "Oh, you know. Not okay, but as expected. The ashes were immersed last month and Jatin's family was able to fly in to Nagpur to be there for it. I was so shocked when it happened. And then I felt so guilty . . . What are those stages of grief everyone talks about? I should look them up to know what I'm in for next." Heena Mavshi chuckled, but it wasn't a happy chuckle. Her eyes were starting to well up.

I knew what the stages were, thanks to a picture book about a lemming that Heena Mavshi had given me years ago when my aaji on Baba's side had passed away: denial, anger, bargaining, sadness, and acceptance. But I didn't feel like I could say that to Heena Mavshi right now. What if it made her even sadder?

"We're here for you," Aai said, squeezing Heena Mavshi's arm as Aaji put her shaking hand on Heena's head comfortingly.

"Always," Aaji added.

"I could help you with your yardwork this summer," I offered.

"That's so sweet of you, shona," Heena Mavshi said, blinking back more tears. "I think I'll do it, though. It will keep my mind off things. And, you know, I actually feel like painting again, for the first time since Jatin died."

I watched as she made some quick circular outlines and energetic lines on her side with her finger, drafting in her mind.

Heena Mavshi nodded, like she had finally figured out what her new art would look like. "I was imagining it on the flight. As soon as I'm over the jet lag, I'm going to make you a mini version and drop it off. Okay?"

"What a lovely gift," said a short auntie with cheeks as round as Alaap's as she wheeled her bag toward us.

"Oh, I almost forgot," Aaji said. "This is Naaglata. She kept me company on my flights too. We were all in the middle seats together."

It took two eight-hour-long flights to get from India to Michigan, plus a layover. So Aaji, Heena Mavshi, and this new auntie had flown to Europe, waited a couple hours at the airport, switched planes, and then landed here almost a full day after they'd left India.

"And she comforted me anytime I started thinking about

what life will be like in Michigan with Jatin gone," Heena Mavshi said. "She's a lifesaver. She even offered to stay with me to help me get used to . . . you know."

Heena Mavshi's voice dropped. Aai put her arm around her as I eyed the new auntie, who had deep-set dimples like she laughed all the time. She was in a shiny green sari, and a large gold band was on her thumb with a huge, blue stone the color of the Arabian Sea on it. I could smell her sweet, jasmine shampoo. And she had a cozy tan cardigan on; she was probably still feeling cold from the airplane and its overly enthusiastic air-conditioning, just like Aaji.

"What are friends for?" Naaglata Auntie whispered, her eyes welling with tears for Heena Mavshi's pain. "You inspired me with all the international traveling you and Jatin*ji* did. My mom always wanted me to see the world. I didn't get to travel with her before she passed away, but I'm glad I got to travel with both of you."

She turned to us. "My cousin lives here, in Plymouth. I was supposed to stay with her, but she had a family emergency in India and had to go back. I didn't want to cancel my ticket and lose all that money, so I thought I'd be brave and fly here by myself and go on a little adventure. I just met Heena on the flight, but we got to talking and it turned out Heena and I were together in first standard in Nagpur," she added, using the British-Indian term for "first grade." Her fingers grazed a milky-white stone dangling on her gold necklace. "Anyway, such an old-fashioned name my mom gave me. You can call me Lata Auntie." She smiled at me, warm creases forming in her face despite the harsh ultraviolet airport lights. "And you must be . . ."

"Geetanjali," I answered quietly, with the same unconfident, high voice. Only, I didn't pronounce my name right, which is probably why I saw a small cringe cross Aai's face. I said "Gee-TAN-jelly," ignoring the *t* sound that wasn't in the English alphabet, made by putting your tongue behind your top front teeth, and totally mispronouncing the last syllables.

I used to say my name right when I went to a Montessori school that had lots of Indian-American teachers. But then I went to Deadwood Elementary School for first grade, and when the teacher mispronounced my name, I was too scared to correct her or anyone else, so the new name stuck. I didn't mind. It was easier to butcher my name and change my ways instead of asking anyone else to change theirs and pronounce my name right. Besides, it was no different than when the word processor at school put a squiggly red line under my name, trying to tell me there was something wrong it. And I didn't see Aai frowning at Microsoft Word every time that happened.

"Geetanjali," Lata Auntie said, gently saying my name the correct way, "your aaji told me all about you. It's so nice to meet you, dear." She shivered, despite the cardigan. "The air-conditioning was blowing right above our heads the whole flight," Lata Auntie added as if needing to justify her chills as she rubbed her arms.

"It was awful," Aaji said, preparing to vent about the plane being unnecessarily cold, like all our relatives did when they came here.

Lata Auntie laughed. "Geetanjali is going to think we're such wimps. Defeated by air-conditioning! Don't listen to us. Be strong and brave like the powerful young girl you are."

I gave her a small smile, thinking of how much she reminded me of the way Aai was before Alaap was born. Before she got stressed and hangry all the time. I wiped at a black scuff on the ground with my shoe. I could be strong and brave. Maybe with the help of Aaji, and even Lata Auntie, I could get over some of my fears before the end of summer.

"You won't believe this," Aaji said. "Lata lived just a few streets away from us in Pune!"

"We lived there when I was young. Then my mom passed away and I moved to Nagpur to live with my aunt. And I grew up hearing all about the two of you. My mom would take me to your shows. And she always told me that you two were the only ones in all of India who could sing that Raag Naagshakti bandish so perfectly you could feel the earth's vibrations inside you."

I watched Aai's polite smile disappear for a brief instant, and she exchanged a look with Aaji. Aaji shook her head ever so slightly, like she was telling Aai not to make a big deal out of it, or like she was telling her it was nothing.

I scrunched my eyebrows. As much as I complained about all the raags, I did know most of their names, and I had never heard of Raag Naagshakti. I couldn't even remember seeing a section on it in Aai's binder full of all the raags that she taught in the basement.

"I'm sure other people can sing that song," Aai said, stroking Alaap's hair, her fingers almost trembling.

"You're being modest, Veena*ji*," Lata Auntie laughed. "Your family wrote that raag." She paused, clenching her necklace. "Everyone in Pune knows. You're famous."

Lata Auntie was right. Our mom's maternal side could trace their fame all the way back to the time of queens and kings in

India. They used to sing in a palace for the local raja and rani. So maybe Lata Auntie was right about them inventing a raag, too.

"I was thinking we'd have a little get-together tonight if your jet lag isn't too bad," Aai said, changing the subject.

"I can't wait!" Heena Mavshi exclaimed, clasping her hands together so quickly, her copper snake bangle got snagged on Aaji's green bag.

"Tonight?" Aaji asked, raising an eyebrow at Aai as Heena apologetically untangled her bangle from the threads in the corner of her handbag. Aai normally made sure Aaji had a couple days' rest to get over the time difference before having a singing party in our basement.

"Unless you're too tired?" Aai asked.

Aaji shook her head with a smile, tickling Alaap's nose and making happy faces at him. "I'm never too tired to sing."

That may have been true before, but I could already see her face looking more sunken in and her eyes had bags under them. I felt a nervous tingle in my palms. There was all this pressure now to make sure every moment this summer was special and important. And now with Aai's recent announcement, everything depended on me not screwing tonight up too. I would definitely get roped into singing with Aai and Aaji. I felt a knot tighten in my belly; my wild imagination had created yet another thing to worry about. There was no reason for me to believe Aaji wouldn't be here again next summer. But I needed to start facing my fears, so I wouldn't end up ruining this summer with her either.

"We'll have fun, right?" Aaji asked, taking her eyes off Alaap for a minute.

I felt our gazes lock, and a surge of warmth flooded me, loosening that knot in my belly.

I nodded at my grandmother. "We always do."

"The fun is already starting, shona," Heena Mavshi said, a little too happily, considering she was almost crying a few minutes ago. She wrapped her arms around me, Lata Auntie, Aai, Dad, and Aaji, smooshing our faces together. Her cold copper snake bangle brushed against Lata Auntie's ring, and for the briefest of moments, the jewel began to glow.

It was an eerie glow that covered my arms in goose bumps. No. I was doing it again. Letting my mind race. I glanced at the bright lights and air vent above us, quickly realizing it wasn't some strange power from a snake bangle and ring merging forces—it was just the gemstone catching one of the ceiling lights and reflecting it.

I exhaled, calming myself down, and stared at my family's reflection in Lata Auntie's brilliant blue stone, determined to make Aaji proud of me. The jewel was no longer glowing, but our family's image still looked warped. Before I could shake the funny feeling the image was giving me, Aai put a hand protectively next to Alaap, and without even trying, nudged me right out of the picture.

CHAPTER 6

As Aaji took a nap up in the guest room, I was in the basement, preparing for the impromptu party Aai had invented just to get Lata Auntie to stop talking about some raag.

With only a couple tiny windows down here, the basement was always a lot gloomier than the rest of the house, and not my favorite place to hang out, especially alone. But Aai was nursing Alaap, while Baba was frantically trying to make kokam saar out of the purple fruits that grew in abundance in his hometown of Konkan. He was boiling the plum-like fruit and adding spices to the drink for the party, thanks to the huge bottle of dried kokam his family had sent from Konkan to Aaji in Pune to bring to Deadwood for us.

It was like a giant game of food telephone. But in the end, you didn't get a funny mixed-up message. You got a delicious, tangy, and sweet purplish-maroon drink.

I crouched below the clock and spread a couple white-and-teal, block-printed paisley cotton quilts from India onto the thin carpet to create some floor seating. I grabbed a rag and dusted off Aai's harmonium, brushing the cotton cloth over the black and white keys, gently unlatching the bellows that folded just like an accordion's bellows, and dusting them off too.

I stopped by the big, tattered orange binder Aai kept by her harmonium for classes. I had a smaller binder full of the raags she had taught me. But the orange binder was the binder full of *all* the raags Aai knew, and their notes and their bandishes and lakshan geets, which were songs from the raags. I blew almost three months of dust off it and turned the pages of the alphabetically sorted raags. What was so special about Naagshakti?

I passed the *M* section and got to the *N*s. But there were several little paper halos stuck to the metal binder rings before the sheet with the first raag in that section, like someone had torn out a raag starting with *N* that was before that page. And I was pretty sure I knew which raag was torn out. But why would Aai do that when this was where she kept the originals of all her class music sheets?

I shut the binder and started to dust the framed pictures of Aai and Aaji onstage that hung on the walls. I brushed off the family photo Aai insisted on hanging down here too. It was one of those mall photo studio pictures, the kind where you pretend like your whole family always wears white shirts and blue jeans at the same time? Except I'd had bad allergies that day and my face was mid-sneeze in every single picture. Baba said we already paid for the package before the photo shoot, so we had to order prints or it would be a waste of money. So Aai picked the only one where I didn't have a vaporized cloud of snot emerging from me. And she thought she was doing me a favor by hanging it in the basement instead of upstairs. But the basement was where all our family-friends parties were, so everyone saw the embarrassing picture when they came down here. I swatted at my face in the picture and headed to the storage area under the basement stairs to pull out the stack of old brown metal folding chairs.

Squeak. As I pulled a chair open, a loud screech cried out from the far side of the basement, from inside the furnace room.

My heart began to thump loudly. Was it garage mouse? No. The squeak was way louder. Was it the furnace? Would the furnace be on in summer? No. Was it a ghost?

"It's just the house settling," a voice said from behind me.

I jumped, my heart now feeling like it was in my throat, and turned to see Aaji standing there, her long, thinning gray hair wavy and damp from her shower. "Aaji! You scared me."

She set down the green cloth bag she was holding and grabbed one of the metal chairs that rested against the storage space wall. "What are you doing down here alone?" Aaji asked, unfolding the chair and setting it up.

I shrugged. "Just trying to help. And you should rest. I can do the chairs," I added, even though I had yet to swallow my heart back down to where it belonged, and I was secretly grateful Aaji was down in the creepy basement with me.

"I know you don't like to be down here alone. So let me help you."

"But . . ." I searched for a respectful way to tell Aaji she looked tired. "How about we open the trunk instead?" I asked, changing the subject.

"It fell out." Aaji pointed to the corner of her thin green hand-sewn bag, right where Heena Mavshi's bangle had gotten stuck in the threads. There was a small hole, just big enough for the long, skinny key to fall out of. "I just noticed it when I was unpacking."

"No . . . ," I said, a sinking feeling released down my shoulders. "I thought the mystery was finally going to be solved."

Aaji clicked her tongue in disappointment. "We can always break open the lock."

"No. We can't hurt the trunk," I said. The trunk was old and mysterious, and I couldn't destroy something that was a connection to my past and my family in India. Aaji was my only living grandparent. And the trunk was the only thing I had that belonged to her mother. I couldn't damage it.

Aaji nodded. "We'll find it. I could feel the key through the pishwi on our drive. I checked the driveway and it isn't there. It must have fallen somewhere in the house," she added, reaching for the next chair in my hand.

I stepped back a bit, hesitant to let someone who had a hurt hip do any work, especially someone older than me.

Aaji put her hand on my shoulder gently. "Don't worry about me. I haven't changed that much from the last time you saw me, have I?"

I shook my head, even though she really had aged a ton.

"Speaking of change," Aaji said, "how are you doing now that Alaap is here?"

I quickly turned my back to Aaji, mentally apologizing to the spiders as I swatted their cobwebs off the ceiling. I hadn't really told anyone how I'd been feeling the past few months but, then again, no one had ever asked either. "Well, Aai is always nursing, or holding Alaap on the baby toilet, or drinking tanks of water, or eating, or napping, or snapping. . . ."

Aaji chuckled, moving the microphones into their places. "When you don't like the way things are, you have the power to make changes too, you know," Aaji replied, almost like she understood that I was a little disappointed in myself these days.

I turned to her. Behind her were framed pictures of Aaji singing onstage in front of the Indian prime minister, Aaji and a young Aai singing together at a concert hall, and an old, yellowed newspaper article from Pune featuring the two of them.

"That's easy for you to say," I replied, not quite ready to tell Aaji *everything*. "You don't have a picture mid-sneeze hanging on the basement wall. You don't get told no anytime you ask for a dog because of the baby. Or get ignored except to be asked math questions. You grew up with so many brothers and sisters, but your mom didn't forget about you."

"I've never been one to shy away from a little attention." Aaji gestured to the pictures on the wall and winked. "But it sounds like things have been a little tough for you lately even before Alaap was born, since Gudhi Padwa."

I ran my fingers across the soft cotton quilts I had spread on the floor, straightening out the bumps, avoiding eye contact again. So, she did know about the concert. Aai must have told Aaji what had happened. I felt ashamed, but a part of me knew Aaji wouldn't judge me the way my mother did.

"I froze up onstage that day," I said. "I saw Baba and Jatin Kaka laughing earlier, and I thought they were laughing at me. Even though I knew they wouldn't laugh at me before I was about to perform, and I got so in my head . . . I messed up and embarrassed Aai," I explained, conveniently leaving out the part before the Gudhi Padwa performance when I'd stood by as a bunch of kids had laughed at Lark.

Aaji shook her head. "Everyone makes mistakes, Geetanjali.

It's okay. And your aai wasn't embarrassed. She was probably worried. She has been doing that a lot since the pregnancy. She worries about you and Alaap. She worries about how she will be able to start teaching her singing class again with Alaap nursing so frequently. She thinks about how we come from a line of strong female singers. And how I'm getting older. And she doesn't know what will happen to that line."

I wasn't sure if Aaji was supposed to be making me feel better, but this was definitely making me feel worse.

"Line" could mean standing in line, or a clothesline, or what connected two dots, or to draw. But the line Aaji was talking about was what connected people to one another, our lineage. Did Aai think I was going to be the end to our family legacy?

"It's hard getting used to a lot of the changes here," I added, trying not to think about how I could ruin our long line of singers. "I have a new brother. My best friend wants to hang out with a new friend instead of with me. And I can't stop thinking about things I've done in the past. All my mistakes . . ." I stopped myself before I slipped to Aaji what I'd done to Lark. I could tell Aaji anything, but I wasn't sure I wanted to tell her about *that*.

I brushed my clothes off, trying to look busy. Maybe my parents should want to spend more time with Alaap. Maybe Penn should want to spend more time with Deepak.

"It's okay if singing isn't your thing," Aaji said, her voice soft. "But if you're silencing yourself because of fear, then we have to work on defeating that fear."

I nodded, feeling hopeful for the first time since spring. With Aaji by my side, anything seemed possible. She once helped me score ninety points in arcade basketball in third grade just by cheering me on. In second grade, we raised almost six hundred dollars for the Deadwood Dog Shelter from a charity singing show in our basement. And last year, when we went to Pune over winter break, we broke the record of how many puran polis anyone in our family could eat in one meal. Of course, Aaji and I felt pretty sick after eating three and a half flatbreads each, filled with mashed chana daal, a kind of chickpea, sweetened with jaggery and topped with melted toop, the clarified butter that helped people digest the meal. But it was still a record broken, a new high, and most important of all, a memory to hold forever with Aaji.

Aaji sat down cross-legged on one of the quilts I had spread out and yawned. She glanced at the clock. "Three-oh-five p.m. That's twelve thirty-five a.m. tomorrow in India," she said, and began to massage her hip. "Would you please get my pishwi?" she asked.

I grabbed the green bag she had set down and brought it to her. Aaji reached in and pulled out a little binder that looked like it was bursting from all the things glued to the handmade cotton pages inside.

"What's that?" I asked as Aaji handed it over to me. I could smell the familiar woody smell, which a lot of books from India had, coming from the pages inside it.

"It's so you'll never forget your roots." Aaji's eyes grew a little shiny. "I don't know how many good years I have left. I want to make sure you have all of this with you. It's our traditions, and customs, and some family stories."

My breath quickened. I didn't like the way those words were making me feel, so I focused on the book instead. On the cover, slipped behind the plastic sheet outside the binder, Aaji had made a picture of me out of scraps of Indian wedding cards and splatters of paint.

"I know we might not be able to go all the way to Ann Arbor to our favorite bookstore this summer, so think of this as a book present from me," Aaji added.

Under the collage, in her shaky handwriting, it said *Geetanjali*. Below that, it said something in Marathi. I recognized my name, but that was it. I put my finger under the Marathi letters and slowly began sounding out the rest. "Ek . . . sh . . ."

"Geetanjali—Ek Shoor Mulgi," Aaji said. "It's like saying Geetanjali the brave."

I felt a flush spread across my face. I knew it upset Aaji that I couldn't speak Marathi properly, let alone read and write it.

"Some pages are in English. And some are in Marathi. You'll have to work on your Marathi so you can understand it all. Once you understand who you are, you'll be confident. You'll be fearless. You'll be unstoppable." Aaji squeezed my shoulder. "You'll be everything I already know you are."

I nodded, flipping through the pages where Aaji described our family's traditions and customs for every holiday we celebrated. There were pages of memories about her childhood in India. She had illustrated it all with her collages. I recognized my cousin's neon-pink wedding invitation being used as a flower for prayers in one of the puja pages.

"It's beautiful, Aaji. Thanks." I gave my grandmother a hug.

"I've been working on it all year," Aaji said.

"Aai has been saving old invitations for you all year too. Heena Mavshi, Maya Auntie, Ashok Ajoba, and some of the other neighbors also sent old ones over for you. They're all on the counter," I said, pointing to the island by the furnace room door.

"Oh," Aaji said, starting to rise from her spot on the floor.

"I'll get it." I got up quickly and headed over to the wobbly stack of cards next to a bottle of glue and scissors.

"Aah, well, that's just what we need." Aaji began to sift through the cards.

She handed me some sparkling brown invitations.

I looked at her blankly.

"Cut four faces out. We're going to start making some changes around here."

CHAPTER 7

I couldn't believe what I was staring at. Aaji had redone the old family picture that was hanging on the wall. Except she hadn't taken a new picture of us. She had made a collage out of the old cards, cutting our outfits out of the paisley and floral handmade wedding invitations and block-printed arangetram invitations, for when a kid graduated from their bharatanatyam dance classes, and a bright-pink invitation to Maya Auntie's Bollywood movie night in two weeks.

"Is it straight?" asked Aaji, tilting the frame ever so slightly as the dehumidifier groaned behind us.

Unlike earlier, this basement noise didn't scare me so badly. I felt safe with Aaji. I nodded in response to Aaji's question, taking in the picture. We were all smiling, one happy little family before Alaap was born, thanks to the smiley faces I had drawn. And I wasn't sneezing in this family picture.

"See?" Aaji dusted her glue-covered hands off. "You can change things. You just have to approach things from a different angle. We may not get to go to the bookstore, but you still got a book. Aai and Baba are busy with Alaap because babies are helpless and need older people to do things for them. So, what if you help your parents with Alaap? Then you can spend more family time with everyone that way, right?"

I nodded. "You're going to spend some family time with an irritated Aai soon," I said, briefly considering the ways I could help my parents with my brother. "Because you know Aai is not going to like this." I grinned, wondering if Aai would even notice the new family picture at the party tonight.

"I'm not afraid of anyone." Aaji beamed. "Now come on. Let's rest our voices and get changed before the party starts. Maybe the three of us can sing one of your favorites. How about that Raag Yaman bandish you used to sing to me on the phone when you were little? I love the way you sing those notes and make them your own."

I twisted my lips. As much as I wanted to be fearless, I wasn't sure I was ready to sing in front of a packed basement.

Aaji shook her head. "Your voice is powerful, Geetanjali. And the three of our voices together? They can change the world. Like Tansen. Remember the stories I told you about him?"

I nodded, remembering Aaji's bedtime stories about the singer from my trips to India.

"Emperor Akbar's courtiers were jealous of how much the emperor favored Tansen. So, they told Akbar if Tansen sang Raag Deepak, he could make their lamps light up with fire, and Akbar just had to see it. The courtiers knew if Tansen sang the raag, he'd catch on fire too. But they weren't the only ones who knew that. So did Tansen. Do you remember the name of the raag he taught his daughter?"

"Megh," I replied. I had been studying raags my whole life. Of course I knew the answer.

"Right!" Aaji smiled, pointing to me. "So, Tansen sang Raag Deepak, and the whole palace grew hot. People were sweating. Their throats dried up. Their palms felt as hot as the sun."

I nodded, thinking that Raag Deepak was as bold as Penn's new best friend, Deepak.

"And then the lamps began to burn. And just as Tansen himself was about to catch fire from his song, his daughter began singing Megh and a thundering rain cloud doused the flames. That's how powerful one voice can be. Let alone three."

"But that didn't really happen, did it? It's just a story, right?" I asked.

Aaji raised her eyebrow and patted my head. "Stranger things have happened. But how will you know the power of your voice if you stop trying?" Aaji pointed to our new family picture. "None of those cards is like the other. They're all from different people, with different tastes, for different occasions. They're different colors, textures, and patterns, too. But look how perfectly they go together."

Aaji was right. Our family picture looked great, and all it took was a few changes. I could start approaching things from a different angle. I would learn to sing in front of people again and maybe try some of the things Penn was interested in, even help Aai and Baba with Alaap. One step at a time.

CHAPTER 8

Aaji's left hand was pumping the harmonium bellow as her right played the keys. Aai was rapidly playing the tabla, the Indian drums that could make every note on a scale, as she belted out tune after tune with her mother. They sat cross-legged, backs straight, on the thin paisley sheet on the basement floor. Aaji had insisted on sitting the traditional way, despite her hip. A backdrop made of a draped deep-purple sari with shimmering gold polka dots sparkled behind them. Before them were about a dozen family friends who were able to come over on short notice. They were keeping the beat on their laps, rocking their heads to the music, and every so often someone would shout, "Wah!" or, "Kya baat hai!" in appreciation of the performance.

I sat in the back, sipping on the last of my tiny serving of kokam sarbat, smacking my lips at the bits of kokam sediment that were left at the bottom, trying to lick up every last tangy drop since Aai wouldn't let me drink more than one cup of it before dinner. Alaap squirmed before me on his honeybee-themed play mat, knocking one of the books next to him down. I picked it back up. "Gah," I muttered as I caught sight of the page it was on, showing a closeup of a honeycomb.

I had a fear of circles. Not by themselves. Like the clock

on our basement wall. I was cool with that. Not two circles. Like googly eyes in a doodle. Not even three of them, like in a Venn diagram. Bring on the Venn diagrams. But when they were clustered together, like, with fungus, or in a honeycomb, or the scales on Gertrude's skin? *Gah.* That was the only way to explain it. One giant *gah*.

I gingerly picked up Alaap, who began chewing toothlessly on my shoulder, soaking my shirt. Here was my first baby step toward helping with Alaap. I sifted through the board books on the mat and the old picture book I had about the lemming who goes through the stages of grief and grabbed Baba's faded old book of Aesop's fables. I flipped the pages until I got to the illustration Alaap loved to stare at, of a rabbit resting on the ground as the tortoise beats him, slow and steady, to win the race. Kind of like the tortoise's own version of baby steps. I waved the page before my brother's face as I looked around at everyone enjoying the show. There weren't any other kids at the party other than Deepak, who was sitting cross-legged on a quilt next to his big sister Shilpa, who was home from college.

I didn't blame my other family friends for skipping this. They all found classical singing to be super boring and preferred Bollywood music, even the ones who'd taken Aai's classes. I was one of the few kids who liked both forms of music equally. And there was no way I'd invite Penn. These parties were loud and boisterous, and he'd have trouble understanding half the jokes being made with so many conversations in Marathi and Hindi and Gujarati going on all at once. At times, I almost wished I were upstairs solving the math problems Baba had written for me in my notebook. Almost.

As Aai hit an especially high note, Deepak's mom raised her hand and exclaimed, "Wah!" loudly. Baba let out a whistle from the back. Everyone was clapping. Everyone except Heena Mavshi. Her "wah"s and "Kya baat hai"s were usually the loudest during these parties. But tonight she just sat silently by Lata Auntie, looking unimpressed, the only person in the room not in the mood for a party.

Well, the only person other than me. I loved hearing Aaji sing, but her voice seemed weaker than normal. Last summer she was the one hitting the high notes. It made me feel a little sad to see Aai singing that part instead this time.

As the song came to an end, Ashok Ajoba, Deepak's great-uncle in the back of the room, shouted out a request: "Tum Ko Dekha To Yeh Khayaal Aaya!"

"You always ask for that song." Aaji smiled playfully.

Ashok Ajoba swept his white curls to the side and laughed. "I'm spending the whole summer organizing all our photos and books and junk. Lots of changes happening. I want something old and comforting like I'm used to!" he chuckled.

"Change isn't always bad," Aaji said, looking at me with a knowing nod. "How about something new?"

Lata Auntie waved her hand hesitantly. "Raag Naagshakti?" she asked, a little shyly, her voice higher than it was when I had met her, like she also had a high-pitched, timid, talking-to-grown-ups voice like me.

Aai's hand slipped, tilting one of the tablas over, knocking down her microphone. She steadied it quickly and cleared her throat. "Tum Ko Dekha it is."

"Veena, didn't you hear Lata?" Aaji asked softly, her hand over her microphone, but we could all still hear her.

"I'm not singing that," Aai whispered back to Aaji. But again, being a small basement, I heard her and I was certain a lot of other people had too.

Lata Auntie's ears burned pink as she gave a small smile to the people around her and then quickly looked down as Aai started the other song. I ran my fingers through Alaap's silky curls. I knew what it was like to be humiliated by my mom, even if Aai wasn't trying to be mean.

"Geetanjali? Do you want to join us?" Aai asked, some of the flustered flush leaving her cheeks.

There it was. The invite I had been dreading all evening. I looked at Aaji's encouraging eyes. I wanted to take that step forward. To make up for the Gudhi Padwa fiasco. To feel the hope I had felt when I made the new family picture with Aaji. But I was scared. The aunties and uncles here could still laugh at me. I mean, I knew they wouldn't be that cruel, but what if one of them got the giggles like Baba and Jatin Kaka had at Gudhi Padwa? I shook my head.

"Ye, beta," Aaji added gently, patting the spot next to her as she asked me to join them.

It was just a few steps away. And I was supposed to take baby steps, wasn't I? I could do this. For Aaji.

I took a step forward and my stomach dropped as all the aunties and uncles in the crowd, and Shilpa and Deepak, turned to look at me with eager smiles. Just then, Alaap began to squirm in my arms, making a frustrated grunting sound. Baba motioned for me to give the baby to him, but I shook my head.

"Alaap has to go to the bathroom," I said quickly, knowing that all my brother wanted was to see the rabbit in the book dance when I jiggled the page. "I'll be back," I added, making a dash for the stairs. I wasn't giving up; it was just going to take a few more days before I was ready to make these new memories. Slow and steady wins the race, or something like that.

CHAPTER 9

I unbuttoned Alaap's onesie and held him on the plastic baby potty on the white-and-gray quartz bathroom counter. The vibrations from the party below were muffled, thanks to the gray tiles on the floor, allowing me to sort of forget about what was going on downstairs. "Ssss," I said, and immediately on cue, Alaap did his business.

"That's fascinating," said a voice from behind me.

I turned. It was Deepak, standing around the corner to give Alaap his privacy.

"Does he poop in there too?"

I nodded, skipping over the part about how it sounded like an exploding fart when he did.

"I mean, it makes sense. Humans are mammals, and mammals don't like to sit in their own waste. You don't see dogs sitting in their poop," Deepak continued, apparently really into showing off more of his knowledge. "But we make babies do it and then tell them it's wrong a few years later. And if you think about it, there was a time when diapers didn't exist."

I cleaned up and washed my hands, not in the mood for this doo-doo discussion. Of course Deepak was an expert on the history of human poop. He was an expert on everything. "This is how Aaji took her kids to the bathroom when they were babies."

"Probably how a lot of people around the world used to do it too, or still do," Deepak hypothesized. He hung around while I put Alaap's diaper back on, snapped on his onesie, and then carried him to the family room. "Shilpa didi doesn't get how much there is to learn from animals," he continued, using the Hindi title for big sister. "I wanted to shadow Ashok Dada at Reptile Rescue Center. He started working there after he retired from Ford, you know," Deepak said, talking about his great-uncle, Ashok Ajoba. But since Deepak wasn't Marathi, he used a different word for "grandfather" than we did. "She only wants me to learn about science and math and robotics and engineering . . ." He trailed off.

I looked at Deepak. Maybe we did have more in common than I thought. This was almost like Baba thinking what I could do with words wasn't as important as doing math. Maybe Deepak wasn't a show-off. Maybe he was just good at certain things and wasn't embarrassed to let the world know it.

Deepak continued, deep in his own thoughts. "But here's a prime example of nature being just as important. This probably saves on diapers, too, helping the earth out in the process."

I shrugged, putting Alaap down on his play mat in the family room, the carpet muffling the sounds of the party.

Deepak looked up like he was calculating something. "If you think a baby is using, like, eight diapers a day, times three hundred and sixty-five days . . . and this saves you two years of diapers . . . you can save . . . five thousand, eight hundred and forty diapers!"

"Yay, math," I muttered.

"Oh, I've been meaning to ask you," Deepak went on,

changing the subject and pulling something out of his pocket. "I found this rock in your front yard, near the rosebushes. Would it be okay if I kept it for my rock collection?"

I looked in his palm at the white-and-rust-swirled polished stone. "Go for it."

"Thanks," Deepak said as he dug into his pocket and opened up a little satchel made out of an old olive-green sari and a gold drawstring.

We got those bags all the time when we went to weddings. They were usually filled with small silver lamps to hold the cotton wicks for our devghar, our home temple, or chocolates, or sparkly mirrored jewelry boxes. But Deepak's was filled with rocks.

He sifted through them to find a dull rock with black splotches on it like a speckled egg. "Did you know seafloors are made of lava that turned into volcanic rock? It's called basalt." Deepak examined the rock closer. "I'm going to Boston for camp later this summer. The only good thing is it's by a lake, so there will be some interesting rocks over there."

"That's nice." I started to organize Alaap's board books around his play mat, wondering if Penn and Deepak had a ton of fun without me climbing the wall. Did Penn enjoy all of Deepak's random facts?

"I can show you some more cool rocks in my yard when you all come over for my mom's Bollywood movie night," Deepak added, when loud footsteps were suddenly heard coming up the basement stairs.

"That sounds fun," I replied, trying to be kind, even though I wasn't interested in looking at rocks, like Deepak was.

"I'm so embarrassed. Do you think I bothered them?" asked a shaky voice around the corner where the basement stairs were.

Curious, I picked Alaap up and walked toward the sound, hoping he wouldn't decide to wail and give us away. Deepak tiptoed behind me as the muffled voice grew nearer and I recognized it as Lata Auntie's.

"My mother used to tell me how much she loved that song. How it filled her soul with music and made her want to dance to the earth's vibrations. I guess I kept asking for them to sing it because I miss her."

"You're fine," Heena Mavshi replied coolly, almost like she was annoyed with Lata Auntie. I'd never heard that tone out of Heena Mavshi's mouth in all the years I'd known her, which was my whole life. She seemed to be a totally different person than the one I'd seen a few hours earlier at the airport.

From the kitchen, I watched as a shiny-eyed Lata Auntie, pulling her tan cardigan tightly around her like a much-needed hug, and a frowning Heena Mavshi emerged from the basement. I took a step back, bumping into the kitchen counter. I knew how Lata Auntie felt, being so upset when my mom used that tone of voice with me too, but I didn't want to get caught eavesdropping.

Lata Auntie smiled when she saw us, though, acting like everything was fine. "I'm sad we didn't get to hear you sing tonight, Geetanjali," she said. "But your aaji told me you'll be singing at Bark in the Park next month?"

I nodded, rocking Alaap in my arms so he'd fall asleep.

"I volunteered to help the stage crew set up, so I'll see you there. I used to really be into singing and stage shows as a kid.

Thought it would be a fun thing to do while I'm here for the summer."

"Oh," I said, smiling politely, thinking of what I could say to ease the tension between the two aunties. "Heena Mavshi, did you start on your mini painting yet?"

"Have you ever heard of jet lag?" Heena Mavshi snapped, turning her back to me. She ignored Alaap, too, and headed for the pile of shoes that were present at every one of our parties by the front door.

Lata Auntie looked embarrassed by how Heena Mavshi was acting but quickly gasped at the pictures in front of her of the lush greenery in Baba's ancestral home. "Wow, is that Konkan?" she asked.

I nodded. "My dad's family is from there. That's his parents' place."

"Lucky family," Lata Auntie said, smiling. "You're missing a good show downstairs," she added, stepping into her sandals. "Your aaji and aai are so talented. We're getting tired, otherwise we'd stay, but we'll see you around." Lata Auntie turned to leave but then paused, turning back to me. "I hope one day I'll be lucky enough to hear you sing too, Geetanjali."

The door slammed in her face as Heena Mavshi exited and headed down the walkway. Lata Auntie timidly rushed after her, gently shutting the door behind her.

I looked at Deepak. "That . . . was weird."

Deepak nodded, his mouth open. For once, the boy who always had something to say was speechless.

CHAPTER 10

That night, as Aaji sipped some hot water with cinnamon in her room, I was swinging my legs off her bed, watching her, feeling so happy she was home, but also feeling a little weirded out by Heena Mavshi snapping at me, perhaps mad at what I'd said. Maybe she had entered the anger stage of grieving. I'd be angry too, if someone I loved died suddenly, I thought.

"Aaji, what's Raag Naagshakti?" I asked, forcing myself to play it cool and stop kicking the bed with all my nervous energy. I wanted to know more about this raag and why Lata Auntie wanted to hear it so badly.

Aaji set her teacup down. "It's a very powerful raag."

"I don't remember Aai ever teaching it to us in class before," I asked, getting up to help Aaji organize the bottles of Ayurvedic, homeopathic, and allopathic medicines on her dresser next to her green bag.

"She wouldn't have. Your aai is not a fan of that raag," Aaji said, sitting next to me.

"Why?" I asked, my hand accidentally knocking whatever was in the green bag over. "Oops," I said, reaching out to put it upright. I peeked inside. "Why is there a bottle of candied buddishep in here?" I turned to Aaji, my mouth watering at the colorful, sugar-coated fennel seeds that were a tasty treat, a digestive aid, and a mouth freshener all in one.

Aaji's cheeks flushed a little. "Your aai is getting so worried about what I eat. She's afraid everything is going to make me sick. I just have this upstairs so I can enjoy it without her worrying."

Aai had just gotten upset at Baba for questioning her food choices earlier, and now she was worrying about what her mother was eating. I raised my eyebrow at Aaji. "Secrets aren't good, Aaji."

Aaji looked at the wall of pictures behind her, which had more framed newspaper pictures of her performing onstage back in the day. "If I tell you what your aai was hiding about Raag Naagshakti . . . will it scare you? I don't want her getting upset at me because you can't sleep."

I brushed my bangs out of my eyes. It didn't feel good to know that Aai had been broadcasting my fears to Aaji like a list of complaints.

"I won't get scared." Besides, I thought, pulling the extra blanket on Aaji's bed over my pajama shorts, what could be scary about a raag? Other than having to sing it in front of people when you might have stage fright?

Aaji took a moment to decide if she should proceed and then nodded. "Well, a long time ago there was a woman and her daughter who were singing Raag Naagshakti. It's powerful because it creates the same pattern of vibrations as the earth's vibrations. And because of that, you know who's attracted to it?"

"Saap," I said, trying to earn a bonus point for using the Marathi word for "snakes."

"Not just any saap. Naag ani naagin. Cobras."

I nodded, thinking about that time I had seen a snake charmer going door to door in India with a cobra in his basket, asking for money. I only saw it for a few seconds and was covered in goose bumps. I would definitely not want to sing something that attracted cobras.

"The woman opened her eyes while they were singing and saw a cobra swaying to the music before her daughter," Aaji continued. "She had to get a kersooni to shoo it out of the house, but there was no way to get up," Aaji said, mentioning the Indian broom made out of long dried grass that was bound on one end to make a handle. "She was afraid if she did, the snake would get nervous and bite her daughter or her. So, she screamed for her husband. He grabbed the stick we hang our clothes on the line to dry with and tried to guide the naag out. But the cobra arched back, hood out, like it was going to strike, and the husband accidentally killed the cobra while trying to defend himself."

I pulled the blanket over my shoulders, the hairs on my legs standing up at the thought of that heavy, tall wooden stick being used to hurt something. I didn't like snakes, but I didn't want them to die. I remember, as scared as I was of the cobra in India, I still felt sad because one of my cousins said the snake charmer must have yanked the snake's fangs out to tame it. And I knew that probably hurt, and that the snake shouldn't have been trapped in a basket for its whole life instead of being free in the wild.

"You know what happens when you kill a naag or naagin, right?"

I shook my head, my bangs flopping around.

"They have a mate. And the mate vows revenge on you. After the incident, the family was terrified the cobra's mate would come after them. That he would take the form of a human to do so."

"An . . . ichchhadhari naag?" I asked, searching for the phrase, remembering an old Hindi movie I had seen about the subject.

Aaji nodded. "And that snake-person could curse them."

"Was the family cursed?"

Aaji shrugged. "Nobody knows. But just the thought of this story, this curse, naag, naagin, it made your aai want to never sing Raag Naagshakti."

I swallowed hard, my heart beating in my throat. This *was* a scary story.

"What's with that face? Are you scared?" Aaji asked.

I straightened my back. "Of course not. There are no cobras out in the wild in Michigan," I replied, trying to sound as brave as I wanted to be.

"Right," Aaji said. She untied a small thinning cotton handkerchief pouch in her dresser. It had her emerald ring, her nath, the traditional Marathi paisley-shaped nose ring of pearls and jewels, and her mohan maal, a necklace of strings of gold beads. She sifted through the jewelry with her wrinkled fingers until she found a milky-white stone dangling from a knotted gold chain. She unraveled the tangled necklace.

"It's a naagmani."

I felt the cold stone in my hand. It reminded me of the necklace I saw on Lata Auntie at the airport.

"It's a stone, formed by a cobra," Aaji said. "It's very rare. And it keeps snakes away. My panji gave it to me when I was around your age." She folded my fingers over the stone her great-grandmother had passed down. "And now I'm giving it to you. Keep it, and you'll have nothing to be scared of."

I nodded; the cold stone felt like I was holding a small clump of hail that would never melt. "Good night, Aaji. I'm glad you're here."

Aaji gave me a hug. "Good night, Geetanjali. I'm glad I'm here too."

CHAPTER 11

I headed across the tiny dark hall to my room and hurriedly flicked on my dinosaur-patterned table lamp next to the silver trunk. I wasn't scared, but I wasn't happy about being alone in the dark after hearing Aaji's snake story. I organized all the notebooks on the trunk, part of my nightly routine, getting everything into place for the next day, and paused. Maybe that little binder book Aaji made had some more information about Raag Naagshakti. It was a creepy story, but I had to know more. Kind of like when I read a spooky book that was way too scary for me but I had to keep going to know what happened.

I plopped down on my bed, skipping the opening chapter, which was all about Aaji's favorite raags, and began leafing through the book. That's when I saw it—Aaji *had* told me all about a naagmani in her wobbly handwriting:

Very few people believe that naagmani—cobra stones—even exist. But they do. A naagmani is formed when the conditions are just right. The right temperature, during the monsoon, on the night of a full moon. It can be found in a cobra's nest by only the bravest of the brave. Mine was given to me by my great-grandmother. She had found it in a nest and told me it will always keep me safe from poisonous snakes. I kept it because I loved my panji. But I've never felt scared, with or without it. So it is yours now. Keep your naagmani close always, and I hope you will feel the courage you've always had within.

The next two pages had a collage of a scary snake and a poem: Beware the Ichchhadhari Naagin—my ajoba used to say this rhyme to me whenever he caught me whistling at night, since you know superstition says that attracts snakes. It's a loose translation, but I think I did a good job with the rhymes!

What did Aaji mean by "Shambhar is the number"? I grabbed a pencil and my notebook that sat beside my thesaurus and dictionary on my nightstand and jotted the line down. Aaji hadn't fully translated the poem from Marathi. Maybe because she liked the rhyme in that line. I knew what shambhar meant, though. It meant one hundred. But I didn't quite understand what the poem meant. After a hundred, her light would be eternally bright?

One hundred what? And would the naagin then be immortal? I was suddenly covered in goose bumps, my arms rougher than snakeskin. I pulled the covers over my shoulder. I wanted to sleep and forget about what I had just read. But it was ominous and scary and gave me a creepy feeling, like it was foreshadowing something bad.

I shuddered, then reminded myself that Aaji had an imagination even wilder than mine; she read those Marathi horror novels written by authors with pseudonyms. Aaji had written an entire section in this book about how to spot Indian ghosts, whose feet were backward. And she had already retold the tall tale about Tansen almost setting a palace on fire because of a song.

I slammed the binder book shut and put it on my nightstand, but it was too close. So I stretched my arm and put it on the silver trunk on the ground. I could still smell the woody pages. I grabbed the little binder and headed to the bookshelf by my window full of my old childhood picture books. One day I'd read them all to Alaap, and a few of my new books, too. I shielded my eyes from the solar-powered spotlight on our patio that always shined through my thin curtains on summer nights. I placed the naagmani and book on top of the shelf, next to the wooden statue of Ganpati that Baba had given me. That was better. The book blended in with my old Indian comic books and new graphic novels. And I couldn't smell it from my bed from this distance.

A hiss in the room startled me and I bumped a book off the shelf, stepping on it with my foot. I bent down and did a quick namaskar to the book, touching it with my right hand and then putting that hand to my chest, to apologize. Books gave us knowledge, and in our culture we weren't supposed to ever put our feet on them. It was disrespectful. So if we did, we did namaskar to it.

The hissing grew louder as I stood up. I turned toward the sound. It wasn't a snake. It was my bedroom window, the curtains flapping from the breeze. I guess I didn't shut the stiff, old window properly and there was a tiny gap for the wind to hiss through.

I swung the curtain to the side, jingling the two wooden puppets in sparkly red-and-orange clothes from Rajasthan that hung on the curtain rod. I pushed down hard on the frame until the window slammed shut and the hissing stopped. I locked it and started to move the curtains back when a light flashed outside.

It was hard to see with the reflection from my bedroom lamp bouncing off the windowpane, but I was certain I wasn't looking at a deer. No. There was a person standing in front of our patio spotlight, staring straight at our house. They swayed ever so slightly, like a leaf fluttering in the wind.

I squinted into the light.

It was Heena Mavshi.

CHAPTER 12

What was Heena Mavshi doing outside, in the dark, and in our backyard? Was she sleepwalking? Or was she taking the hundred steps my ajoba on Baba's side used to take after his dinner? (Although, it was pretty late for that.) Was she still in a crabby mood and trying to walk it off?

Heena Mavshi bent down by the garden bed right next to our patio and began frantically clawing at the soil. Was she gardening?

Just then, a shorter woman rushed up to her. It was Lata Auntie. She stepped right on whatever Heena Mavshi was doing in the dirt. Something then caught Heena's attention; she pointed, and Lata Auntie walked away from the garden lights. I could barely make out her shadow, turning her back to the house as she bent down by our mock orange plants, grabbing whatever it was Heena Mavshi was pointing to.

My heart began to beat in my ears. Heena Mavshi suddenly turned her head in my direction. I swung the curtain shut, hoping she hadn't seen me, and booked it out of my room, down the hall, straight to Baba and Aai.

I yanked their door handle down and swung the door open. It banged against the wall, startling my parents, who were fast asleep, and waking up Alaap, who started to sob.

"Geetanjali?" said Baba, sitting up with a start.

"What's going on? Everything okay?" asked Aai as she nursed Alaap back down to sleep by her side.

I nodded, catching my breath. "I just . . . It was a bad dream," I said, unsure how to explain what I had just seen or if I had even really seen it at all. "Can I sleep in here?"

Aai shook her head. "Geetanjali. We've been over this," she said crossly. "I told you when Alaap was born that you couldn't come running in here every night when you got scared. We can't risk you rolling onto the baby and accidentally hurting him."

"But Baba's here. He's not rolling on Alaap."

"That's because of the way we are sleeping," Aai said, pointing to how my dad was perpendicular to her. "My feet would stop him from rolling anywhere near the baby. I did the same to protect you when you were a baby too, Geetu. You're a big girl now. There's nothing to be afraid of, okay?" she said gently.

I nodded, backing out of the room and shutting the door. I'd just have to sleep in my bed with all the lights on and deal with Baba's lecture in the morning on how much electricity costs. I started to head back when I remembered there *was* a room whose door was always open to me.

I crawled into bed next to Aaji. She was breathing noisier than she normally did, but it was comforting to hear her breath moving in and out. Her gold bangles jingled against one another on the loose, wrinkly skin of her arm as she reached out, half-asleep, to hold me. And although my heart was still thumping faster than I thought it ever could, I felt less scared. My eyelids grew heavy, and I finally drifted off to sleep.

CHAPTER 13

The next morning the sounds of chirping sparrows, chattering chipmunks, a lawn mower rumbling, and the hammering of our resident backyard woodpecker filled the air through the patio screen door.

I peeked outside and saw Baba and Aai sitting at our patio table with Alaap, eating breakfast next to a plate of freshly cut Kent mangos. I inhaled deeply, grateful it wasn't the stinkier hapoos amba variety.

Several feet past them, sitting on chairs in the middle of our lawn, was Aaji with Penn and Deepak. What were they doing here, and why had no one woken me up to let me know they had come over?

I stepped into my chappal, swung the stiff patio door open, and headed outside. "Good morning, Alaap," I said, tickling his soft toes that were basking in the morning sun. He gave me a big smile, and I returned it before I grabbed the koi of the mango and began to suck the fruit off the big seed.

Aai shook her head. "I bet Aaji didn't have a good morning or night, squeezed into a twin bed with you."

I frowned, tucking the naagmani into my shirt. When I saw the necklace on my dresser this morning, I figured I should start wearing it. It was too nice to just sit and collect dust.

How had Aai figured out I'd gone into Aaji's bed instead of back to my own? Baba handed me a plate of pohe, flattened rice with potatoes, peas, onions, lemon juice, and spices, next to a little bowl of homemade yogurt.

"It's not my fault," I responded, chewing on a piece of spicy green pepper. "Heena Mavshi and Lata Auntie were in our yard. And Heena Mavshi was digging in our dirt like a puppy, which by the way, I'd love to get at some point now that Alaap is here."

"No puppies, Geetu. We've been over this," Baba said. "And Heena might have needed some fresh air; it's perfectly normal for her to have some trouble sleeping after Jatin's death."

"She probably spotted a weed and plucked it for us," Aai said.

"At night?" I questioned.

"Grief makes people do strange things," Aai responded. "And you can't keep going into Aaji's bed," she added, looking at my grandmother. "What if you roll onto her in her sleep?"

I shoveled bites of the steaming hot pohe into my mouth. What was with Aai thinking all I did was roll onto people at night to suffocate them?

I set the plate down and headed farther into my yard, toward the boys and Aaji. As I got closer, I could hear Deepak singing an old Bollywood song over the hum of the distant lawn mower. It was about a woman counting down the days until she could see someone again. "Ek, do, teen," he sang loudly, counting from one to three in Hindi in the Bollywood hit.

Penn's head was twisted to the side again, like he was disturbed by the music.

"Why didn't anybody wake me?" I interrupted, wiping my sticky mango hands on the side of my shirt.

"Oh, you had a tough night," Aaji replied, before the boys could. "I wanted you to sleep in. Besides, I invited them over."

I raised an eyebrow as I took a seat in the grass; there wasn't an extra chair out here for me, and Aaji needed to sit comfortably for her hip. "You did?"

Aaji nodded. "They were playing in Penn's yard, and I remembered how much Penn liked Indian food and invited them over for breakfast."

I roughly pulled some rubbery grass seeds on a blade, watching them go flying chaotically. Penn and Deepak were already hanging out together this morning. And unlike the other times they'd gone to the wall and asked me to come along, I wasn't even invited this time.

"We just started playing antakshari," Deepak chimed in. "Want to join us?"

Did I want to play one of my favorite games from India, where someone sings a line and whatever Hindi letter they end on, the next person has to sing a song that starts with that letter? Yes! I just wasn't sure I wanted to play with Deepak and Penn right now.

"Deepak ended on *na*," Aaji said, stating the Hindi letter.

I glanced at Penn. His favorite Skye Suh-Oliviera song started with that sound. "Do you want to go?" I asked, even though I was a little annoyed at him. Penn was my best friend. Shouldn't he have wanted to call me first? "You can sing 'Nothing but Gray Rainclouds,'" I suggested.

Penn turned pink. "You can go."

He must have still felt a little embarrassed after Rohan compared his singing to a dog howling.

"Did you know 'gray' has a lot of meanings?" I asked, trying to make the song seem less daunting to Penn. "It can mean the color, of course, but it can also mean having to do with getting old, it can mean being tired or sick, when you're talking about money it can mean something not officially counted, and it can mean something dull."

"Penn told me you're really good with words," Deepak said.

"Thanks," I replied with a small smile. "You can think about which version Skye was referring to when you sing the song," I said gently to Penn.

But he just shook his head again. "I'm good."

I cleared my throat, trying to think of a Hindi movie song that started with the letter *na*.

"Need help?" Aaji asked.

I shook my head, standing up. I took a few steps back from everyone. Maybe a little distance would make this easier. And then I remembered a really old song from a black-and-white movie that Baba liked to play that could work.

"Nanhe munhe bachche, teri mutthi mein kya hai," I sang softly, starting the song that I was sure Aaji could just barely hear over the neighbor's lawn mower. I avoided eye contact with the boys as I repeated the line. But, just then, the lawn mower stopped.

That meant everyone would hear me clearly.

I sang the next few words, my ears turning hotter. I shifted my eyes, glancing at the garden bed around our patio, wishing I didn't feel so self-conscious, when I noticed something in the dirt and suddenly stopped the song, midsentence.

"Would that ending letter be *tthi*?" Deepak asked Aaji.

"Look over there," I interrupted, pointing to the lines in the dirt as I headed closer, grateful to end my performance.

Aaji, Penn, and Deepak followed.

"I saw Heena Mavshi digging here last night," I continued. The lines didn't look like the work of someone weeding, but, rather, something frantic. And it had footprints over it.

I crouched down for a closer examination by the patio. It was like a big letter *C*, except stretched out. And there were two beady eyes in the middle. I gasped. It was the same shape as the painting in Heena Mavshi's living room.

"It's a cobra!" I exclaimed.

"Where?" Aai yelped from the patio table before quickly catching herself. "I mean, there are no wild cobras in Michigan, Geetanjali. You and your imagination."

"You're the one who just jumped," I said, walking up to the patio table to eat more breakfast.

"You know I had all these incidents as a child, where I'd see a cobra out of nowhere," Aai said, finishing up her usual, which today was made of sprouted mung. "I'd be playing with my friends in an old fort and one would be in the stairwell. I'd play by the mango trees in our backyard and a cobra would be hiding in the groundcover. My fear doesn't come from imagining things. It comes from reality."

I sighed, taking a spicy bite of my pohe from my plate by Baba. "Heena Mavshi drew a cobra in the soil here last night. I'm not imagining it. I saw her do it. I just didn't know what it was until now."

Baba got up and inspected the lines in the soil, kicking

some dirt over my proof as he looked. "Those are just marks from when I was using the weed whacker last weekend," he said, looking at my disappointed scowl. "I want to believe you, Geetanjali. But remember when, just a few months ago, you made a presentation on sharks for school that was so thorough, you started screaming in the shower that a shark was going to come out of the drain?" Baba laughed.

I glanced at Penn and Deepak from the corner of my eyes and saw them exchange a look. Were they trying not to giggle at this story that half the Maharashtra Mandal had been laughing about since winter? I felt hot all over.

"And then you ran out in your towel, Baba ran in, and slipped on all the water you had left on the floor in your quick escape," Aai added with a little chuckle that stung even more than the pepper in my mouth.

Aaji clicked her tongue, putting her hand on my shoulder. "Don't laugh at her."

"My friends are right here," I whispered through gritted teeth at my parents.

"I'm sorry," Aai said, trying not to smile. "Really. But you have to admit it was funny, wasn't it?"

"Hilarious," I muttered, blinking fast so no tears would fall from my eyes. "Just like when Baba and Jatin Kaka laughed at me at Gudhi Padwa."

"What?" Baba turned to me, his grin disappearing. "I never laughed at you. Neither did Jatin Kaka. Before your performance, he was telling me this story about how he heard from his sister in LA that Costco had keshar on sale. You know how expensive keshar is."

I nodded, still irritated, as Penn and Deepak stepped a little closer to me. Saffron was an orangish-red threadlike spice used in our food. It was the stigma of a flower, and it took thousands and thousands of flowers to make a tin of saffron. It was the most expensive spice in the world, and we always bought tins of it here to give to relatives in India, even though it came from India, because it was an expensive gift.

"Well," Baba continued, "Jatin Kaka was in such a rush to see if the Michigan Costco had the same sale, he ran for the mailbox to see if the Costco coupon book had come, slipped on a tiny patch of ice, and ended up spraining his foot. He told me he had to pay tons more for his insurance deductible to get treated than he would have saved on the saffron for his trip to India. That's why we were laughing."

I felt a little less sweaty. It was a relief to hear they hadn't been laughing at me that day.

"Geetanjali, why don't you go drop this food off for Heena and Lata?" Aaji suggested, changing the subject and motioning toward a fraying jute bag full of glass containers and repurposed yogurt containers full of Indian food on the table. "It will be a nice way to help Heena out, don't you think?"

I sighed. Heena Mavshi needed us right now. I had to think about her in this moment and not my own feelings. So I picked up the bag and turned to the boys. "Do you want to come with me?" Unlike them, I knew how to include my friends.

Penn gave me a little shrug. "We actually were going to do something for Gertrude. That's why we met this morning. I figured it wasn't something you'd be interested in."

"Oh," I said, my palms feeling a little sweaty. Even if

hanging out with a snake or climbing a dangerous wall wasn't what I was interested in, it was still nice to be invited. "Well, tell her I say hi," I replied as I turned to leave.

Tell a snake I said hi? I felt my skin crawl with embarrassment. That was a line I'd be remembering for quite a while, adding it to my list of humiliating things to replay in my head. But I shook it off. I was on a mission to help our neighbor. And maybe I could ask her what she had sketched out in our yard last night so I could finally stop being the butt of my family's jokes.

CHAPTER 14

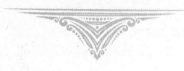

I crossed the black path that cut between our yard and Heena Mavshi's, the heavy jute bag full of food in my hands, dewdrops on the grass tickling the sides of my feet. I ran across Heena Mavshi's messy patio, with wicker furniture still covered in tarps from when she'd left for India in spring, and a garden hose strewn about haphazardly. I paused to lift some plastic chairs that had fallen over in the wind, when Lata Auntie slid the patio door open to the stormy-gray house.

"Geetanjali!" she exclaimed sunnily. "Come in. Come in!"

I gave her a polite smile as she ushered me inside. "My family sent some food over for you and Heena Mavshi. They felt bad you left early," I added, even though Aai was probably relieved Lata Auntie was no longer at our house asking questions about Raag Naagshakti.

"Oh, how sweet," she said, her dimples showing.

"How's Heena Mavshi?" I asked gingerly, stepping out of my sandals on the doormat.

"See for yourself," Lata Auntie replied, motioning toward the sunroom that extended from the navy-blue-and-white kitchen behind her.

I took a few steps toward the kitchen. The sunroom was my favorite part of Heena Mavshi's house. It wasn't just because of the amazing breeze from the wall-to-wall screens. The sunroom was Heena Mavshi's art studio. I loved seeing all the different paintings in progress, the bright colors that made me miss India, and even the messy globs of paint splatter on the old newspapers coating the tables. It was all part of one big, beautiful masterpiece.

But today the sunroom didn't feel cheerful. It felt off. That was the only way to describe the funny feeling it was giving me. Heena Mavshi was in an olive-green-and-purple cotton bandhani salwar kurta, with white tie-dye diamonds forming the shape of paisleys. She was crouched over a long rectangular table in the middle of the sunroom, instead of standing or sitting in front of it. She had an agitated frown as she slashed at the canvas before her with a paintbrush, almost tearing it.

"Hi, Heena Mavshi," I said timidly.

Heena Mavshi barely glanced my way as she mumbled hello. I looked below the table. There were about fifty note cards of mini practice paintings down there. And they all were of the same thing.

A cobra.

Their hoods and beady eyes looked just like the partial cobra I was positive she had scrawled into our dirt last night. *I was right*, I thought, wishing Baba were here.

"Are you over your jet lag?" I asked uncertainly as Heena Mavshi splattered drops of blood-red paint onto the cobra's mouth.

"I'm exhausted," she replied, throwing her hair out of her face.

The sudden movement caused her odhni to fall off her shoulder, revealing a bloody, crusty circular wound on her upper back.

"Oh, Heena, your birthmark is showing!" Lata Auntie rushed forward to fix Heena Mavshi's odhni so the scarf covered her again.

A birthmark? I knew I had never seen that gash there before, and Heena Mavshi wore backless sari blouses all the time. Besides, birthmarks weren't supposed to actively bleed.

Heena Mavshi jerked her shoulder, shaking Lata Auntie's hand off her.

Lata Auntie looked embarrassed as she stepped back. "She must have cut it on a branch or something last night when she went for a stroll in the garden," she said softly to me.

"Are you replacing the living room painting with a new cobra painting?" I asked, trying to figure out what this pile of cobra paintings could possibly mean. They weren't like the living room cobra-and-mongoose painting. Heena Mavshi always said I understood her art. But I had no idea what any of these chaotic cobra canvases were saying. All I knew is that they gave me an uneasy feeling in my gut. Like something was wrong.

"Not sure," Heena Mavshi said, too busy painting to look my way.

"Well, thank you for the food. We'll stop by later to thank your parents and aaji," Lata Auntie said, leading me back toward the patio door. "I think we're both still so tired, our moods are all over the place. Your aaji is probably handling it with grace. Wish we had more of that in us!" she laughed, a little too hard.

A tiny white butterfly tickled my hand as I ran from Heena Mavshi's yard to my own. My family was no longer out there, probably all inside fussing over Alaap.

I jumped around the mock orange plants in the center of our backyard and came to an abrupt stop.

There in the grass, a few feet from the back of the garage, was a dead mouse. I guess my parents didn't need to worry about trying to catch it anymore. Unless this was garage mouse's cousin. I quickly checked the bottoms of my chappal to make sure I hadn't stepped on it on my way to the garden. Nope. My sandals were good.

But the mouse wasn't. Two tiny ears protruded from the grass, cold and lifeless. The mouse's mouth was open in an agonizing silent scream. Its eyes were frozen wide with panic, like the last thing it saw was so terrifying, it would forever be etched in its rodent face.

I took a step closer. A gentle morning breeze twirled around my toes, the tall grass blades swaying side to side. That's when I noticed the two holes in the poor little mouse's back.

CHAPTER 15

I ran across the street to Penn's, to let him know what I had just seen, but practically skidded to a stop across the hot concrete at the end of our driveway. Penn was sitting in his front yard by the curb at the little yellow table we used to paint on when we were in preschool. He wasn't painting, though. He was selling lemonade, something we hadn't done in years, and tending to a kid customer. Deepak was sitting next to him, lost in another book.

A lemonade stand was the thing they were planning to do for Gertrude? It didn't make sense. Besides, I would have loved to have made lemonade with them, sell it, and collect money. That was the kind of math I found interesting.

I scrunched my face up, irritated, but quickly forced the frown off my face. I was already jealous of a baby and Penn's pet snake; I didn't want to be jealous of Deepak's growing friendship with Penn, too. I didn't mind him so much. Plus, he was the only person other than Lata Auntie and me who'd witnessed Heena Mavshi being so mean. So, I took a breath and walked toward the boys and their customer.

"Heena Mavshi's acting really—" I stopped abruptly when I noticed the customer was on a shiny blue bike with a stegosaurus helmet.

My stomach dropped.

"Did you know the only thing that scares my dog, Dottie, is snakes? How many of these do you need to sell to get Gertrude a new terrarium, anyway?" Lark asked, in between sips of her lemonade.

That was the connection between lemonade and Gertrude. It was like a fundraiser.

"Like, two hundred of them," Penn said, looking disappointed. "That's why we have to win at Bark at the Park, right?" he asked, looking my way.

I cleared my throat. "Right." I turned to Lark hesitantly, since I didn't know if she would appreciate me being near her when the last time she'd seen me I'd stood by as she was bullied. "Hi, Lark. Are you still singing?" I asked softly.

Lark turned and looked me up and down with her hazel eyes, seeming unbothered to see me again. "Of course I am. My mom says I'm unstoppable."

I breathed easier. She was okay. She was super brave and wasn't going to let one setback stop her. I wished I had some of that in me.

"Mayor Conovan is right," Deepak said to her, looking up from his book.

"I'm singing right after you at Bark in the Park, you know," Lark added, giving me a small smile as she dug into a little bag tied to her handlebars to get her portable microphone out.

"I'm sure you'll do really well," I said, trying to be extra kind to make up for before.

"Thanks. You too." She waved and sped off on her bike, humming loudly and totally off-key into her microphone.

I envied her level of confidence, even if it was ridiculous to not be bothered by what anyone else thought of you. It was sort of how Deepak came across about the things he was interested in, whether it was the history of human poop or a rock collection. It must be nice to be so sure of yourself all the time.

"She told us she's been practicing every day. Should we practice too?" Penn asked. "I don't want Lark to rob us of our first-place ribbon. I need half that prize money. Gertie needs a new terrarium."

"Maybe Deepak can take my place," I sputtered to Penn, desperate for a way out of this. So much for breaking the cause-and-effect chain.

"I think you need to do this," Deepak said.

"Yeah. You know how strict they are about the sign-up," Penn replied, even though when Deepak said I needed to do this, I think he meant conquer my fears.

"Besides," Penn continued, "we wrote all the words after you were mad at your parents for saying no to getting a dog. 'Happy bark day to you' has special meaning to you, so you should sing it," Penn added.

I took a sip of the sour lemonade.

"Gertie deserves more space. Plus, my parents actually took time off work to come to this. And I want our song to be *really* good for them. That means we have to practice." Penn cleared his throat and started to sing. "Bark is for trees. Trees line the park. Dogs like to bark at . . ."

He looked at me, encouraging me with a raised eyebrow.

There was no cobra dirt art to save me from singing this time. I opened my mouth and sang softly, ". . . Bark in the Park."

A flush of sweaty embarrassment crept across my torso, and I quickly stopped, remembering why I had come over to Penn's house in the first place. "I forgot I have to tell you something important. Heena Mavshi was acting super bizarre when I dropped the food off. She was painting cobras over and over. Just like what I saw in our garden bed."

Deepak shrugged. "Art is how she expresses herself. Maybe it's helping her get out some of her feelings about Jatin Uncle's sudden death. Plus, she does have that gigantic painting of a cobra and mongoose in her living room. Maybe she likes them."

"But that's not all," I interrupted, a little irritated. Obviously, I knew about that painting. I had known her way longer than Deepak had. "I'm not sure you're going to like hearing this, Penn, but there's a dead mouse in my backyard and I think Gertrude is the one who killed it."

"Oh no," Deepak said, his eyes growing shiny. "Do you think the poor thing suffered?"

"It has two bite marks in its back, like a snake's fangs, so I'd think so," I said, a little snappier than I had intended, like Aai when she was hangry.

"There's no way Gertrude could escape," Penn said loudly, his face growing red like he was upset for the mouse but even more upset at the allegation.

"It could happen. Remember last summer when someone's pet snake got loose by the Commons, and Reptile Rescue Center caught it eating a mouse?" I countered.

Deepak nodded. "It was before I moved here, but Ashok Dada told me. He handled the rescue and rehab of that snake. But snakes swallow mice whole and digest everything, even their bones. Their stomach acid and enzymes are really strong. The mouse you're describing was not swallowed, just killed. Snakes kill for food and if they're threatened. There's no way the mouse threatened a snake. And if it were a snake, why didn't the snake eat the mouse?"

I pointed at the doggy door in Penn's front door that the previous owners had installed and we had dented, ignoring Deepak. "Remember how mad your dad got when we busted that, pretending it was a soccer goal? What if Gertrude squeezed through and got out?"

Penn shook his head. "Even if she did that, which she didn't, Gertrude doesn't eat mice. She eats eggs."

"Come on," I said, shooing a bug off my forearm. "Whoever heard of a snake who ate eggs instead of animals? Besides, 'snake' has lots of meanings. It's a reptile, but it's also someone who is deceitful. Eating an innocent little mouse is pretty deceitful, and the snake didn't even eat the mouse. It just killed it for fun," I said softly, pretty certain Penn wasn't going to forgive me for pointing the finger at his snake.

"Penn's telling the truth," Deepak said. "Gertrude is an egg-eater snake. They don't kill rodents for fun. It has to be a snake from the woods back here or at the Commons."

"Besides," Penn added, "Gertrude is in my room. She couldn't have escaped just to bite a mouse and then head back into our house and get into her tiny terrarium all by herself."

"If she didn't, there's a vampire running loose around here," I snapped again, before taking a breath. I guess I was still pretty upset at not being included in the lemonade stand.

Penn sighed. "It is so hard convincing you you're wrong

when you want to believe something. This is like when you didn't believe me that paper beats rock when I first moved here."

I paused, remembering how we had gotten into a screaming argument at the playground when we were five over rock, paper, scissors, and our embarrassed dads had to pull us apart. And even though I still felt sad and a little mad that the boys hadn't thought to include me in setting up the lemonade stand, I knew I had to do the right thing and admit my mistake here.

"I'm sorry I jumped to conclusions and thought Gertrude bit the mouse," I said.

Penn looked at me, his eyes softening. "Thanks," he mumbled. "And hopefully that dead mouse is just a one-off thing and there's not really some evil snake slithering around our neighborhood, killing mice for fun and not even eating them."

"Your wish might not come true," Deepak said, stopping just shy of the crow with missing feathers who was walking around something at the very edge of Penn's yard, the side that was in front of half of Heena Mavshi's front yard.

Penn and I exchanged a quick look and hurried over to Deepak's side, startling the crow, who cawed loudly as it flew away.

As it flapped out of view, we could see what Deepak was staring at: another dead mouse with two fang marks in its side.

CHAPTER 16

There were now two dead mice with the same markings. The only time we'd had dead animals in our yards before, they were birds that Paneer, Ashok Ajoba's white cat, attacked. But Paneer died a couple years ago.

Who had hurt them?

I pondered this as I stress-bit the salty, sour, avalyachi supari, made from dried, shredded Indian gooseberry. I gripped the side of my car door. My hands had turned white, sweating and scared, as I sat next to Aaji and Alaap, while Aai drove our family across the Ambassador Bridge to Canada for the chance to eat a mango.

This was something we did every May or June when stinky hapoos amba came into season. The Indian stores in Windsor would get a few crates of the mango from India that was only in season for a couple weeks in a year. We would drive thirty minutes to another country for the chance to bite into one.

The only problem was, to get to Canada, you either had to go in a tunnel, which I was positive was going to collapse on us and fill our car with water from the Detroit River, or you had to go across the Ambassador Bridge. This was by far the worst option out of the two, I thought, as Baba played his Hindi music loudly and Aai kept using her steering wheel controls to lower the volume for Alaap.

"Look how close we are to the side of the bridge," I said. "All it would take is one strong gust of wind to cause us to skid to the edge and flip over. And it would be impossible to get out of the car underwater. Plus, remember a few years ago when they caught a lake sturgeon in the Detroit River and it was the same size as a small shark? That means a small shark could very well get into the Detroit River too and—"

"Not another shark story, please," Baba chuckled.

I frowned, looking at Alaap, who was sleeping next to me, unaware that we could plunge into the river with just the slightest mistake.

I tried to block my scary thoughts and focused on the fact that I was going on an adventure with Aaji.

Aaji was massaging her left hip as Aai went over a bump on the bridge.

"Aai, drive slower, please," I whimpered, swallowing the supari. "Remember Aaji's hip?"

"I'm okay," Aaji said, squeezing my knee. "But thanks."

"I'm glad. Because we have to make good time," Aai replied. "You know they're going to delay us on our way back through the US border to search our car as they let all the other families zoom by. And we had enough of a setback this morning when Baba got rid of the dead mouse."

He shrugged. " I took care of the one in Penn's yard for them, too. I just hope there isn't some wild animal with rabies roaming about, killing those poor mice and then leaving them."

"Rabies? Can we catch that?" I asked. "Because I'm sure Aaji doesn't need that," I added, watching her flinch after the car went over a particularly pothole-filled section of the road.

"What if there's a legion of rabid raccoons living in the woods and coming into our yards at night and then they bite one of us when we come home late from a party and it's dark and—"

"Geetanjali, let's get your mind on something else," Baba said.

Oh no. This meant math problems. I looked at Aaji desperately, hoping she could read my mind and know that the panicked look on my face was equal parts from the fear of heights, the fear of drowning, and the fear of math.

Aaji winked at me, no longer tending to her hip. "Actually, I think we all need to rehearse for our show."

That sounded worse.

"She's right," Aai said. "And while we're at it, you should probably practice your Bark in the Park song, too. I don't think you've practiced once with Penn since you two wrote that song, and it's in less than two weeks."

Aaji's smile disappeared for a second into disappointment. But she caught me looking at her and quickly beamed again.

"That's not right, beta," said Baba, lowering the music's volume for once.

"I did practice. I practiced with him yesterday," I said softly. "I swear," I added.

Aai nodded. "Good," she said, and then began to sing an old Hindi movie song as we finally got off the bridge and went through the Canadian border.

I slowly let go of my grip on the door and wiped my sweaty palms on my shorts, relaxing. That was until Aaji joined in the singing and looked at me.

I had sung yesterday during antakshari and at the lemonade

stand. I could do it again. I took a deep breath, opened my mouth, and sang the next stanza. My voice was shaky and soft, and Aaji put her hand to her ear, gesturing for me to be louder.

Aai took a sharp right at a light at the last minute and turned into a parking lot.

Saved by the mango, I thought, as we piled out of the car and into Mumbai Grocers, a tiny Indian store in a strip mall full of restaurants, a used bookstore, and a nail salon.

The smell of cumin and chili powder greeted us as we walked around the store. Baba went straight to the produce aisle and grabbed three hapoos ambas from the tower of mango crates that people were gravitating toward.

Instead of hanging out by the mango mayhem, I ran my fingers down bottle after bottle of pickles as Baba stood in the long line to check out. There was sweet lime pickle, my favorite, spicy raw mango pickle, stuffed red chili pickle, onion pickle, ginger pickle, a pickle made with raw mango and lotus root and limes, a pickle made from green berries in mustard seeds and oil that tasted sort of like olives, a pickle made of turmeric rhizome . . . I frowned, looking at some of the slivers of turmeric that looked almost snakelike, frozen mid-slither in brine.

"I thought your aai was exaggerating when she said you barely sing these days," Aaji said, reaching above me to squint at the label of the syrupy sweet chhoonda pickle she always made from scratch.

I could feel my cheeks blush warmly as I looked down at my shoes.

Aaji put her arm around me. "I know you have much more to say inside than just that."

I leaned into her frail frame. I felt shy and scared, but I didn't know why. I thought it was just this spiraling outcome of not standing up for Lark and then messing up onstage. Like the American version of the Indian concept of karma. Even though that's not how it really worked in our tradition about karma. In that, your karma from one life affected your next life, not something you did a few hours later.

I just didn't want to experience what I went through at Gudhi Padwa, ever again. If only I could explain that to Aaji. But that would confirm what everyone thought of me, that I always feared the worst and let it get the best of me.

I was opening my mouth to try to find some way to tell my grandmother just a little of what I was feeling and why, when someone bumped into me with a shopping cart.

"Ouch!" I yelped, rubbing my ankle where the wheel had hit me. "Sorry," I added quickly in my high-pitched talking-to-grown-ups voice.

"You don't have to say sorry when you're not at fault, you know," Aaji whispered to me as I started to turn to see who had hit me. "Part of being brave is standing up for yourself."

I paused, frowning. I did say sorry a lot when it wasn't my fault. It just seemed to make the situation easier. I guess confrontation was yet another thing I was afraid of.

But when I saw the scowl on the person who had bumped into me, I felt I had a right to be the tiniest bit afraid.

CHAPTER 17

Are you following us, Heena?" Aaji joked with a smile, gently putting her wrinkled hand on Heena Mavshi's shoulder. I rubbed my right ankle with my left until the stinging stopped.

"How are you feeling?" I asked, scared she might snap at me again like she had when I'd come to her house.

Heena Mavshi shrugged. "Jatin used to call Mumbai Grocers every day mid-May to find out when the hapoos amba would get here," she said, almost like her old self. "Thought I should continue the tradition."

She reached by me to grab a bottle of dark maroon, sweet lime pickle. "Jatin loved my homemade lime pickle," Heena Mavshi said, her right finger now moving rapidly on her thigh like she used to do when she was figuring out a painting. "I used to tell him to just buy it. It was easier. When he collapsed at the airport, I begged and pleaded and prayed so much, hoping he'd be saved. I whispered to him as the medics worked on him. I said, 'Just make it. Live, and I'll prepare the biggest bottle of that lime pickle when we get home . . .'" She trailed off.

I clenched the soft cotton pockets on the sides of my shorts, feeling awful for Heena Mavshi even if she didn't look particularly sad while she told us this story. This was clearly the bargaining stage. I remembered from my picture book that not all the stages happened in the same order for everyone. If Heena Mavshi got the bargaining stage done with already, maybe this chilly anger stage she was in was going to be extra long.

Aaji nodded. "I know what it's like to lose your husband when you're young."

I looked at the Y-shaped lines by the outer corners of Aaji's eyes. I always thought they came from laughing. But my grandfather had died when Aai was about my age. It must have been hard on Aaji. Maybe those lines weren't just from a lifetime of laughing. Maybe they also came from sadness.

"I'm always here if you want to talk," Aaji said quietly.

Heena Mavshi put her arm out like she was going to hug Aaji. That was what I expected from the old Heena Mavshi. Maybe she did just have a few off days. Aaji started to hug Heena Mavshi back, but before they could embrace, Heena Mavshi dodged her and reached for a bottle of ayurvedic chyavanprash behind Aaji instead.

Aaji looked a little confused as Heena Mavshi breezed over the ingredients of the sticky sweet herbal jam. She then jolted her cart away, in a not-sweet-at-all motion, drawing on her thigh with her right hand.

"She's really not acting like herself," Aaji commented, more to herself than to me. "She seemed so fine on the plane, despite what had happened to Jatin. We must be extra kind to her."

Aaji was right. I shouldn't be judging or making up things about her in my head, like I had done with Gertrude and the mice. She was still our family friend. I followed Aaji out the door to join Baba, Aai, and Alaap in the parking lot.

Lata Auntie was there too, and she greeted us with a huge smile and a hug full of the warmth Heena Mavshi was missing. Lata Auntie must be desperate for some kindness after living with Heena Mavshi, I thought as I watched Alaap reach for the mangos and whimper when they were taken out of his reach.

"Poor baby," Aai said, kissing his head. "Next year. You can have it next summer when you're eating solids and it's in season. Okay?"

Apparently, it was not okay. Alaap began to sob.

As Aai nursed him back to sleep, I braced myself for the smell of the hapoos amba. It was strong, like a regular mango about to spoil, and I hated it. Ever since I was little, I was afraid to tell the members of the mango cult this. Especially the life-time members, a.k.a. my family, who traveled to another country just to get a bite of one.

So, I held my breath as Baba cut the mango in the parking lot on the steel plates we had packed. I imagined I was about to eat a nonstinky Kent mango as Aaji passed me a plate. And I reminded myself to just say "mmmm" after I bit into it, to blend in with the rest of the club.

I closed my eyes and bit into my slice as Aai, Baba, and Aaji went on and on about how tasty the mango was. I got ready to suppress the gag that was going to lurch up my throat.

But strangely, I didn't feel like spitting it out. I actually liked the taste. It was sweeter than I remembered. And the smell was kind of nice, less like stinky feet than last summer.

Aaji smiled at me. "You like it?"

I nodded. Maybe my taste buds had changed. And if my taste buds had changed, I was more certain than ever that I could change too.

CHAPTER 18

The next morning I stood before a wall of turtles, tortoises, and lizards at Reptile Rescue Center with Aaji and Alaap, who was starting to fuss in his stroller.

"Almost all of these are rescued pets that people owned and then abandoned in Deadwood and neighboring towns," Ashok Ajoba said, approaching us. "There were so many snakes, we have three rooms full of them."

As a six-lined racerunner with a scar on its tail scampered back and forth in its tiny glass tank, I frowned. I'd never rescue a dog and then dump it in the woods.

Aaji shook her head and clicked her tongue. "I wish people would make sure they can handle the responsibility of pets before getting them."

"Yeah, it's awful. Remember how we helped all those stray dogs in front of your bungalow in Pune?" I asked her.

Aaji grinned. "You were so good at rolling the poli we made them."

"Dipped in milk, of course. And they had the cutest little milk mustaches when they ate."

Aaji laughed. "You are always so caring and thoughtful, Geetanjali. It makes me proud."

I beamed, trying to soak in this moment, and hoping the

next time we went to India and saw a lizard scooting up the walls in Aaji's bungalow, we'd be laughing about how cute the reptiles at the Reptile Rescue Center were.

Alaap frowned and whimpered louder as he squirmed in the stroller. Determined to prove to Aaji I was as caring for my brother as I was for animals, I scooped Alaap up and pointed to a veiled chameleon, hoping Ashok Ajoba wasn't going to take us into a snake room next. I felt bad for the reptiles here. But I could also empathize with the snakes without hanging out next to them.

"Have any mice-eating snakes ever escaped from here?" I asked Ashok Ajoba, trying to see if I could solve the mystery of the murdered mice before any more dead ones showed up.

He shook his head. "The only snakes that leave here go to other rescue centers or to a foster home." He straightened the informational sign next to a map turtle named Cupcake who had a big crack across the top of his shell. "I'm afraid the center isn't going to be able to keep up with the costs this summer," Ashok Ajoba continued. "We have so many fosters taking care of animals we don't have the space for. But we have to cover the costs of the rescue animals' food and medicine and care, even when they're not on our grounds."

Alaap began to whimper like he was going to cry. I swayed with him. "Look at the chameleon. Can you say 'chameleon'?" I asked, but he just fussed louder.

Suddenly, the veiled chameleon began to relieve itself. "Look!" I said to Alaap, even though it was pretty disgusting. "Can you say 'poop'?"

Alaap's eyes widened and he smiled. Had I just discovered

a way to keep him happy? I looked at the squirmy baby in my arms who seemed to be lighting up with delight just by hanging out with me and hearing me say a funny word.

"Poop!" I repeated, and he giggled. "Poop means sheeshee," I said, using the Marathi word for "excrement," and Alaap beamed again. "But poop also means to be tired or stop working, or up-to-date info. So if you were doing a big research project about feces and you were exhausted you could say, 'I'm so pooped from looking up all this poop about poop!'"

Alaap gurgled happily.

"You're a good tai," Aaji said, using the Marathi title for big sister. "And you can be a good neighbor to Reptile Rescue Center."

"How?" I asked as the veiled chameleon did another massive poop.

"They need money. Remember when we raised all that money for the Deadwood Dog Shelter? What if you, Penn, and Deepak did something together to raise funds for Reptile Rescue Center? I couldn't help but notice things were a little . . . different between you and Penn the other morning," Aaji added.

"That's a wonderful idea," Ashok Ajoba exclaimed. "Everyone here would be so grateful for any money you raised for the animals."

I glanced at Ashok Ajoba's bushy white eyebrows, furrowed with concern for the reptiles before him. Then I looked at the map turtle with its cracked shell. I was glad he had a home here and people to care for him. I watched the racerunner flick her hurt tail and felt a lump in my throat. I glanced at the veiled chameleon, who had finally finished emptying her bowels. It was gross. But she was a rescue too. And there were other animals like her who needed help.

"Maybe," I began, with a little hesitation, as Alaap swatted my naagmani necklace. "Maybe we can go door to door and collect cans and donations," I sputtered.

Oh poop. Had I just volunteered us to knock on doors and ask grown-ups to give to a cause? That involved speaking to strangers. That involved a level of confidence I didn't seem to possess at the moment. And that involved hanging out with my best friend and his new friend even though I wasn't sure there was now space for me.

But I had to flush this feeling of dread down the drain. Sure, these animals weren't cuddly bundles of fluff like a dog, but they still deserved a safe place to live and rest and heal. It would just take me using my voice. I could think of it as a practice round for singing in front of a big audience again.

CHAPTER 19

On Saturday, the hottest day of the week, I pulled an old orange wagon whose rusty, wobbly wheels loudly announced themselves on every inch of concrete they rolled over. Penn pushed his own pink plastic wagon, which seemed in much better condition than mine. Deepak carried several cotton tote bags with sayings like BE AN ALLY and I'M A FEMINIST on them.

"I'm burning," I complained as we headed up the driveway of one of the large homes on the far side of our neighborhood.

"We just started," Penn replied, fanning his face. "Besides, I'm hot too. And I could be collecting cans for Gertrude's housing upgrade, but instead I'm here helping the other reptiles. Sometimes you have to be a little selfless for the greater good."

I squeezed the scruffy plastic handle of my wagon, feeling the loose shreds of plastic dig into my palm. What was that supposed to mean? Wasn't I being selfless right now? Raising money for helpless animals? This whole thing was my idea. Well, it was Aaji's idea and sort of a ploy to get me to hang out with Penn and Deepak and make things better in our friendship, but it was still *my* idea to do a can drive.

"Who's going to ring the bell?" I asked, changing the subject. "And what do we say?"

Deepak shrugged, ringing the bell like it was no big deal. "We'll just say what needs to be said. No need to overthink it."

The door opened, and an old lady with gray hair tied up in a bun answered. "Well, hi, kids!" she said enthusiastically. "What can I do for you?"

"Did you know that there's only one population of the six-lined racerunner found in all of Michigan?" Deepak began. "Well, only one population that's known. According to Michigan State University's website, their breeding period just ended and now it's their nesting period."

The woman nodded politely, but her scrunched-up mouth betrayed her confusion. "So you're running a race?" she asked, scratching her head and causing her bun to wiggle.

"Oh no," Deepak replied. "Although I do like running. Did you know a rising sixth grader once ran a mile in five minutes and one second in 2014?"

The woman's face was getting more wrinkled by the moment as her frown deepened. This was not going well at all. My heart began to thump nervously. We had to fix this. I looked at Penn. He needed to say something to get us back on course. But unlike what happened last spring at the park with Lark, this time it didn't feel like Penn and I were on a team. Penn looked at me for a second and then turned away in uncomfortable silence.

And I did the same. Was Penn wishing he was climbing the wall with Deepak instead? Or selling lemonade with Deepak instead? Or doing anything with Deepak instead of me?

"That was the fastest recorded time ever for a ten-year-old," Deepak continued. "I'd have to look up what the average speed is for someone our age, though. I don't know that fact off the top of my head. I do have a good book on sports facts, though."

The woman turned back toward her kitchen. "I have tea on the stove I need to tend to."

"Money!" Penn blurted out.

"Excuse me?" the woman asked.

"Sorry," Penn replied, face flustered with sweat. "We're collecting cans to raise money for Reptile Rescue Center."

"Oh." The woman's face softened. "Well, why didn't you say so earlier? I have a bunch. Hold on."

She shut the door to go retrieve them, and my heart rate started to slow to a less frantic pace.

"We have to come up with a better way to ask for cans," I whispered to Penn and Deepak, pretty sure I was going to upset them with my constructive criticism.

Deepak blushed a little. "Yeah. My way might not have been the best approach. After I told you we don't need to over-think it, I think I began to overthink it."

I paused. Deepak was good at admitting when he was wrong. It seemed a lot easier for him than it was for me when I'd apologized about accusing Gertrude of mouse murder.

Penn's shiny face turned pink. "Did I . . . did I scream 'money' at her?"

I looked at Penn. And in an instant, the distance I was feeling between us temporarily dissolved as we burst into laughter.

The door swung open, and the old lady handed us a paper grocery bag full of cans. "Good luck. Hope you get a lot more!" she said, and waved.

We thanked her and ran off the porch, the cans rattling in the bag.

Penn put the bag in his wagon, glancing inside. "There have to be, like, fifty cans in here!"

"That's five dollars!" I said in a quick feat of math that would have made Baba proud.

"It's a good thing we live in Michigan, where cans are ten cents each. Did you know not every state has bottle bills?" Deepak asked.

Penn and I shook our heads, and we headed up the driveway of the pink brick home next door, with gardens full of pink roses, gold irises, and purple hydrangea bushes.

"So, do we just shout 'money' again? It seemed to work," I joked.

Penn laughed as we left our wagons and stepped up onto the wraparound porch with hanging baskets of ferns, in view of the video camera doorbell. "Let's come up with a better plan this time."

"Why don't you impress them with one of your word definitions?" Deepak asked.

My palms grew sweaty at the thought of sharing them with strangers. "They might think it's weird," I replied, remembering the old lady's face as Deepak bombarded her with lizard facts.

"Just try it," Penn suggested. "Besides, their doorbell is already recording this whole conversation. They'll be disappointed if they don't hear your word definitions."

The door swung open. "He's right," said Lark, standing on the other side of it.

My stomach sank a little. We were at Mayor Conovan's

house. That's why everything looked so fancy. "Okay," I said with a small smile. "Um . . ." I racked my mind for some definitions. Was there one for "money"? Not that I knew off the top of my head. "Reptiles!" I shouted, sounding almost as bizarre as when Penn had shouted "money" at the last house. Or maybe stranger.

Lark raised an eyebrow at me.

"Reptiles mean the animals who are reptiles, of course," I said shakily. "But reptiles can also mean a person no one likes."

"Neat," Lark said. "So, what about reptiles?"

"Reptile Rescue Center needs our help. They don't have enough money to care for all the animals," I stated.

Mayor Conovan rushed to the door. "That's awful!" she said, her hands to her chest. "That place is a Deadwood staple."

I nodded, suddenly remembering another reptile-themed word. "Cold-blooded means an animal that can't regulate their temperature from the inside, like we do. Reptiles are cold-blooded. But cold-blooded also means acting without caring," I said quietly. "And a lot of people acted in a cold-blooded way when they dumped pets they couldn't care for. And those pets don't know how to survive in the wild anymore. Reptile Rescue Center is feeding and helping as many as they can."

I stood up a little taller at the last word I said—"can"—as I made a quick definition-connection. "But we need *cans* so they *can* do the rescue work." I beamed.

Mayor Conovan smiled. "Ooh, I see what you did there. Nice wordplay. And I'll tell you what, in addition to cans, which we *can* give you"—she winked—"I'm going to give you something else to help. One sec."

She disappeared down the marble hall and around the corner, leaving us with Lark.

"I have no clue what she's doing," Lark told us. "Maybe she has one of those giant award money checks stashed away somewhere. Although you'd think I'd have noticed a four-foot-long check leaning against the vacuum or resting on the couch."

Just then, Mayor Conovan returned. She handed us two large garbage bags. "There are at least two hundred cans there," she said.

"Twenty dollars!" Penn whispered.

"And be sure to give the center this," she continued, handing us a familiar-looking neon-green piece of paper.

Deepak took the page, and I glanced over his shoulder. It was the Deadwood Community Grant flyer that Rohan had knocked out of place at the park this past spring.

"It's a ten-thousand-dollar grant to a deserving Deadwood business in need," Lark's mom said. "And we haven't had many applicants."

Penn, Deepak, and I raced down the hilly black path from the Commons toward our homes, cans rattling noisily in our wagons and clinking against one another in Deepak's bags. We had collected over nine hundred cans. Almost a hundred dollars for Reptile Rescue. That would help with at least some of the food and medication costs. And we had done it as a team, and by me speaking up and using my words to help people understand the cause.

Maybe I needed to speak up more and tell Penn I wished he had invited me to make lemonade for Gertrude too. I had proven I could help reptiles, after all. But we'd just had so much fun together. We were all laughing and running and shouting "money" and having the perfect summer day, like we used to. I didn't want to set us back by bringing up my feelings. So, I swallowed hard, shoving those words back down so they couldn't escape.

"I can drop the cans off at the store with my mom on our way to Ashok Dada's for dinner tonight," Deepak offered, holding up the green flyer. "And I'll give him this, too. If the center wins, all the animals will be okay. And we'll know we played a part in helping them."

"That's awesome," Penn replied as we neared my backyard and Heena Mavshi's.

I spotted her in her sunroom, painting away. "I could see why some people find turtles and lizards kind of cute," I said, looking away from Heena Mavshi's house. "But I never quite got why you liked snakes."

Penn's face fell.

"I am kind of warming up to them now, though, after today. It feels good to help. Even snakes. Who knows, maybe when I see one out in the woods, the first thought that jumps into my mind won't be to wonder if it killed a mouse lately."

Penn nodded. "And I'm glad there haven't been any more dead mice."

"Except that one," Deepak said dejectedly, pointing at the grass on the left of the path, in Heena Mavshi's yard.

We walked toward a patch of clover to see a little mouse frozen on its back, eyes wide open, mouth wide open, with two fang marks in its side. Just like the others.

CHAPTER 20

It was two days before Bark in the Park, and I was feeling confined next to Deepak in my dimly lit, cold basement.

Aai was finally easing back into teaching, and we were sitting in a circle around Aai and Aaji with seven other little kids, in a shortened afternoon mash-up class of beginners and seasoned singers.

There were Trisha and Ami, eight-year-old twins. You could only tell them apart because Trisha's thick hair was parted to the left and Ami's hair was parted to the right. Mona, a nervous-looking six-year-old who seemed to have a voice softer than mine, sat next to them. And by her side were Apoorva, Sachit, Deepti, and Divya, inseparable second graders who were wearing shirts with female scientists on them from some cartoon they were all into. Aai played the harmonium as Aaji sang the raags and everyone repeated.

"We for sure have a predator roaming our streets," I whispered to Deepak during a break between songs. He was organizing his raags alphabetically in his pink binder.

"It's weird, that's for sure." Deepak snapped the rings on his binder shut.

"What's that hanging on the family picture?" Aai asked as she reached for her binder.

Busted.

"Aaji made it because I was sneezing in the old one," I said hesitantly as Aaji gave me a reassuring wink.

"It's really cool," said Deepak, admiring the art. "I noticed it at the party."

"Thank you." Aaji beamed; I fiddled with the dangling strings at the bottom of my jeans, waiting for Aai to get mad.

"It's like how Heena Auntie expresses herself through art. We express ourselves through singing. And you express yourself through art *and* singing," Deepak hypothesized to Aaji. "Although I guess I sort of express myself through scientific facts, too."

"It looks funny," laughed Trisha; wrinkles spread across Aai's forehead.

"Yeah," said Mona. "Like a kid made it."

I frowned a little at Mona's comment. I could see how irritated Aai was getting from the way she dramatically cleared her throat. I knew I had to do something fast, or else I'd be in trouble and Aai would lecture Aaji and me all about how much she paid for the photo studio package. "What's Raag Naagshakti?" I blurted out.

"What?"

"Naag-shakti?" asked Ami. "Like, snake power?"

"Oh yeah," Deepak added. "I was curious about it too after Lata Auntie requested it at the party. I didn't find anything about it online when my mom and I looked it up that night."

"I can play it for you," Aaji said, scooching toward the harmonium. "Help ease your curiosity."

But Aai wasn't budging from her spot in front of the instrument. "It's a very complicated, rare raag. So, let's sing an easier one. Hum Ko Mann Ki Shakti Dena in Raag Kedar."

Aai began playing the harmonium, and we all started to sing the prayer that asked for our minds to be strengthened and to make us free from dishonesty and full of forgiveness. (But every time Aai taught this song to her youngest students, a few kids giggled anytime they said "mann ki." They didn't need my love of looking up word meanings to know what "mann ki" sounded like in English.)

"Monkey?" asked Deepti, smiling.

A sharp look from Aai stopped her. "Mann. Like our minds," she added, pointing to her head, saying the word that definitely rhymed with "run." "Ki. Possessive," she continued. "As in apostrophe *s*. It doesn't sound like monkey if you pronounce it right. This is a serious song. Let's not make it silly, okay? I don't want to see any of this next month during our performance at Accent Mark in the Park." She did a flourish on the harmonium before whispering to me. "And *you* are lucky enough to get to practice onstage this Friday, Geetanjali." The smile slipped from my face.

Aai went back to singing, and all the kids managed not to smile and join in. All except for me. Every time the class sang "humko mann ki shakti dena," I thought of singing "humko *monkey* shakti dena," please give me monkey strength. Before I could help myself, I began to laugh, louder than my voice had ever been in class today.

"Geetanjali," Aai begged.

I almost frowned, thinking about how Aai would have probably laughed at how similar "monkey" and "mann ki" sounded before Alaap was born.

"Make good choices, please," she continued. "There are younger kids watching you." But I couldn't stop. It was the silly giggles. The kind you couldn't finish until they were all laughed out. The kind Baba and Jatin Kaka got about the Costco coupon book at Gudhi Padwa. And Aai was not happy.

"I think you should take a break from the class for today, Geetanjali."

"But . . . ," I said, wiping away a happy tear from my eye.

Aai just nodded her head toward the stairs, dismissing me.

Deepak gave me a sympathetic look. The rest of the kids observed me in shock. Sick of all the stares, I quickly stood up and ran up the basement steps, sad tears stinging my eyes.

"Geetu . . . ," Aaji called after me.

"It's okay, Aaji," I called back, although it wasn't. I was embarrassed and mad at Aai for kicking me out of class, even though class felt like torture since I didn't enjoy singing anymore.

I shut the basement door and blinked away my tears. This wasn't worth crying over. This was a lucky break. I didn't need to sing with a bunch of little kids and Deepak to prove to myself that I could sing with Aaji onstage before she left. And I didn't need to be belittled by a grumpy mother who spent all her time taking care of my little brother.

Baba, home from work early to take care of Alaap, was pointing out the birds outside to my brother from the kitchen table. "Bathroom break?" he asked.

I shook my head. "Aai break," I said as I stormed out to the garage.

CHAPTER 21

I grabbed my helmet, stepped around the empty mouse house (stale cracker still inside), and found my beat-up bike that we had bought at a garage sale. I furiously rode down the driveway, pausing by Penn's just as he kicked a soccer ball into the wobbly doggy door on his front door, scoring in our makeshift goal.

"Do you wanna play soccer?" I asked him.

Penn shook his head. "I was just trying to get it out of the grass so the LawnBot didn't hit it."

"Do you want to ride bikes?" I asked, hoping he could see I really needed a friend right now. Hoping it would be just like when we did our can drive and laughed and hung out all day like we used to.

"I'd love to, but I actually have to make sure the robot mows the grass right, and then I'm meeting Deepak at the Wall of Doom after your class," Penn said, bending down to start the round lawn-mower robot his mom's company was developing.

He didn't ask if I wanted to come to the wall, just like he didn't invite me to help with their lemonade stand. I was already mad at Aai. I didn't want to be annoyed with Penn, too, especially not after the progress we had made this week. So I quickly changed the subject. "Have you seen any other dead mice?"

"Nope. I was practicing for Bark in the Park. You know. Since it's in two days."

I gripped the bike handles tightly. "Of course, I know that," I said. Why was Penn in such a rotten mood? "Did you think I wouldn't show up?"

"Well, you haven't wanted to practice with me," Penn said softly, keeping his eyes trained to his lawn.

I sighed. "We already practiced at the lemonade stand." Why did Penn want to practice so much? It was just a little town concert, and he hadn't uttered a word about practicing when we were doing our can drive.

"You sang one line!" Penn replied.

I scraped a tiny wood chip out of the heel of my shoe on the hot concrete below. One line was almost the entire one-minute song! Besides, I sang the whole thing at the park in spring, and before that when I wrote it, hadn't I? "Why are you trying to fight after we had so much fun with our can drive?" I muttered.

"I'm not trying to fight," Penn said, louder than I expected. "I just looked at the calendar this morning and realized how soon the performance is. I'm nervous and just wish I had a little support here before we go onstage. I'm not a professional like you, you know."

I looked down, opened my mouth, and sang quickly: "Bark is for trees. Trees line the park. Dogs like to bark at Bark in the Park. So park yourself in this spot. While Spot wags his tail. Because in this tale he's happy, so happy bark day to you." Finished, I looked up and gave him a smile that was almost as icy as Heena Mavshi. "How's that?"

Penn shrugged, confused. "Good, I guess. A little fast. But

I'm glad you still remember the words. I'll see you Friday." He didn't smile like he normally would have. He just followed the LawnBot to the strip of grass by the woods in his backyard and waved bye.

A hot flush spread across my neck. I pushed aside everything that was going wrong this summer and pushed equally hard on my bike pedals. I rode my bike up the sidewalk, avoiding the spot three houses down where a concrete square was inches higher, thanks to some tree roots. I was in no mood to wipe out, even if I did have a helmet on.

I took a deep breath in, the sun warming my face, until I was finally feeling a bit of confidence seep back . . . and then the bottom of my jeans snagged on the pedal. My bike fell over, taking me down with it.

The concrete scraped my palms. I knew there would be little pebbles to wash out of my beat-up hands. My jeans were torn too, white denim strings tinged in red from the blood oozing out of my raw kneecaps. Black spots fluttered before my eyes. My ears were ringing. Everything stung, and I knew if I stood up, I would fall right back down.

"Oh no! Let me help you!" a voice called out from behind me.

I wiped my nose and turned to see Lata Auntie returning home from a walk with Heena Mavshi. Heena Mavshi was listening to Hindi movie music from her phone and swaying to it as they strolled.

Heena Mavshi passed by me without a hint of the concern, the opposite of how she'd acted backstage at Gudhi Padwa. The wound on Heena Mavshi's upper back peeked out just above the collar of her peacock-colored kurta. The gash had a dark purple scab over it that was perfectly round. She caught my eye, a look of annoyance flashing across her face, as she tossed her sheer yellow odhni over her neck so the scarf dangled over the gash. But I could still see it.

I glanced down at the cuts on my knees, stinging with fresh blood. Forget calling me "shona"—Heena Mavshi didn't even ask if I was okay.

"That looks messier than the red paint I spilled all over the sunroom," Heena Mavshi muttered, entering her house and slamming the door shut.

How was I supposed to go about my summer, making memories, when things were so terribly off?

CHAPTER 22

With Heena Mavshi tucked away in her house, I sat on her porch with Lata Auntie, watching cars pull up in my driveway to pick up the kids from Aai's singing class. Deepak was already heading down the path with Penn to the Wall of Doom. I watched as each little kid emerged from our house with a huge smile on their face at the sight of their moms and dads. I used to have the same look, before Aai was crabby and sleep-deprived.

"Better now?" asked Lata Auntie as she put the last Band-Aid on.

I nodded. She was being so nice, totally different from the way Aai had been with me earlier. And I knew she understood what it was like to be embarrassed by Aai.

"Thanks for helping me," I replied. My voice was high and shaky as I pretended to yawn; I wanted to stretch back and look inside the house for any signs of what Heena Mavshi was up to, but I couldn't see her.

"All set to sing at Bark in the Park?"

"Yeah," I said, my voice wavering.

"Must be nice to sing with a friend. Strength in numbers and all that. I'm lucky Heena agreed to help me volunteer at Bark in the Park. I'm scared of dogs."

I tried not to react to this confession. But something about the fact that even a grown-up could get scared and nervous made me feel better. Made me feel less alone. Maybe that's what Lata Auntie meant by strength in numbers.

"Is Heena Mavshi's bite okay?" I squeaked uncertainly, figuring if Lata Auntie could tell me about one of her fears, maybe I could ask her about one of mine.

"What bite?" Lata Auntie asked.

"On her back."

"Oh, her birthmark," she said quickly, just like she had the other day when I had seen it while Heena Mavshi painted cobras in her sunroom.

I normally wouldn't have pushed back to an auntie or uncle. But I had to speak up. Heena Mavshi would have done the same for me if something was wrong with me. "Birthmarks don't bleed, though," I said softly.

Lata Auntie leaned against the brick wall of the porch. "You're right." She sighed. "I saw bedbugs in her room."

I shuddered.

"I think things have been hard for her, being alone without Jatin, keeping up with all the improvements the house needs." Lata Auntie shook her head. "I know you offered to help her with the yard and she turned it down, but she does need help. The house is a mess. She told you about the spilled paint. There's dust everywhere. I'm trying to clean and help her. And then the bedbugs . . . I've already called someone to take care of them. And her bite is okay. I've talked to a doctor about it. It's just that every now and then her clothes rub up against it and irritate it."

I nodded, feeling for Lata Auntie. She was so nice to take care of her childhood friend like this. I remember when my aaji on Baba's side was sick, my atya in India was exhausted taking care of her. Baba had felt so bad for his sister. He'd said being a caretaker is really tough.

"She's been so irritable lately," Lata Auntie said, maybe feeling good to finally have someone to talk to. "And probably really sad, too. I don't know how to even talk to her about what she's dealing with." Lata Auntie crouched down to pack up the box of Band-Aids. "I suppose being brave has never been my strong suit."

I tried to take another look for Heena Mavshi, but Lata Auntie quickly stood up again, blocking my view. "Can I walk you home, dear?"

I wondered if Lata knew more about Heena Mavshi than what she was telling me.

Before I could respond, I spotted Aai at the top of our driveway, bouncing Alaap in the wrap. Then she noticed me and Lata Auntie.

"What happened?" she asked, rushing toward me, putting her hand on my elbow in concern.

"She fell off her bike," Lata Auntie replied, standing up to walk my bike over.

"Those are a lot of Band-Aids. Are you okay?" Aai asked, hugging me tight and leading me back to our house.

I nodded, still a little annoyed that Aai had made me leave earlier.

"Poor thing. It was a bad fall," Lata Auntie said, following Aai into the garage to park my bike.

"Thanks for taking care of her. I was in class and . . ." Aai trailed off, probably remembering how she had kicked me out just for laughing and having a little fun. "I'm sorry, Geetanjali," she said, opening the door. "I know you and Aaji are helping. I'm so tired these days, I . . . I didn't mean to take it out on you."

I shrugged, embarrassed Aai was apologizing to me in front of Lata Auntie. "It's okay."

"What's that sound?" Lata Auntie asked. "Is someone singing?"

I turned my head toward the den, across from the laundry room, where Baba recorded his radio program.

"I'm surprised you could hear that," Aai said, opening the laundry room door so I could hear the faintest sound of my dad's radio voice. "Abhishek is interviewing my mom."

Lata Auntie beamed, stepping inside. "Well, I couldn't hear it that well, but the floor was vibrating, so I felt it." She looked down at her feet. "Um, I hate to bug you, but . . . can I take a peek?"

Aai nodded, and Auntie followed the sound to the den door.

Aai stayed back with Alaap, who was making way too many cooing noises to be around the microphone recording in the den. I followed curiously, though, trying to ignore my throbbing knees and stinging palms. I watched as Lata Auntie put her ear to the den door and smiled, eyes twinkling. "No one can tell a story like your aaji." She nodded. "They just finished." Lata Auntie cracked the den door open.

"Lata! What a wonderful surprise," Aaji said.

Baba turned to us, his headphones on next to the big black

machine he recorded interviews with. "We just have to wrap things up," Baba said, putting a finger to his lips so we'd be quiet.

I nodded, blowing on the tiny scrapes on my hand that Lata Auntie had neglected to bandage.

"This was a fascinating interview," Baba said into his microphone. "But we're unfortunately out of time. I hope next time we can chat a little more about what it was like when you went to the Filmfare Awards. Thank you for doing your son-in-law such an honor and gracing *Geetanjali* with your voice."

"Just make sure you tell everyone how wonderful I am when they make mother-in-law jokes," Aaji retorted in Hindi.

Baba and Aaji laughed and he pressed a switch. "All set." He smiled, taking his headphones off.

"Wow. So this is where the interviews happen, huh?" Lata Auntie said, eyeing the hundreds of old Hindi movie records, cassette tapes, and CDs lining the shelves.

"When I can't get to the studio, yes," Baba said anxiously as Lata Auntie rubbed her fingers over his priceless old record covers.

"Do you take requests?" Lata Auntie asked a little hesitantly. "I was hoping you could play one of your mother-in-law's most famous songs for my birthday. It's on July fourteenth."

"The day after Accent Mark in the Park!" Aaji exclaimed as Aai entered the room with Alaap.

Lata Auntie nodded. "And it's a big one," she added.

"Fifty?" asked Aaji.

Lata Auntie laughed. "I wish!"

"You can't possibly be older than that. Now, which song do you want?" Aaji asked.

Lata Auntie bit her lip and gave an apologetic cringe. "You won't be upset?"

Aaji groaned playfully.

"I know. I'm sorry I keep asking to hear Raag Naagshakti. I just know how much it would have meant to my mom, and I'm missing her as my birthday approaches. After she passed away, I moved to Nagpur to live with my aunt. I only made a few trips back to Pune, but you weren't performing it then. You must be so annoyed by me asking so many times. It's just that I grew up hearing how only two people alive today could still sing that song." Lata Auntie turned to me. "Unless you can sing it too, Geetanjali? That would make three people alive today who can still sing it."

"No." I giggled awkwardly, even though there was no reason to be laughing.

"Then my only hope is you and Veena*ji*," Lata Auntie said, putting her hands in a namaste to beg Aaji. "Please say yes. Please?"

Aai smiled politely. "July fourteenth is a couple of weeks away still. Let's see what happens."

CHAPTER 23

The next morning, as my knees healed from the bike accident, I bounced Alaap in my arms in the kitchen, occasionally whispering "poop" to him in a funny voice to get him to giggle. Aaji sat at the kitchen table, sorting lentils on a plate for our dinner.

I watched as her gold bangles slid down her wrinkly arms, trying to soak in the sound of the melodious clanging. I wanted to keep that sound with me forever. It reminded me of watching Aaji wave down a rickshaw to take us to see the latest Hindi movie in Pune. Or of Aaji bowling a cricket ball to me in her yard there. It reminded me of her showing me how to make rangoli designs outside the front door with colored powder as parrots and bulbul birds called out all around us. Or even of her swatting at the hungry mosquitoes that buzzed around our faces in the evening outside her home when we were trying to smell all the different kinds of jasmine Aaji grew in her garden.

I had to add more memories to this list before the summer was up.

"Aaji," I asked. "Remember when we won the puran poli eating contest?"

Aaji laughed. "How could I forget? We both had stomachaches all night!"

"But we had stomachaches as winners," I said with a grin. "That was all that mattered. I know we can't do that again. Aai would for sure get mad at me for making you eat a bunch of puran poli. But I thought we could still have some together. And maybe you can teach me how to make it?"

Aaji looked up from the plate of orange and green lentils. "Now, that sounds like a fun summer day."

We spent the rest of the morning cooking Bengal gram into a paste with sugary sweet jaggery and cardamom. I helped Aaji mix wheat flour with water to make the dough. We scooped the sweet filling into the balls of dough, and then we rolled the dough out, like we'd done for stray dogs in Pune without the filling, and cooked it on an iron tava.

When it was time for our family lunch, I watched as Baba spooned toop onto a steaming hot puran poli for Aai. The clarified butter began to trickle like liquid gold all over the sweet flatbread. Aai gobbled her puran poli down, pausing every now and then to tell me how good it was and how proud she was of me for making it.

"I'll make this for you next year," I said to Alaap, who was curiously eyeing our lunch from Aaji's arms.

"It's good, isn't it?" Aaji asked, taking her last bite. "And we didn't even get stomachaches this time."

"I kind of want to eat more even if I do get one," I said, licking the sweet specks of cardamom and jaggery off my teeth.

"Tond dhua," Aai said, finishing off her puran poli as she instructed me to rinse my mouth like we always did after eating.

I nodded, getting to my feet and taking Aaji's empty plate to the sink. I inhaled deeply as a breeze from the patio screen door carried in the smells of the mogra outside. "This feels so much like Pune, doesn't it? We're just missing the sounds of parrots and bulbuls."

"Makes me think of all the fun we had there together," Aaji said, handing Alaap to Baba and rising to wash up.

"I know we can't play cricket, but we could watch a Hindi movie tonight and make some rangoli outside right now. Just like we used to. I even have that old book you had given me last time I came to Pune, the one with the rangoli patterns in it."

"Just when I thought this day couldn't get any better." Aaji smiled.

As the scent of jasmine and puran poli swirled around me, mixed with the chirping birds, Alaap's laughter, and the jingling of Aaji's gold bangles, I had to agree.

CHAPTER 24

On the front porch, Aaji drew a bunch of white dots with the rangoli powder bunched up in her hand until it formed a grid. Kind of like when you'd draw a bunch of dots to play dots and boxes.

I squatted next to her, feeling the sticky beginnings of a scab on my knee stretching a bit. I thumbed through the rangoli pattern book, the one with thin, yellowing pages from Aai's childhood that Aaji had given me the last time I had visited her in Pune. I found a rangoli design with geometric flowers in the corner and lots of diamonds in the center.

"How about this one?" I asked.

"Perfect," Aaji replied.

I took a handful of white powder and, in sync with Aaji, started drawing the outlines of the shapes on one half of the grid as Aaji did the other side.

"Maybe we can squeeze in some ice cream later this week?"

Aaji yawned as she grabbed some bright pink powder and began filling in a flower. "That sounds like a plan."

As I filled the remaining half of a diamond outline with purple powder, I wished that this perfect day with Aaji would never end.

• • •

Later that afternoon, as Aaji napped, I decided to stop by Penn's house. Penn didn't answer the door, so I cut across the creek in his yard and tried Deepak's home, but no one was there, either. Knowing the boys and their obsession with a certain wall, I knew where they had to be if they weren't home.

I sprinted up the black path toward the Commons, ignoring the pain in my bruised knees, eager to fix things once and for all. I was certain an invitation to make rangoli together on one of our porches or a leftover puran poli treat would be just the thing to get us back to how we used to be. I wanted Penn to know that he was still my best friend and that he could count on me too.

I got to the top of the hill, my bangs flopping in my face, and then came to a stop at the playground. As expected, Penn and Deepak were at the top of the wall. They didn't notice me, though.

They were too busy singing.

Why would they be singing here after what happened with Rohan and his friends? I looked around. No one was at the shelter or on the playground. I chewed on my cheeks and walked quietly toward them, trying to hear what they were singing over the songs of birds.

"Bark is for trees," sang Penn shakily.

I crouched behind the slide, out of sight.

"Louder," Deepak said enthusiastically. "You've got this. No one is going to accuse you of howling. You can do it!"

"Trees line the park," Penn sang, a little steadier, before stopping. "I can't. Can you just sing it with me?"

"You can. But, yes, I'll sing it with you here," Deepak replied. "But you're on your own at Bark in the Park."

On his own? What about me? Did I just not count anymore?

"Well, hopefully not really on your own. Geetanjali will help you through that performance tomorrow," Deepak added. Then he sang with Penn, so loudly, I could barely hear Penn's voice under his: "Dogs like to bark at Bark in the Park. So park yourself in this spot."

I felt a hot burning sensation in my throat. This was the song *I* had written. To sing with Penn. I knew I hadn't been great about practicing with Penn. But seeing Deepak sing my part of the song made my throat hurt and tears sting my eyes.

Deepak spread his hands out in a Bollywood pose for the grand finale: "While Spot wags his tail. Because in this tale he's happy, so happy bark day to you!"

I needed to get out of there.

Cheeks burning, I ducked under the slide and raced toward the black path.

"Is that Geetanjali?" I heard Penn ask faintly over the birds.

But I didn't look back. I just kept running, composing a new song as I raced away from the boys: *Bark is for trees. Trees line the park. Penn's at a park. Pens are for writing. Looks like Penn's written our friendship off.*

CHAPTER 25

The next day, Aaji, my parents, and Alaap went over to Deepak's house to have tea with his mom. That was the last place I wanted to go, so I decided to try to help out with Heena Mavshi's yard. Perhaps neater plant beds would put her in a better mood. And maybe helping out would put me in a better mood about Penn and Deepak.

I crouched down by her front garden bed with a bucket and some weeding tools. I gently moved a roly-poly out of my way and scooted down around the patio, plucking weeds, rehoming earthworms, avoiding centipedes, until I finally neared the sunroom.

The crow with the missing feathers was sitting on its roof, cawing loudly at a hawk that was circling above, when I saw a sudden movement in the open window above me. I cautiously walked toward it. The crow took off with a start as I got close enough to see inside. Heena Mavshi's fingers were covered in red. I gasped, dropping the dirt-covered trowel. Heena Mavshi turned toward me. Without breaking eye contact, she put her finger to the canvas behind her and started drawing squiggle after squiggle. I picked up the trowel and reminded myself it was just finger paint and not blood.

"I like your painting, Heena Mavshi," I said, lying through

my teeth. What was there to like about bloody squiggles all over a canvas?

Heena Mavshi scoffed at me through the screen. "You'll like it a lot more when it becomes your reality." With that, she turned her back to me and continued painting her squiggles off the canvas, over and over, with the same frenetic energy she had the first day I'd seen her paint since she'd come back from vacation.

It was creepy and unnerving and so odd. *Why was Heena acting this way?* This didn't just seem like the stages of grief. I backed away, grabbed my full bucket of weeds and tools, and booked it toward my house.

Safely in my room, I sat on my bed, trying to figure out what Heena Mavshi was talking about. A bunch of red squiggles was going to become my reality?

I opened my notebook, flipping past the facts Baba and Aai would make me memorize every summer, like the state capitals and the world capitals. It was time to write down everything I knew about the weird things happening on my street.

- *Heena Mavshi is in the middle of her stages of grief (she's mean and not her usual warm self), but it seems like it is something more than just that.*
- *She has a bloody, round gash on her back.*
- *She's obsessed with painting snakes.*
- *She said the squiggly lines she painted would soon be my reality.*
- *Three mice found in our yards were dead and had fang marks.*

• *Snakes have fangs.*

I sighed. This wasn't helping me solve what was going on. Nothing here made any sense or even seemed connected except for the fact that Heena Mavshi was drawing snakes and I had suspected a snake had killed the mice. Even though, as Deepak said, snakes kill mice and eat them—they don't just kill them for fun—so maybe it wasn't a snake at all.

I wished I could figure out what Heena Mavshi was trying to say through her art this time. Maybe that would give me a clue about how to fix this.

I turned to my bookcase, where I always went for answers when I was stuck on something for school. Well, unless it was a math problem, in which case I'd be asking Baba for help.

I crouched down and ran my finger across the hundreds of titles in my bookshelf, seeing if I had a book on snakes. There was a picture book about a fictional snake named Slither and a hilarious graphic novel about a snake who goes to outer space. Neither of those would be helpful. My eyes widened as I stood up. There was one book that might help.

Aaji's book.

I grabbed the little binder and got to the section on the naagmani. The page was slightly less scary in the daylight than the first time I'd tried to read it. I turned to the next page to see the poem again, but it was just the words to a Marathi nursery rhyme Aaji had sung to Alaap the other day, about the peacock sitting on your hand, eating a seed, drinking water, and flying away.

I looked back at the naagmani page. In between it and the

nursery rhyme, in the crack, was a torn halo of paper still bound to the middle ring of the binder.

Why was my family ripping pages out of books? We didn't destroy books. They gave us knowledge. They had to be respected. Although I guess this was technically a binder full of things Aaji had written down, so it wasn't exactly a book, but still. It had a story in it, like a book. Where were these mystery pages and what was on them that they needed to be removed?

I set the little binder down and headed across the hall to Aaji's room. I could hear her snoring loudly. The shrikhand we'd had at lunch, made by straining homemade yogurt in a cheesecloth until it is as thick as Greek yogurt and then sweetened with sugar and spiced with cardamom and saffron, was so heavy it must have really knocked her out.

I reached my hand out to wake her but quickly stopped. Aaji looked exhausted, the wrinkles on her face looking deeper than ever before. It wouldn't be nice to wake her. I could ask her about the missing page when she woke up.

I was turning to head out when I spotted the green pishwi on the dresser. Aaji hid the sugary fennel seeds she didn't want Aai getting upset about in the bag. It seemed like the perfect hiding spot for other stuff too.

I bent down, my bruised knee aching a little, and looked into the opening in the frumpy green cloth tote. Sure enough, there were pages in them. Pages with three holes.

I reached my hand toward the opening but stopped. Was this stealing? No. Aaji gave me that binder. And the pages hadn't been in the bag when I'd seen the buddishep in them the day her flight had landed, so they must have been taken out after. So they were almost stolen from me. Except my aaji would not steal from me. I was certain it was more like she was trying to protect me from being the family joke again in case the pages scared me and activated my imagination.

I'd just borrow them to help Heena Mavshi and could put them back before Aaji even noticed they were missing. I reached into the bag, pulled out the pages, trying not to make a sound. And then I tiptoed as fast as I could, back to my room.

I opened my window, letting the fresh air in, and sat on the carpet in the yellow prism full of warm sunlight. "Bring on the snake stories," I whispered before looking at the first page. It was the poem I'd already read.

> *Beware the ichchhadhari naagin*
> *and her vengeful bite*
> *She wants to stay human*
> *She's full of spite.*
> *The cobra's song*
> *Will fill you with fright*
> *She'll take what's yours*
> *Maybe even tonight*
> *Shambhar is the number*
> *after which her light*
> *will eternally be bright*
> *And you'll forever be a saap*
> *Much to her delight*

This didn't seem to relate to any of Heena Mavshi's snake drawings. Or any dead mice. I flipped to the next page.

Her body is cold
Cold-blooded
Cold-hearted

Her anger is fiery
forked
un-guarded

Her bite is venom
Poison
Darted

Once in possession
Of teen dear things
It's too late
to stop what she's
        started

None of this made sense. It was just a chapter full of creepy snake poetry.

"Are you enjoying the book?" Aaji's voice asked from behind me with a little yawn.

I gasped, looking up at her. "I found the pages you took out," I said, the confession slipping out before I could even stop it.

Aaji smiled, taking her time to sit cross-legged on the floor next to me, her knees cracking as she rubbed her hip. "I decided to edit the book after I published it. Your aai was a little upset with me that I had told you . . . so many things. She said it would just give you nightmares." She patted my head and tucked my bangs to the side. "I hope you're not scared?"

I shook my head. "No. I mean, a little. But there aren't ichchhadhari naagins in Michigan."

"No. They're not," Aaji said gently. "I got worried the weekend I landed, when you were talking about being up at night and seeing Heena in her yard. I thought if I could hide scary things from you, maybe you'd get out of this fearful phase faster."

A phase. "Phase" had a lot of meanings. It could be the way a planet or the moon looked based on how much of it could be seen. It could mean to do something slowly. But it could also mean one part of a bunch of events. A stage. Like the stages of grief. And if it was a stage, that meant I'd be over it eventually.

I scooted a little closer to Aaji, letting more of the sunbeam fall on my legs, warming me. I opened the binder rings and slipped the pages back into their place, proud of myself for reading the entire ichchhadhari naagin story. But I couldn't do this alone. As much as I hated to admit it, I needed Penn and Deepak's help. I needed us to get out of the weird friend phase and back into our normal friendship phase, before it was too late. It was going to take the three of us to figure out what was going on with my next-door neighbor.

CHAPTER 26

On Friday, I gobbled up a lunch of kala channa, the tiny, dark-brown variety of chickpeas, a spicy and tangy cauliflower pickle Aaji made, broccoli bhaji, poli, and aamras, my favorite summer treat made by blending sweet mangoes and spicing them with keshar and cardamom. Then Aaji and I split a pint of ice cream from the freezer and headed out with Alaap while Aai and Baba stayed home to catch up on their mail and bills.

"Are you ready to perform this evening?" Aaji asked as we walked around our neighborhood.

I shrugged, still tasting the mint chocolate chip ice cream on my back teeth. "Bark in the Park will be quick and easy," I replied, trying to convince myself this was true. In reality, I was still nervous about singing with Penn, especially because I was so upset with him, even if I should have practiced with him more.

"I'm glad to see you're being so helpful," Aaji said to me as I pushed Alaap's car-seat stroller up the black path to the Commons.

"I'm trying," I huffed, a little winded. "I want to help Heena Mavshi, too."

Aaji nodded, putting a hand on the stroller to help me. "I

know. I'm proud of you. Your baba told me that you weeded there."

"I figured she'd like help her with her yard," I said slowly, unsure if Aaji would believe me if I started talking about the other things Heena Mavshi had said to me or all the creepy snakes she'd drawn, or if she'd just blame it on my imagination. "I think something is wrong."

"What do you mean?" Aaji asked as we got to the top of the hill where the path split into three routes.

In the distance the sound of kids laughing at the Commons could be heard. I glanced at the Wall, but Penn and Deepak weren't there. The Bark in the Park talent show would start in a few hours. Were they hanging out at one of their houses, singing my song again, practicing together?

"Let's go this way, Aaji," I said, leading her down the path to the left, which opened up on the east side of our neighborhood, near the shops in downtown Deadwood. "I mean, Heena Mavshi is acting strange."

"I've had chaha with her a few times now. She seems fine. Sad, and not as talkative as normal, but okay. She has emotions she must sort out within herself to deal with Jatin's death."

I shook my head as we exited our neighborhood and headed down the street. "It's more than that. She isn't making me paintings anymore."

"Give her some time," Aaji replied.

I sighed as we took a turn and passed Good Doggy. Should I tell Aaji what Heena was painting? Only scary cobras and not the pretty art that she used to paint? I had no concrete proof to convince the grown-ups in my life that Heena Mavshi wasn't herself and that it was more than just grief. They were too busy with Alaap to pay attention, and too eager to blame my inventive, fearful mind for anything I did notice.

"Let's go in here," I said, motioning toward Reptile Rescue Center a few buildings down. "I want to check out their library." Aaji followed me in as I continued. "This is more than just her moods or her not giving me a painting, Aaji." I pushed Alaap past the room full of lizards, pointing to the green signs with a boa constrictor wrapped around a book. "Heena Mavshi *is* making art."

As we entered the small room with six bookshelves on reptiles and a couple tables and chairs, we saw Ashok Ajoba behind the counter, talking to a redheaded woman with glasses. Her name tag said MRS. CHARTERS: DIRECTOR. He gave me a wave and greeted Aaji with a namaskar as we passed.

"I saw her making cobra paintings at her house," I continued. "And she had dozens and dozens of practice cobra paintings on note cards," I added. "And I'm pretty sure she's been drawing squiggles on her leg with her finger, *and* she's got this awful bite on her back."

"Your ajoba used to bend his arm over and over again anytime he was riding his scooter. It was just a habit. He started doing it as a kid and was never able to stop. And perhaps she scraped her back on something or it's a bad bug bite."

I shook my head. "She's never painted just one thing before. And in the same color." I grabbed a book called *Snake Facts* and rested it on a table near Aaji, when I suddenly remembered something Heena Mavshi had said. "Aaji, Heena Mavshi said no one understood her art like you and me. Any idea what a canvas full of red squiggles could mean?"

Aaji scratched her head. "Red usually means something dangerous or powerful. Sometimes blood, maybe death—" She looked at me and quickly stopped. "I mean, red could also just be a pretty color. And a bunch of squiggles could just be a pattern."

"Or a basic way of drawing a snake," I added, pointing to the page I was on that had a snake drawing by the author's toddler next to some facts. I flipped through the book, skimming the pictures, and came to a stop on a page about venomous fangs. There was an image of a human leg with two round bloody holes in it from a snakebite.

I shivered. "This looks just like the bites on those mice," I said, changing the topic from Heena's drawings. "Aaji. I think our street has a snake problem."

CHAPTER 27

I stood on Penn's porch, frantically ringing his doorbell, ready to have a big, scary talk with him about fixing whatever was going on so that I could then have a scary talk with him about our scary snake problem.

"Geetanjali, honey?" Penn's mom's voice called out from their video doorbell. "A little easy on the doorbell, please."

"Sorry, Mrs. Witherspoon. Is Penn home? I need to talk to him."

"I think he's gone to the movies, sweetie," she replied. "But I know he's excited to see you at Bark in the Park this evening."

I nodded. "Thanks, Mrs. Witherspoon." My belly dropped. I had assumed we would walk to Bark in the Park together, like we did every summer. But things were clearly different this summer.

A few hours later, I was surrounded by dogs. There were scrappy little Chihuahuas, big dogs with paws that demanded shaking, and furry lap dogs with wagging tails and slobbery tongues. Despite all the stinky breath, I had the hugest grin on my face as Aaji and I petted as many dogs as we could at Bark in the Park.

"You know my mother used to say dogs could sense when a cobra was nearby and would start to howl?" Aaji asked as a shaggy gray dog jumped up to lick her hand. "It's why your aai insisted on getting a dog after she saw a cobra slithering her way growing up."

"Limca," I said, recalling Aai's dog's name as I crouched on my knees to scratch an old white dog's chin. "So Aai got a dog when she was my age, but I don't."

Aaji gave me a sad smile, when suddenly Lark Conovan's face was in front of mine, startling both me and the dog. I yelped, almost losing my balance, my hurt knee stinging as I grazed it across the grass.

"I heard you're a famous singer in India," Lark said, turning to Aaji as I gathered myself.

"I do love to sing," Aaji replied. "Do you?"

Lark nodded. An unleashed dalmatian came running up to her, and I recognized him as Mayor Conovan's dog, Dottie. "I can sing anything. Watch. Here's opera."

I twisted my lips as Lark began to sing the highest note she could in vibrato. Her dog panted happily, unbothered by the noises.

"And I can hit the lowest of lows." Actually, Lark could not. She sang an octave above, unable to hit any of the low notes.

"That was a good warm-up," Lark said, snapping at the dalmatian so it followed her. "See you onstage, Geetanjali. I bet I can be as famous as your grandma one day," she added, waving to Aaji.

"I'm sure you will be." Aaji smiled as Lark headed through the crowd.

"You lied to her," I said, picking up a little shih-tzu mix, thinking for a moment that if someone had told Lark she wasn't singing in tune, maybe she'd stop, and then bullies like Rohan wouldn't get a chance to laugh at her.

"Her voice matters, Geetanjali. As does yours."

I felt a bunch of anxious butterflies body-slamming my insides. "I know, Aaji. I'm going to be fine onstage today, and in a few weeks at Accent Mark in the Park when we sing together," I assured her, even though my nerves were telling me that was far from the truth.

"Good." Aaji gave me a little hug from the side, and I felt her hand tremble against my arm more than I had remembered it doing last summer. "Because the world would be an awfully quiet place if everyone was scared into silence. Don't you think?"

I nodded, twisting my hair into a braid, feeling bad about what I had just thought. Lark wasn't frozen in fear by their laughter. I was jealous that she was sort of unstoppable. I was afraid to sing again, when no one had laughed at my singing. They'd covered their ears because the microphone had screeched, sure. But I think they'd felt bad for me when I'd messed up onstage. They'd wanted to hear me sing, because, like Aaji said, my voice was important, just like Lark's. So, maybe instead of baby steps, today was the day for one big leap. And maybe I'd be able to make up with Penn after singing my heart out with him onstage.

We passed Ashok Ajoba as we headed for the tent with the stage. He was next to the iron clock tower in the park, sticking a sign up on the trunk of a vibrant pink beech tree.

"Did you find what you were looking for at our library?" he asked me.

"I'm going to finish reading the book later today," I told him, when I caught sight of what the sign said:

WARNING—COBRA SIGHTING. WATCH YOUR PETS AT NIGHT, ESPECIALLY IF YOU LIVE BY THE WOODS. IF SPOTTED, DO NOT ATTEMPT TO HANDLE. CALL REPTILE RESCUE CENTER.

I looked at Aaji. "A cobra? On the loose? Here?"

"We got a couple phone calls last night that one was spotted near the woods by the Commons. We're thinking it must be someone's pet who escaped."

"Baapre," Aaji exclaimed. "Is it even legal to own a pet cobra here?"

Ashok Ajoba shrugged. "Not sure. We're looking into that at the center. But a few years ago a man in Michigan was bitten by his pet cobra, and he needed many vials of antivenom before he recovered, so we want to make sure we catch this cobra before it bites someone."

A breeze caused the grass blades around my ankles to tickle my skin; I suddenly jumped.

Ashok Ajoba let out a small laugh. "It's okay. It's just the grass, not a cobra. They like to stay hidden and are nocturnal hunters."

I nodded. "Oh, I knew that," I said, trying to play off my reaction. "Over the past few days, there have been some dead mice on our street with fang marks on their backs," I added, since I hadn't shared the information with him yesterday when checking out my book. "They looked just like the snakebites in the library book."

Ashok Ajoba scrunched his face up, looking perplexed. "That's odd. I don't know why a cobra would have let three mice go after biting them instead of eating them immediately. Maybe they were bitten by something else?"

I shrugged.

"I'll make sure to let the center know. Just in case they're related to this," he said, pointing to his sign.

Aaji patted my back. "We have to get going. Geetanjali is singing in the talent show soon."

Ashok Ajoba nodded. "If I finish hanging these signs on time, I'll be sure to stop by. Good luck!"

"Thanks," I replied, smiling politely as Aaji and I walked past a purple tent full of pet beds for sale, and an orange tent for Deadwood Dog Rescue.

Was it just a coincidence that yet another strange sighting involving snakes was happening in Deadwood? Maybe. Or maybe someone's pet cobra was escaping and biting the mice in our area. And Heena Mavshi just happened to be dealing with her grief by painting snakes.

Or maybe doubting that there was something more to Heena Mavshi than just grief because of what everyone else told me was another way of silencing my voice.

We neared the yellow tent for Good Doggy. Through the open flap, where the stage was set up next to the racks of leashes and collars, I could see Deepak and Penn, standing in line with seven other talent show participants, including Lark.

Aaji nudged me forward as Aai, holding Alaap, and Baba neared. "You're going to do great."

Baba waved his phone. "I'm ready to send it to everyone in India."

CHAPTER 28

The seats were starting to fill up. Baba, Aai, Alaap, and Aaji sat in the first row next to Maya Auntie and Mayor Conovan, whose gray bob was bouncing along as she cheered on Lark. Lark was practice-singing "me-me-me" a bunch of times and blowing raspberries and doing whatever other strange exercises her voice teacher had taught her while Dottie lay by her side, ignoring the painful noises she was making. Lata Auntie was fixing the shiny gold fabric that was hanging lopsided for the stage's backdrop. Deepak was with Penn, spinning a name-tag rack while irritating the shopkeeper.

"Not 'Dee-pack.' It's *dee* like 'My country, 'tis of *thee*.' Well, actually your tongue is a little farther back than *thee* but it's pretty close. And it's definitely not *pack*. It's more like *puck*," Deepak said.

The man behind the table started to turn red. "Well, however you pronounce it, I don't have a name tag for a dog like that. I just have American names."

"That's a microaggression," Deepak said, having no trouble telling an adult that his words were hurtful and kind of racist since we were American, too. "And now that we're on the subject, who do I talk to about changing the name of Accent Mark in the Park? It's kind of othering. Things need to change around here." He looked back, noticing me. "How about her?" Deepak asked.

"What about me?" I ignored the urge to scratch the scabs on my knees and avoid their conversation.

"See if they have your name," Deepak replied.

Penn snorted.

"You shouldn't laugh, Penn. They have 'Penn' right over there." Deepak pointed to Penn's name, right between Penelope and Penny.

Penn's smile disappeared.

My voice went high and super polite. "Gee-tan-jelly."

The man shook his head. "Sorry, kids. I've got Cooper, Duke, and Bailey, though." He took the moment to escape Deepak and organize his leashes in rainbow order with his back to us.

"Why do you do that?" Deepak whispered to me.

"Do what?"

"Why're you afraid to say your name right? It's not *T*, it's *t*," he said, emphasizing the sound that no one in Deadwood could say unless they were desi. "And it's not *tan-jelly*. If you're too scared to say your name right, how will anyone ever get it right? My mom's going to talk about this at her movie night tomorrow."

I looked to Penn, who was staring at us with a wrinkle in his nose. He was clearly just now realizing he had been saying my name wrong his whole life, despite hearing my parents say it correctly.

"Yeah. I'll be there," I said, annoyed at both Deepak for calling me out and at myself. Why did I always mispronounce my name to make things easier for everyone else? I had to stop worrying about being an inconvenience for others. I had to own who I was and my feelings. Maybe I needed to speak up and tell Penn right now that he had been hurting my feelings lately.

Lata Auntie caught my eye as she finished fixing the curtain and waved. "Heena's showing the media around and should be here on time for the show."

"That sounds great," I said politely. I turned to Penn and Deepak. This weird distance that was growing between me and Penn felt endless. I had to fix it. I had to be honest about what I was feeling.

"I have to tell you something," I started.

"Don't tell me you're chickening out of singing with me," Penn said, beads of sweat forming across his forehead.

"What?" I said. It seemed like I wasn't the only one with an imagination that could run wild. "No. That's not it." I took a deep breath, trying to gather my thoughts and find the best way to say it.

Penn's eyes darted to the left and right, like he was trying to figure out what I was going to say.

And that's when I realized, I shouldn't say anything. It wasn't the right time. Penn was clearly nervous about singing onstage. It wouldn't be fair to accuse him of being a bad friend right before he had to perform in front of everyone. So I brought up the next thing that had been on my mind to talk to him about.

"Heena Mavshi has been painting snakes every time I've seen her. First it was the simple dirt one in my yard. Then she made them on note cards and now on canvases all over her house. She used to always be so caring and thoughtful. Now she's snapping at everyone and rude and mean. It's like she has a completely new personality. There's something more going on than her being crabby over Jatin's death."

"I think she's just sad," Penn replied. "My mom was angry and upset after she lost a contract with a big company, and she told me she had to mourn the loss of the project. Mrs. Karwande is mourning something even bigger than that. She could be dealing with it by painting snakes. Maybe Mr. Karwande loved snakes and it reminds her of him."

I scowled. I was so sure Penn would believe me. We were a team. Or at least we used to be. "This is more than that. Trust me."

Penn shrugged. "You're thinking of the worst possible thing again, Geetanjali. You should just let her be sad in peace."

I blew my bangs out of my eyes with an exasperated breath. I wasn't bugging Heena Mavshi. I was trying to make sure she was okay. Why didn't anyone understand that? I didn't bother saying any of that out loud, though. I had to avoid getting into a fight before it was our turn to sing. "Where's your mom, Penn?" I asked, changing the subject. "And your dad. Aren't they supposed to be here?"

Penn sighed. "My dad got called in to work at the hospital this morning when another nurse got sick. And Mom had to go on a last-minute work trip yesterday to an expo with the LawnBot."

That's probably where she was answering the video doorbell from, I thought. "That stinks," I said as a woman with a walkie-talkie whom I had seen at Deadwood library events before walked by us and pointed toward me.

"You must be Gee . . . Jee, sorry. I'm not even going to try to say it."

I caught the knowing look in Deepak's eye, urging me to speak up. To question why she couldn't take the time to try to say my name or to ask me how it was pronounced. But I didn't make a sound. I just nodded.

"Sorry," I automatically said, once again apologizing when I didn't need to. So much for that lesson Aaji had tried to teach me in Canada. "Geetanjali," I added, pronouncing my name incorrectly to make it easy for her.

The woman with the walkie-talkie scribbled something onto her clipboard. "Okay, like I was saying, you and Penn will be onstage first. Is Penn here?"

I pointed to him.

"Great. The mics are on," she said, gesturing to the stage. "And your music is cued. Come up right after I say your names."

"You've both got this," Lata Auntie whispered. "I believe in you." She then headed to the wings just as Ashok Ajoba entered and took a seat in the back of the crowd.

Penn smiled eagerly at me as the woman welcomed everyone, thanked Good Doggy for sponsoring the prize, announced our number, and butchered my name once again. I tuned her out and headed up onto the stage with Penn and looked at the sea of seats before us. Okay, it was more of a puddle than a sea, with only about fifteen chairs fitting in the yellow tent. Fifteen people was nothing. I was going to sing our short song about dogs and it would all be over in a minute. And I would make my parents and Aaji proud.

But did Penn even want me up here with him? He had

been practicing with Deepak. That's who he wanted next to him. I clenched my hands into sweaty fists by my side. No. This was my song. I was the one who wrote it. I had to be the one to sing it with Penn. He was *my* best friend, no matter who he had been singing with earlier.

Our music began. I swallowed down the nerves, jealousy, and irritation, and focused on Aaji's warm face, nodding at me. I was opening my mouth to sing right at our cue when the distant howl of a dog distracted me. It wasn't the normal excited barks that Bark in the Park was known for when dogs greeted one another and potential *furever* families. It sounded scared. It sounded upset. It sounded . . . haunting.

"Bark is for trees . . . ," began Penn, shakily, and barely audible.

He looked at me, desperate for me to join in, but something about the dog cries was disturbing. I'd always thought dogs understood a lot about us. They could sense when we were sad. And they could warn us when something bad was happening. And this sounded bad.

Lark's dalmatian threw his head up and joined in, his eyes squeezed shut, his body shaking. If even Dottie was disturbed, when nothing else seemed to bug him—not the barking dogs at the park, not even Lark's off-key singing—something had to be going on. Besides, what had Lark said? The only thing her dog is afraid of is snakes? Plus, Aaji had just told me dogs howl when they see cobras.

"Trees line the park," Penn added, motioning with his head for me to join in.

Behind him, in the wings, Lata Auntie motioned for me to

sing with her hands. Aai and Aaji motioned for me to sing from
the crowd. Baba's cell phone was aimed at me as it recorded me
not singing.

Didn't anyone else want to know why so many dogs were
howling in the tent? And how could anyone even hear us over
all the howling? What if the cobra that was on the loose was
here and the dogs knew it, but all the humans thought they
were fine because Ashok Ajoba told everyone cobras are nocturnal? What if the snake bit someone in my family? What if
I was the only one who could save them? A few more howls
escaped from the crowd, and I knew what I had to do.

"Snake!" I blurted into the mic, causing it to wobble and
screech almost as bad as at Gudhi Padwa.

"That's not part of the song," Penn whispered to me, but
the microphone picked it up and the crowd began to murmur,
looking around, lifting their feet up.

"There's no snake here, Geetanjali," Aai snapped from
her seat.

Aaji put her hand on Aai's shoulder, like she was reminding her to calm down and go easy on me, especially in public.

What had I done? I wished the stage would swallow me
whole and spare me of yet another embarrassing moment. My
parents looked stunned, and humiliated.

"Sorry," I said, steadying the mic, unable to make eye contact with the people I was apologizing to. I turned to Penn but
couldn't figure out what to say next. I bolted down the stairs,
past Lark and the other participants, past the front row full of
my disappointed family.

CHAPTER 29

"Geetanjali!" Penn called out loudly. Beet red, he ran after me as I rushed out the tent flaps to the open air, passing a bunch of still-howling dogs.

I came to a stop by a cluster of trees, all marked with the loose-cobra warning from Reptile Rescue Center, and took a deep breath. I wiped a small, embarrassed tear from the corner of my eye when Penn caught up to me, his face still flushed.

Sure, I had messed up onstage yet again. But this time my mind wasn't making things up.

"Do you hear that?" I asked as the howling grew louder.

"The howling?" Penn asked, out of breath. "Yeah. We're at a dog festival. It's kind of expected. How could you do that to me?" His eyes were shiny with tears.

"*To* you? I only signed up *for* you. I'd never do something to purposely hurt you," I said, my voice trembling.

"The song was just one minute long. Just one minute of your time, and then you could have gone off to investigate what was making dogs do what they naturally do—howl. But you couldn't even spend one minute doing something *I* wanted to do."

I dug my shoe into the soil around the tree's twisted roots. I *had* enjoyed having an excuse to get off the stage, just like I had enjoyed using Alaap to get out of singing at the basement party. But if Penn was really my best friend, shouldn't he have understood all that? "You're the one who was making me sing after everything that happened the last time I was onstage," I snapped. "You know I was upset about Lark and it got in my head that day. I wasn't ready to be onstage again today. That should have been apparent to you."

"Oh, it's apparent, all right," Penn retorted. "You barely even practiced with me."

"So, you practiced with Deepak instead. I saw you." My voice rose and my head felt hot all over. "I saw you singing the song I wrote for us with him."

Penn's cheeks flushed. "If you wrote it for us, why didn't you sing it just now? Oh, right. Because you were busy being a dog detective. Geetanjali and the case of the howling dogs. Why are the dogs howling? Oh, that's right. Because they're dogs!" he yelled.

"This isn't some silly dog investigation," I snapped. "Look at all the pieces to this puzzle. They're all pointing toward a snake. And I can't believe I'm the only one on our street who can tell something is off!"

"I'm confused," Penn said sharply. "Are you concerned about Mrs. Karwande acting weird or are you worried about a loose cobra?"

"Maybe they're connected," I said, my mind starting to race with the possibilities. "After all, it's pretty weird that Heena Mavshi comes back and then dead mice start popping up—"

"You're just looking for an excuse not to sing," Penn interrupted, a few tears rolling down his cheeks. "Lark wasn't the only one Rohan and his friends laughed at that day, you know. They laughed at me, too. I was scared they'd be here tonight, ready to laugh again. You didn't stick up for me that day. And you weren't here for me today."

"The dogs weren't just an excuse," I asserted, trying not to cry. "And if you want to sing so badly, go up onstage and ask for a do-over with Deepak. He's practiced enough—he has to have it memorized by now."

"You're so jealous of him. Well, you should be. Because he's better at being a friend than you."

I gasped and couldn't stop the tears from spilling out.

But Penn kept going. "Besides, you know you can't switch contestants at the last minute. There are rules," he squeaked angrily. "I'm used to my parents ditching me, but I never thought you'd be the one to ditch me. You're scared of every little thing and make it all about yourself. I should have known this would happen." Penn practically spat the words out as he stormed away. "And, news flash, dogs howl for lots of reasons, even when they have to poop!"

"Penn!" I called out, my stomach sinking as he walked away from me. "Wait!"

Another loud, haunting howl interrupted my thoughts. It was followed by the sounds of dogs whimpering and crying. I looked back at the canines I had passed. They were all shaking with their tails between their legs. One puppy was so terrified, it had peed on itself.

The dogs all had their eyes trained on one person: Heena Mavshi, leading the Channel 12 camera crew through the festival.

CHAPTER 30

Penn refused to talk to me the next day, and as sad as I was about it, I was also mad. Aaji kept telling me how important my voice was, but when I finally did use it to warn my family and friends that something wasn't right, no one listened to me. Now I had humiliated myself again and hurt my best friend's feelings and I was pretty sure he owed me an apology, too, for icing me out and hanging out with Deepak without me.

On Sunday afternoon, despite Aaji's homemade apple and onion pickle that Penn would have devoured on a normal day, I was friendless, hanging out with Alaap in the backyard instead. I had been extra helpful all morning, doing the dishes, the weeding, and now taking care of Alaap, so my parents wouldn't lecture me about ditching Penn onstage and tell me to stop accusing our family friend of provoking the dogs at the park.

I shook a silver rattle from India at Alaap, who I was wearing in Aai's rainbow-colored linen wrap. It was overcast, and the smell of rain could be detected just under the scents of the peonies and mock orange bushes. I blew into the whistle built into the rattle's handle. "Read any good books lately?" I asked Alaap, knowing all I would get was a gummy, drooly smile.

A crow started cawing from Heena Mavshi's yard by the black path that divided our properties. I turned toward the sound. It was the crow with the missing feathers, and something in its beak was glistening in the tiny sliver of sunlight coming from behind the gray clouds above me.

I put a hand protectively over the back of Alaap's head and creeped as slowly as I could toward the crow. When Penn and I were in second grade, we used to tiptoe toward any robin we saw to see how close we could get to it before it flew away. I frowned, thinking about my fight with Penn, and continued to move forward.

The crow bobbed its head as I extended my hand. "What do you have in your mouth?" I asked quietly.

Apparently not quietly enough, though. The crow startled, dropped the thing in its beak, and took off into the air.

I squatted down so Alaap wouldn't fall out of the wrap and grabbed the latest gift from the crow. Thankfully, it wasn't a dead mouse.

It was a key. A long, skinny, dark-gray key. And I knew just what it belonged to.

As the rain pattered our windows, I sat on the floor next to Aaji in the family room, my great-grandmother's trunk before me. Baba was on the recliner behind us, listening to his tablet with headphones as he edited his radio program. He had spent the day fielding phone calls from someone in India who wanted to buy his family's land in Konkan and turn it into a resort, and his siblings who wanted to consider the offer.

The conversations were making me feel a little nauseated.

It was like losing another connection to my family back home, even though I'd never gotten to go to Konkan, and now probably never would.

Baba was getting so many calls that he finally booked a flight to India in ten days so he could be there with his family to talk to the buyer. I felt sad thinking about the lush green mangroves where his family grew up being torn down, but Baba said he had to hear the offer out. Unfortunately, or fortunately, that meant he would be missing my performance at Accent Mark in the Park with Aai and Aaji.

Aaji hummed to Alaap, who was cooing on the play mat by us.

"Ready to solve the mystery?" I asked Aaji as Aai entered the family room and lay down next to Alaap.

"Ready," Aaji said as I put the key into the lock and turned it. It stuck a little before giving way, and the trunk popped open a crack. I gasped and quickly lifted the lid, ready to come face-to-face with a pile of gold jewelry.

But it was completely empty.

"There's nothing here," I said, slouching.

Aaji reached her hand in. "Aha!" she exclaimed. "A bobby pin!"

I smiled a little as Aaji put the bobby pin in my hand. "I guess you were right." I took another peek inside. On the bottom of the empty trunk, I saw a bit of paper stuck in the corner. "You might be right about the hishob, too," I said, using the end of the bobby pin to try to pry the paper out. But instead of paper, the whole bottom of the trunk popped up.

"It's a false bottom!" I gasped. Underneath the metal was

a thin memo book made of super lightweight and fragile lined paper. I opened it up and carefully turned the pages. Aaji's mother had written a book.

"Mysteries," I read in English. "What is this?"

Aaji smiled. "I remember that. My mother wanted to write a book that she said would be better than Kipling. She didn't like how everyone idolized Rudyard Kipling's books about India. She said they made Indians sound awful, and if someone should tell an Indian story, they should be Indian. She said she would publish it in Marathi and English."

"The Howling Dogs," I read, turning to the first page. I skimmed my great-grandmother's handwriting. "This is about a man who acted mean for no reason. And the dogs in the town kept howling anytime they went near him." That sounded familiar.

"I told you, dogs can sense a lot of things we can't," Aaji said, grabbing a bottle of coconut oil from the bottom shelves of the changing table. She began to massage the clear oil into Alaap's head.

I read the English words at the bottom of the page. "The man was . . ." I felt a shiver go down my spine, as if it was winter, when the coconut oil in Aaji's hands would be cold and solid white. I turned the next page. ". . . an ichchhadhari naag." I felt uneasy. "He hadn't transitioned fully to his human form. He was still thinking like a cobra, full of anger and frustration and—"

"Okay, I think that might be enough of this book," Aai said, putting her palm out, preventing me from reading any more.

But the events of this summer all seemed to click. Heena

Auntie's anger. The odd bite mark on her back. The mice in everyone's yard. The creepy art. The dogs at Bark in the Park.

"Aai, I think Heena Mavshi is—"

"Enough. Please. You know Alaap was up all night with a stomachache, crying so much he could barely nurse," Aai interrupted. "We have to go to Maya Auntie's tonight for her Bollywood movie night. It'll be a late night, and I want to sleep without you having a nightmare about an ichchhadhari naagin in Michigan, of all places."

"Sorry I'm such an inconvenience," I muttered, although I couldn't help but smile inside. Aai confirmed what I was thinking without me even saying it. I didn't know if this should make me happy or even more terrified.

"That's not what I meant." She burrowed her head in her hand. "When I was young, I was known for being the most fearless kid on our street. I'd jump into the stepwell to go swimming," she said, talking about the ancient, swimming-pool-size wells with intricately designed stairs leading down to them, sometimes in geometric patterns. "I'd lead everyone into the ruins of the fort near us to play. The only thing I was afraid of was cobras, who'd startle me at least once a year by jumping out from the stairwell of the fort. Or lunge at me on the way out of the stepwell when I was soaked and not on guard. I swear it was the same cobra, however impossible that may be. I know how hard it is to battle your fears. I don't want you to live in fear all the time. I want to help you fight these battles. You're my everything," she concluded, looking at me.

I pulled a strand of carpet loose. "Even though you're mad at me for not singing at Bark in the Park?"

"You're my everything, Geetu," Aai repeated, emphasizing each word, her eyes shiny. The rain suddenly died down and a beam of sun filtered in through the window, making Aai glow. "Even when you accuse our family friend of being a naagin. You're not an inconvenience. Not ever." Aai threw her head back with a groan. "I'm just so tired," she said in Marathi, but somehow I wasn't convinced.

"I don't understand," Baba interrupted, taking his headphones off.

That made two of us.

"My interview with Aaji," Baba continued. "The ending didn't record. It's all static." Baba pulled the headphones cord out of the tablet and pressed play. Aaji's voice floated out of the speaker. She told a story about being nervous the first time she had to sing for the music directors. It must have been the story Lata Auntie commented on when she was over.

And then, the radio program's closing music started as Baba began to thank Aaji for being on the show. "See?" Baba said. "It's all static."

Sure enough, a loud sound had taken over, masking anything else that was being said. Only, Baba was wrong. It wasn't static.

It was hissing.

CHAPTER 31

I ran outside with the tablet. I needed to show Penn. "I have proof," I yelled from the end of my driveway, waving the tablet. I knew Penn and I still had a lot of things to talk about, but I also desperately wanted him to be on my side, to believe me about Heena Mavshi.

Penn glared at me and continued to kick his soccer ball hard toward the doggy door, pretending I didn't exist.

"Bark what you mean," he sang loudly. "Don't be average, that's mean."

A math pun. Ugh. That *was* mean. "Real mature, Penn. I'm trying to tell you about you know who." I turned toward Heena Mavshi's house, making sure she wasn't outside.

"Ditching someone onstage is mean." Penn drew out the last word, singing it high for everyone on our street to hear.

"Penn!" I lowered my voice. "There's hissing on my dad's radio show. Like a snake."

"So?" Penn shouted back loudly.

"Shh!" The tablet almost slipped out of my now-sweaty hands.

Penn scowled. "I won't 'shhh.' Unlike you, I'm not afraid of people hearing me." He gave the soccer ball one more angry kick. It ricocheted off the brick of his house and flew back across the street, toward me.

I jumped up to catch it, clenching the tablet tight to my chest with my left hand, hoping I could use the soccer ball as an olive branch with Penn, but it sailed over my head.

I turned to grab it, but Heena Mavshi was there, a few steps from her porch, the soccer ball on her front lawn. "You kids having fun?" she asked, without a hint of warmth in her voice or on her face; she sounded like a robot.

"Sort of," Penn replied from his yard.

Why couldn't Penn tell this wasn't the Heena Mavshi we knew? The old Heena Mavshi would have invited us over for sweets or talked about the nice weather.

Heena Mavshi extended her arms and handed me the ball.

"How . . . how are you, Heena Mavshi?" I asked, hoping to find a sliver of my old neighbor left. If there was a bit of her kind, human self in there, maybe we could reverse whatever transition she was going through.

I held out my right hand. I wanted to help her, but I was still a little afraid of getting too close. I didn't want to end up like one of the mice. "Do you need help?" I asked softly. "You were always there for me. Is something happening to you?"

I hesitantly took the ball just as Heena Mavshi twisted her head to the side and whispered, "It's all amiss." Only she didn't just say the word "amiss." She hissed it, holding on to the *s* sound at the end way longer than a human would.

I gasped, dropping the ball to the ground, and ran toward my front door. But, once again, I was the only one who noticed the hiss in her words, just like the sound in Baba's radio show.

"Oh, *real mature!*" Penn shouted as he crossed the street to grab the soccer ball rolling down my driveway.

I didn't bother responding, though. I fiddled with the door, my perspiration-slick thumb slipping repeatedly until I finally got it open.

I slammed it shut on the neighbor I was fighting with and the other neighbor I was terrified for and of.

CHAPTER 32

There was only one way to show my family that Heena Mavshi really was an ichchhadhari naagin: facts.

I sat in my room, ready to approach this from a different angle and read every page of the snake book I had checked out from Reptile Rescue Center, writing down anything that could prove my hypothesis. Snakes hissed. So did Heena Mavshi. Snakes were cold-blooded, meaning they couldn't regulate their own body temperature. Heena Mavshi was freezing cold after she got off the plane. (Although Aaji and Lata Auntie were too, so maybe this wasn't the strongest fact.) Cobras are venomous. Venomous meant poisonous, but it also meant behaving nastily, and Heena Mavshi was doing that.

There was one thing I'd found in my research that wasn't quite working with my theory. Cobras don't actually dance to music. They sway to keep track of moving objects. So when a snake charmer is playing and moving his instrument, the snake sways because of the instrument, not from the notes the musician is playing. Heena Mavshi swaying as she listened to music on her walk may have just been a coincidence, then.

And then there was the nonscientific evidence, that gut feeling I couldn't ignore. The copper snake bangle Heena always had on. A cobra had been sighted by the woods at the

Commons. *Was it Heena Mavshi transforming?* There were dead mice in our yards. Snakes like to eat mice. Plus, dogs howled at cobras. And the dogs at Bark in the Park howled at her, including Dottie, the dog who only was scared of one thing: snakes. And I think Heena Mavshi first drew the cobra in the soil of my yard just for me. I always understood her art and she wanted to tell me what was going on, but it was too early for me to figure it out.

"I still can't believe you made a list of evidence that our neighbor is a mythical creature," Baba laughed that evening as we walked down our driveway. My big plan was a failure and we were heading to Deepak's Bollywood movie night like everything in the world was normal and we didn't live next door to an ichchhadhari naagin.

"You have to leave her alone," Aai said, holding Alaap in the linen wrap. "She's going through a lot, and the last thing she needs is you saying she's a cobra. She thinks of you as family. Think of how hurt she would be by this accusation."

"It's not an accusation," I whispered, remembering another fact from the book: that snakes couldn't hear well but they could sense vibrations. I wasn't sure how loud the vibrations from my family talking were. "I'm just . . . exploring the possibility."

Aaji let out a tiny groan as we stepped off the driveway onto the street.

"Are you okay?" I asked her.

Aaji nodded. "My hip's giving me a little trouble, that's all."

I grabbed Aaji's frail arm, trying not to look at Heena Mavshi's house. "Aaji, you told me to use my voice," I said, desperate for her to believe me. "And when I do, everyone just laughs at me."

"We're not," Baba said.

"You just laughed about my list," I snapped, turning back to him.

Baba gave me a sympathetic smile. "How about a math problem? If we're walking at the rate of three miles per hour and—"

"Baba, please." I stepped on a branch and it snapped in two with a loud crack as I followed my family across the logs over the creek. I was pretty sure Ashok Ajoba had mentioned avoiding the woods until the cobra was caught. I picked up my pace.

"I'll add it to your summer notebook. That way you'll still get to keep up with math when I go to India," Baba replied, reaching for Aaji's left hand as I grabbed her right to make sure she didn't fall.

I held on to her hand extra long, still thinking about getting bitten by the loose cobra in the woods. At the clearing in the trees, we could see shadows of our neighbors gathered on folding chairs in front of the large outdoor screen.

Aai whispered into my ear, "No more stories or false snake sightings tonight, please."

I looked at Aai, who seemed to be blinking back tears in the darkness; she quickly grabbed Aaji's hand from mine and walked ahead with her and Alaap to the back row, where Lata Auntie was sitting, alone.

I swatted at a mosquito and caught up with them. I smiled at Lata Auntie, thinking she must have felt lonely since her only friend here was at home. Baba slowly joined us after whispering hello to a bunch of family friends. And Deepak and Penn were two rows up, eating makhana and popped jowar together as they watched the movie.

My tongue watered at the thought of the puffed lotus seeds spiced with chaat masala and the popped sorghum seeds that looked like shrunken popcorn kernels.

"Are you and your friend fighting?" Lata Auntie asked softly, eyes still locked on the screen.

I shrugged.

"Because of Bark in the Park?"

"Yeah. Among other things," I added, keeping the part about his not believing my ideas about Heena Mavshi to myself.

"It can be hard when a friend suddenly becomes . . . less friendly," she said with a knowing look.

Was she talking about Heena Mavshi? Surely the person living with Heena Mavshi would have noticed all the changes in her behavior even more than I had.

"Have you noticed anything strange about Heena Mavshi?" I asked.

Lata Auntie paused, eyeing me up and down, like she was trying to figure out if she could trust me. "Is that why you screamed 'snake' at Bark in the Park?"

"Watch the movie, Geetanjali," Aai said sternly. "You know the songs."

Lata Auntie gave me a polite smile and turned her attention back to the screen.

I sighed. Maybe this wasn't the place to try to figure out if Lata Auntie had noticed any snakish things about Heena

Mavshi. I focused on the film. Aai was right. I did know the songs. As a bunch of actors began to sing onscreen, I couldn't help but softly sing along. In the dark, with everyone around me singing at the same time, I didn't feel self-conscious or awkward, and I made it a point to lean forward while singing so Aaji could see me. She beamed, singing along with me. I settled back in my spot, feeling like I was making up, even if it was just a little bit, for all the times I hadn't sung the way Aaji would have liked this summer.

I glanced ahead at Penn while singing the catchy refrain, knowing we'd have to talk at some point and make up. I expected him to have the same horrified look he had when Baba blasted his radio program on our way to get Aaji from the airport. But he was tapping his fingers on his knee and rocking his head from side to side like he was really into the music.

I turned back to the screen and almost screamed. Heena Mavshi's silhouette was projected onto it, looking like a lurking monster, her shadow swaying side to side.

CHAPTER 33

Heena Mavshi must have just gotten to Deepak's yard and decided to stand in front of the projector in the aisle, looking for a seat, not caring that she was rudely blocking the movie, just as the word INTERMISSION flashed on the screen.

Lata Auntie rushed to Heena Mavshi's side, and I could hear Heena Mavshi loudly complaining about how she couldn't see anything in the dark and the volume on the film was loud and disorienting. She didn't sound sorry at all for blocking the movie.

This was no anger stage. Even if Heena was grieving, I'd never seen her so irritated before, and she'd been this way for weeks. No, this was a venomous ichchhadhari naagin. I rushed to the brick patio, along with most of the other guests, trying to find Penn and Deepak.

Maya Auntie had laid out a spread of typical Indian snacks from her childhood under the twinkling solar lights. Based on what I saw on the table, her childhood was 80 percent cookies, and it was glorious.

I chewed on a rectangular Parle-G glucose biscuit. I wasn't sure what glucose was, but this was my favorite sugar cookie. I used to dip it in steaming hot chaha in India and eat the soggy, tea-drenched biscuit before it dissolved in the cup.

"Do you like the movie so far?"

I turned. It was Deepak. I nodded. My throat was sticky and clogged with the biscuit, but that was okay. All the things I wanted to say to Penn, who was standing behind Deepak and now glaring at me, were lodged in my throat. And this gave me an excuse not to say anything.

"See what I mean?" Penn muttered to Deepak.

I frowned. "What you mean about what?" I asked with a full mouth.

"Penn thinks you can be a little . . . self-centered at times," Deepak said, grimacing as he said the hurtful words. "I think you both just need to talk it out. . . ."

I felt tears sting my eyes. I was trying to warn everyone about Heena Mavshi to keep them safe. How was that selfish? Plus, I was the one being left out. That made Penn selfish, not me. He just didn't understand me the way he used to. Maybe I didn't do a good job expressing myself behind all of my catastrophic thinking. Maybe it was easier for Penn and Deepak to think I didn't want to climb the wall at the Commons because I only wanted them to do my ideas, when, in fact, it was because I was petrified of heights.

"We always do what you want to do," Penn said. "And you don't just do it to me. I bet you don't even know what camp Deepak is going to because you're too busy trying to give snakes a bad reputation."

"Of course I do," I said, getting a little annoyed at all the accusations. "It's . . . it's . . . about . . . math?"

"Robotics, actually," said Penn.

Deepak shrugged. "Robotics does use some math, so technically she's—"

"And does he want to go?" asked Penn.

"Why wouldn't he? He loves that stuff," I said.

"I'm right here," Deepak said, gesturing with his hands. "Why are you both talking about me like I'm not here?"

"Because he isn't sure he wants to do robotics," Penn replied, ignoring Deepak. "He doesn't want to be exactly like Shilpa. He wants to do his own thing. You'd know that if you listened. And you'd remember that I didn't grow up getting to sing onstage all the time, like you. You'd know it was a really big deal for me to go up onstage yesterday, especially after Rohan laughed at me at the park. I only had you, Geetanjali, and I was counting on you to be there with me!" Penn began to cry.

I looked down at my feet. I had no idea Deepak liked things outside of rocks and math and random facts. And I had no idea Penn felt any of these big things about my singing with him. And he's right, I should have. I heard how softly he was singing. I saw how sweaty he was. I knew deep down that he was as nervous as I was up there, but instead of getting through it together, I'd just ditched him.

"You're right," I said softly.

"What?" Penn asked, wiping his tears with his shirt collar.

"I'm sorry," I said, this time really meaning it. "I'm sorry I didn't speak up for you at the park that day. And I'm really sorry I used the dogs howling to bail when I should have just stayed and sang with you. I did the same thing at Gudhi Padwa. I used my guilt over Lark as an excuse for freezing up onstage. But I just made a mistake, like everyone does at times. I had never messed up with my singing before and I decided to stop doing it instead of facing my fear." I swatted at a mosquito by my neck. "I wasn't thinking of you when I ditched you at the talent show, and that was wrong. I was really hurt, though, by you always going with Deepak to the wall, and then I saw you both singing the song I wrote, after you had already planned a lemonade stand without me and gone to the movies without me. . . ." I trailed off. "I was jealous," I said, knowing I had to finish what was on my mind. "And I felt left out. And sad. And mad."

"I didn't mean to leave you out," Penn said, wiping his eyes. "You seemed uninterested in practicing with me. I was scared of singing onstage, and Deepak was being a good friend, helping me feel more ready."

I nodded. "I get that now. But I wasn't lying when I told you that I was trying to warn everyone about a snake." My apology was spilling out of me faster than Penn's tears, and I wasn't sure I was making much sense.

"My parents barely have any time for me with Alaap. And that's fine, because I love my brother and I get that he's a baby and needs them. But I think with them always looking out for him, I started worrying more. Worrying about people staring at me when I'm onstage. Worrying about messing up when singing again. Worrying about disappointing my family. Worrying that there's something wrong with Heena Mavshi and that no one else believes me. So, I'm sorry for what I did to you, Penn. And I'm sorry for not asking you about your camp, Deepak." I blinked fast, but not quickly enough to stop the tears from rolling down my cheeks.

"No worries," Deepak said, offering me and Penn each a cloth napkin.

Penn gave me a sad smile. I dabbed at my cheeks, and he did the same. "I'm sorry, too, Geetanjali—*Gee-taan-juh-lee*," Penn corrected himself, pronouncing my name the right way, the way Deepak always did. "For hurting your feelings. For making you feel left out and all alone. I didn't think you'd be interested in raising money for Gertie. And the movie we went to see was a documentary at Reptile Rescue Center on pythons in the Everglades. I shouldn't have just assumed you wouldn't want to do that just because it was about snakes. I'm really sorry for that. And if you think something is up with Mrs. Karwande, I believe you."

"You do?"

Penn nodded. "And I'll help you. Just don't accuse Gertie of being a part of it. I promise she has never gotten out of her cramped terrarium," he said with a smile.

"Deal." I looked at Deepak. "Will you help too?"

"I believe . . . it's worth investigating," Deepak said, matter-of-factly.

I smiled. "Thanks. Because yesterday, when Heena Mavshi handed me Penn's soccer ball, she said something really odd. She said, 'It's all amiss.' Only, she hung on to the last *s* sound for way too long, and it became less humanlike and more snakelike. Like an animal hiss."

"Weird," Penn said.

"Or maybe that's just how she says her *s*'s?" Deepak wondered.

A sudden wave of goose bumps peppered their way across my arms. I felt like someone was watching us. I turned. Heena Mavshi was standing right behind me.

"Heena Mavshi!" I exclaimed. "Um . . . How are you?"

"It's all amiss," she whispered, barely moving her lips. She held on to that last snakelike *sss* sound again as I backed up into the boys.

"Tell me you're hearing this too," I said softly.

"I did see her lips move," Penn replied. "But what did she say?"

"The same thing as before. With the hiss at the end."

"Maybe we should tell our parents," Deepak said, louder.

Before I could respond, a horrific, guttural scream interrupted me, courtesy of Lata Auntie.

"What's wrong?" Aaji asked from across the patio as a concerned panic began to spread across the crowd.

"*Ss . . . ssss . . .* saanp!" Lata Auntie pointed in front of her on the patio, using the Hindi word for snake.

But unlike when I had screamed about a snake at Bark in the Park, this time there actually was one. In the glow of the string lights dangling across the cedar pergola above, a slithering snake could be seen, coiling its way right toward Aai and my sleeping baby brother.

"Gertie?" asked Penn.

I ran forward to throw myself in front of Alaap. I wanted to get Aai and my brother out of the way. But my feet came to a sudden, terrified stop.

"Is that you?" Penn crouched down to get a better look. "Come here, pumpkin!"

But the snake, who was clearly no *pumpkin* at the moment, started slithering faster toward Aai and Alaap.

Deepak dumped a floral-patterned Corelle serving bowl of cookies out and tried to scoop Gertrude up, but he was shaking and seemed unsure how to put Gertrude in a bowl she wouldn't have fit in anyway.

"Ashok Dada!" Deepak yelled. "We need help with a snake!"

Ashok Ajoba slowly made his way through the crowd from the yard, but before he could get to us, Aaji pushed her way forward, one hand on her sore hip, grabbed a large, empty planter from Maya Auntie's brief gardening hobby, and dumped it upside down, on top of the snake, trapping it underneath.

My heart was pounding in my chest as I turned to Penn, relieved, shocked, and still a little scared. "What was that you were saying about her never getting out?"

CHAPTER 34

After what happened at Maya Auntie's party, I didn't even bother trying to sleep in my room. There was no way I'd be able to go to bed alone after my interaction with Heena Mavshi and Gertrude's appearance. How had Gertrude gone from Penn's front doggy door all the way around the house and then down his backyard hill to Deepak's house? Had the snake been drawn to something?

I ran my fingers over my naagmani necklace (I hadn't taken it off since the day after Aaji had given it to me) and snuggled up close to Aaji, waiting for her to start her nightly prayers.

But before she did that, I had to speak up. I hadn't gone about warning everyone the right way at Bark in the Park. I needed to give it one last try, especially after Aaji saw Gertrude at the party.

"Aaji, I know everyone thinks I'm imagining things," I started.

Aaji slowly turned toward me.

"But Heena Mavshi hissed at me at the party. She said, 'It's all amiss.' Kind of like what I've been saying since she came home." I paused, trying to figure out how to phrase what I wanted to tell her without sounding ridiculous. "What if Gertrude knows Heena Mavshi is an ichchhadhari naagin and came to warn us? What if—"

Alaap began to cry from my parents' room next door.

"Geetanjali! Please be a little quieter," Aai snapped through the wall.

"Aaji," I whispered. "You wrote that book for me for a reason. You wanted me to know where I come from. You know it's not just a story. Ichchhadhari naagins are real, aren't they?"

Aaji let out a breath, like she was filling the room with sadness and disappointment. "If I weren't there, Geetu, what would have happened?"

"What do you mean?"

"Manjhe, saap kunee pakadala asata?"

I pulled the sheet up over my shoulders. I wasn't sure who would have caught Gertrude if Aaji hadn't been there. Definitely not Aai. Deepak had been shaking with that bowl, so he wouldn't have been able to. Maybe Ashok Ajoba?

"You're lucky you don't have poisonous snakes here," Aaji said.

"There's an actual cobra on the loose, remember?" I asked softly, wishing this moment were more like the fun summer memories we had been creating.

"You have to figure out how to harness these fears. I know you're trying, but you have to believe in yourself more and take bigger strides now. I'm not going to be here forever. *You* will have to be the one to save the day. You must be your own hero."

This was like the opposite of Lata Auntie's "strength in numbers" thinking. Aaji was basically telling me I was on my own. Luckily, I had Penn and Deepak on my side again. I cleared my throat, hoping the lump that was forming in it would go away. "I'm trying. I'm trying to warn everyone about what I think is going on."

"I mean, with real-life things," Aaji said.

That meant singing. And putting a stop to my stories, I guessed. I shook my head. "I'm not brave like you and Aai."

"I saw you apologize to Penn," Aaji said. "It takes a brave person to say they are sorry when they're in the wrong. I'm proud of you. I need you to try to believe in yourself more." Aaji groaned a little, massaging her hip. "But it's not something that I can make happen. It must come from inside you." Aaji's bangles jingled as she moved my bangs out of my eyes. "I'm going back to India in a month, and who knows how my health will be next summer. If I'm too sick or too old, your parents can't afford the health insurance for me to visit. I'll have to stay back in India. But I'll worry every day if I don't leave here knowing you're going to be brave enough to handle things without me."

"I'm really sleepy, Aaji. Can we talk about this tomorrow?" I yawned and closed my eyes. It wasn't because I was tired. I needed to stop the tears from falling out. I suddenly felt sadder than ever before and wondered if this was how Heena Mavshi felt from the weight of grieving Jatin Kaka all the time. And Aaji wasn't even gone yet. I didn't want to think about Aaji being not healthy enough to come here next summer. Or the fact that she was disappointed in me and that, deep down, she didn't think I was strong enough to protect my family.

CHAPTER 35

The next morning I stood staring at a million little circles, feeling disturbed, deep down in the pit of my stomach, as Gertrude slithered around inside a plastic box on Penn's lap at the vet.

I had decided to try to be a better friend and accompany Penn and Deepak as they took Gertrude for a checkup to make sure she was okay after going through the woods to get to Deepak's house last night. So, after filling the boys in on all the Heena Mavshi–snake things that had happened since she'd come back to Michigan on our walk over, I was now in a cramped room that smelled like wet dog—the only part about dogs I didn't like—and rubbing alcohol.

But, strangely, I didn't mind. I had spent so much time feeling jealous of Deepak and Penn spending time without me, I hadn't thought about how nice it would feel if I had said yes and just hung out with them at the Commons. It felt good to be included. And it felt good to have two friends, instead of just one, by my side.

I watched as the vet took Gertrude out with the help of a tech, checked her head and eyes, and used a tiny wooden rod to open her mouth and examine her forked tongue, mouth, airway, and nose.

I glanced at a poster of a sad boa constrictor that said, IS YOUR REPTILE FEELING OKAY? DON'T WAIT UNTIL SOMETHING GOES WRONG. BRING THEM IN FOR AN ANNUAL CHECKUP TODAY!

I was pretty positive the reptile next door to me wasn't feeling well. In fact, I was certain she'd be feeling a lot better once whatever it was that was happening to her came to an end. Too bad we couldn't take Heena Mavshi in for a checkup.

It was time to speak up to make sure Heena Mavshi did get better. "Have you ever heard of a snake that kills mice but doesn't eat them?" I asked.

The vet shook her head. "Never. And I've been practicing veterinary medicine for three decades," she added.

I raised an eyebrow at the boys. "What if she was in her human form when she bit the mouse?" I asked softly. "That would explain not being able to eat it."

Penn shuddered. "Creepy," he whispered back.

"Can a snake sense another snake is nearby and want to slither toward it?" I asked, wondering if we could prove Gertrude was there to warn us of another snake at the party.

The vet picked Gertrude up. "Depends. Snakes can actually detect airborne vibrations better than groundborne ones."

Deepak frowned and I did too. I couldn't think of an instance when Heena Mavshi had mentioned hearing something. But maybe Gertrude had sensed the airborne vibrations of the party. And maybe she could detect that one of those airborne vibrations belonged to a snake. A possibly dangerous one.

The vet observed Gertrude as she squiggled in her hands. "She has good muscle movement, her skin is soft and free of bruises, and there's no swelling. I think she's okay," she said, putting Gertrude back in her carrier.

Penn looked at me with a relieved smile.

"And your mom paid the bill over the phone," the vet tech said, handing the carrier back to us, "so I'll check you out and you can take Gertrude home to rest."

"Oh, I almost forgot!" Deepak exclaimed, reaching into his backpack as Penn carried Gertrude. "Ashok Dada and I worked on the grant proposal this morning. We're ready to submit it, but I've read it at least a dozen times and something seems to be missing." He handed me a couple pieces of paper. "I thought, because you're so good with words, maybe you could help?"

I glanced over the pages with a small smile. Deepak thought I was better than him at something, even though he was the expert on most things. I couldn't help but feel a little proud of myself as I zeroed in on the opening paragraph.

"I really like how you opened with a lot of facts and numbers here," I started, remembering how when we were peer critiquing our writing in fifth grade, we always told our critique partners something positive before pointing out what could be improved.

"Facts are important," Deepak said as we took a seat on the bench outside the vet.

"You know most of them," Penn chimed in.

I nodded. "Facts are important. But so is heart."

Deepak's brow furrowed as I continued.

"We want to appeal to the committee's hearts in order to get this grant. Reptiles aren't exactly cute to everyone. No offense, Gertrude," I quickly added.

"None taken," said Penn in a high-pitched voice on Gertrude's behalf as he gently swayed the box she was sitting in.

"When I was at the center before our can drive, I saw all these injured animals that were abandoned pets. What if we start with a story about say, the six-lined racerunner. How there's a colony of them in Michigan, but this one didn't get to live freely with them. She was a pet, stuck in a tiny terrarium."

"We know what that's like," Penn sighed, pointing to Gertrude.

I nodded. "And then the owners decided they no longer wanted the six-lined racerunner and dumped her in the woods, where she didn't know how to care for herself because she had never lived out in the wild." I straightened my spine as more lines started to come to me. "But luckily, there was one group who did know how to care for her! And they came to the rescue. But they can't rescue more without the help of this grant. And then we can put your facts in to help convince the committee."

I turned to the boys, but they were just staring, wide-eyed, their mouths hanging open in surprise.

"What?" I asked.

"That's genius," Deepak sputtered. "You figured out exactly what the proposal needed!"

"You saved the day so that Reptile Rescue Center can save the day!" Penn cheered. "That doesn't exactly roll off the tongue, but that's why you're the word expert, not me."

I beamed, holding my chin up higher than I had in a long time.

Deepak held the grant proposal triumphantly in the air. "This calls for a celebration."

CHAPTER 36

T hanks to the spending money our parents had given us for our trip to downtown Deadwood, we sat at Hungry Hari's, a sandwich shop by Good Doggy that had all kinds of sandwiches, with a large glass of mango lassi in front of each of us.

I finished up my samosa sandwich, brimming over with a spicy mix of peas, onions, and potatoes, and topped with mint, cilantro, and tamarind chutneys, and glanced at Gertrude through the decorative diamond cutouts in the cast-iron outdoor table. She was sitting in her travel box by Penn's feet so other diners didn't get scared away.

Gertrude peeked her head out, and I felt a guilty pinch in my gut, thinking about how Penn didn't win the pet store gift certificate, so Gertrude didn't get the large terrarium.

"Look at all those scales," I said, watching them glisten in the sunlight. "Did you know scale means to climb, something that weighs things, a musical scale, or to remove scales—like when people eat fish—and those tiny little scales all over Gertrude's body." I tried to stop my shudder so Penn wouldn't feel offended.

"That's neat," Deepak said, opening a container in his bag and revealing an egg. "Do you have trypophobia?"

"What's that?" asked Penn, taking the egg from Deepak and placing it in the carrier.

"It's a fear of small holes or circles or a repeating pattern, like in a honeycomb or snakeskin or lotus root."

"Gah," I muttered as we stood up to leave and Gertrude swallowed the egg whole.

Penn took a loud slurp of his mango lassi. "How can someone be afraid of circles?"

"It actually makes sense from an evolutionary perspective," Deepak said. "Lots of dangerous or poisonous animals and plants have those patterns. A wasp's nest, an octopus, a venomous snake . . . Scientists think it could be a leftover response to when we lived outside and encountered wild things more often."

"Huh," replied Penn. Well, I'm glad I don't have that or else I'd be afraid of my own pet."

Deepak had actually made me feel a little better about my fears. Or at least one of them. There was a scientific reason behind it.

"Okay," Penn began, "now that we know Gertie is okay, let's move on to Geetanjali's problem—Mrs. Karwande."

"She might become all of our problems if she becomes a full-on evil cobra-person," I replied, ducking under some of the neon-green wasp traps someone had set on their tree, filled to the brim with dead wasps. "'It's all amiss.' What does that even mean?"

"Is it a saying in India?" Penn asked, drinking the last gulps of his mango lassi.

I shook my head. India was diverse, and I only knew

Marathi and Hindi and could sort of understand Gujarati and Punjabi from some of our family friends. I wasn't good at any of those languages, really, but I was pretty sure it wasn't a saying in any of them or the tons of other languages across India.

Penn licked his orange-colored mango lassi mustache off.

"Well, in the literal sense, she's telling you everything's wrong or . . . out of place," Deepak said. "I feel like that sometimes. Like I enjoy studying and doing high school work. But sometimes I feel like things aren't the way they should be."

"Like what?" I asked, even though I really wanted Deepak and Penn to focus on our neighbor. I reminded myself a one-minute sidetrack wouldn't hurt anyone. That's what a good friend would have done, and I wanted to be a good friend.

"I don't always just want to be doing homework and studying. I think it would be really cool to run an organization like Reptile Rescue one day," Deepak said. "I like learning about reptiles and figuring out how to help them. And I thought it would be a good way to spend the month of August. Maybe I could shadow Ashok Dada and be like the Crocodile Hunter."

I looked at him blankly. "We're vegetarian."

Deepak shook his head. "He wasn't really a hunter. He was this conservationist who helped all sorts of animals. He caught snakes with his bare hands. Or maybe one day I'll be a scientist who helps save some endangered reptile species. But Shilpa didi says that's a job for someone who doesn't think like me. She says robotics are the future and I have to go to this camp in Boston right after Accent Mark."

"I'm sorry," I said as we stood up to throw our trash out.

"You should tell your mom you don't want to go," Penn

suggested, pausing to tie his shoelace and setting the carrier on the ground.

"Yeah," I chimed in. "You're always using your voice to help everyone else. But you should stand up for yourself, too."

"Maybe I just don't want to disappoint her."

I nodded, leaning forward to make sure my own laces were tied, when my naagmani fell out from under my collar.

Gertrude flickered her forked tongue and coiled into a ball away from me.

I paused. The naagmani worked. Did this mean I was safe from Heena Mavshi? Not that I had any idea if she could hurt me or not.

"New necklace?" Deepak asked, watching Gertrude as Penn rose to his feet, the tote in hand.

"It's a naagmani. A cobra stone," I said, clenching the necklace to stop it from swaying around my neck and scaring Gertrude more.

"I read about that when I was researching snakes and trying to convince my parents to let me get one," Penn said, looking at the stone on my necklace.

"You did?" I let go of the chain and tucked the stone back under my shirt. "Did you read anything else about naagmani in your research?"

"I read an old folk story about a cobra who could turn into a human woman and how scared everyone in that town was, so they all got naagmanis to protect themselves. I also heard some really cool songs from all these Hindi movies about cobra-people. I even learned one of them," Penn added, turning a little pink.

I almost smiled but stopped myself, sensing Penn wasn't joking.

Penn began to hum, cocking his head like he had anytime I had seen him listening to Indian music. I raised an eyebrow as Penn sang the old Hindi movie song. Had Penn been making that face every time, not because he thought my music was weird, but because he liked it?

"Oh yeah," Deepak said. "I know that song. You should come to singing class with us."

Penn shook his head as we headed down the street. "Everyone will look at me funny. Like why is this white kid singing Indian songs and saying all the words wrong?"

He looked flustered and embarrassed, like the last times I had seen him sing. "I say the words wrong all the time," I said. "Who cares?"

"That's true," Deepak chimed in. "But you should care enough to try your best."

"I can't even say my own name right," I went on, still trying to make Penn feel better.

"No, you choose to say your own name wrong," Deepak corrected. "Big difference. But the point is, you can come to our class, Penn. Just tell your mom. Like how you told me to do about camp."

"He's right," I added. "You should come. Deepak and I can't sing without you. We're a team."

Penn's eyes brightened a little and he nodded hesitantly.

I tucked my naagmani back into my shirt so Gertrude could relax and turned to my friends. "So, we know something is wrong," I started, bringing us back to the mystery at hand. "But 'amiss' could also just mean how she feels since Jatin Kaka died."

"She never acted like this before she went on her trip," Deepak said. "She was friendly and called us 'shona' and cared about everyone. She'd drop off mithai anytime she made it," he added, talking about all the Indian sweets Heena Mavshi made so well.

I nodded as we turned onto Deepak's street. "She used to make me a painting every two weeks. And she hasn't given me even one all this time she's been back. It's been over two weeks. The only thing I've seen her paint is snakes. In bright red."

Deepak shook his head. "But this still doesn't make total sense. This is a mythological creature we're talking about here. It would be like if I told you a monster truly lived under my bed."

"That's why your family doesn't believe you," Penn added. "And if Mrs. Karwande is an ichchhadhari naagin, why are we just finding out now? Did she just turn into one or has she always been one?"

I shrugged. "You can't just turn into one. Every story I ever heard of them, you had to be born one."

"Those are just stories. Myths. We have to be scientific about this," Deepak said. "But it's tough to do that when there's no research on ichchhadhari naags or naagins because they technically don't exist. It's not like there's a book full of facts about them sitting in the Deadwood Public Library. There's no way even Reptile Rescue Center has one."

I straightened my shoulders. "But I do."

CHAPTER 37

We sat in my room, huddled around Aaji's book, the missing pages back inside. Deepak read the first poem out loud.

"'Beware the ichchhadhari naagin and her vengeful bite. She wants to stay human. She's full of spite.'" Deepak looked at us. "Okay, that's pretty self-explanatory. 'The cobra's song will fill you with fright. She'll take what's yours. Maybe even tonight.'"

"What's she going to take?" Penn asked.

"No clue," I replied.

"'Shambhar is the number'?" Deepak asked, running his finger under the Marathi word to make sure he hadn't misread it.

"That's one hundred in Marathi," I replied.

"Oh, okay. So after one hundred, 'her light will eternally be bright. And you'll forever be a saap.'"

"Snake in Marathi," I translated.

Deepak nodded. "'Much to her delight.'"

"So after one hundred, her light is eternally bright," Penn said, fiddling with the University of Michigan Rubik's Cube he had given me for my eighth birthday. "Sort of sounds like she'll be invincible or live forever."

"But what is it, one hundred days? One hundred mice?"

I asked. "Maybe Heena Mavshi just turned one hundred and that's why all this weird stuff started happening? Like she didn't fully transition into an ichchhadhari naagin until now?"

Deepak examined the page. "I don't think so. When I was staying at my dad's once, he told me that my uncle, Ashok Dada's son, and Heena Auntie went to elementary school together in Nagpur."

"And I assume your uncle isn't one hundred years old?" Penn asked.

"Right," Deepak replied. "But whatever it is, it sounds like the poem is saying everyone around her will turn into a snake once she's successful."

"I like snakes," Penn said slowly, "but I definitely don't want to become one."

I turned the page. "The next poem is even more mysterious."

"'Her body is cold. Cold-blooded. Coldhearted,'" Deepak read. "So she's like a reptile who is cold-blooded."

I nodded. "Either physically or coldhearted, meaning you don't care about others or you're kind of mean, which she has been lately. She walked right past me when I fell off my bike in front of her."

"Her anger is fiery, forked, un-guarded," Penn read. "So like a fiery temper. You said she's snapped at you a lot in the past few days."

I twisted my hair around my fingers. "Un-guarded means not protected, but it also means careless. Like she has no control over it, which seems to be true. She doesn't appear to be self-conscious about anything she says. But what does the 'forked' part mean? Because forked means split in two."

"How can anger be split in two?" Penn asked.

I scratched lines into the carpet. Emotions couldn't be split in two.

"A forked tongue!" Deepak exclaimed. "Snakes have a forked tongue. Maybe it shows when she gets angry."

I frowned. "Maybe . . . but I've never seen a forked tongue when Heena Mavshi was crabby."

Deepak nodded. "Okay, then let's keep going. 'Her bite is venom. Poison. Darted.'"

"Dart means quick. Or to move your eyes around rapidly. Or to throw . . ." I trailed off, trying to make sense of it.

"Or like a poison dart," Penn said. "Maybe it means her bite has good aim?"

"Yeah, possibly," I said. "This whole poem is also a translation from Marathi, so who knows how much of it is accurate," I added. "But at least we have a good starting point." I turned the book. "'Once in possession of teen dear things, it's too late to stop what she's started.'" I looked at the boys. "When I told Heena Mavshi I liked her paintings full of cobras, she said, 'You'll like it a lot more when it becomes your reality.' I think that's a clue. We'll all become snakes and not nice ones, like Gertrude," I added. "So we have to stop what has been started before it's too late. We have to stop her from getting teen dear things. Only . . . what are teen dear things?"

"Zit creams?" Penn suggested. "Texting? TikTok dances? Changing the world for the better?" He set the cube down, all sides completed. "I'm basing this off my fifteen-year-old cousin in Canton."

Just then the echoey sound of my doorbell interrupted us.

We listened as Aaji opened the door. "Oh! Heena and Lata! We were just about to make some chai. Join us."

I snapped the book shut. "She heard us," I whispered.

"How could she hear us from next door?" Penn asked before I loudly shushed him.

"Actually, snakes don't hear the way we do," Deepak said softly. "Remember what the vet was saying? They hear vibrations with their inner ear. But they also can't hear from too far away."

"You sure know a lot about snakes," Penn said.

"Shh! He knows a lot about everything," I whispered, cutting Penn off. "Better to be safe than sorry. And maybe her human ear can hear us."

We heard Lata Auntie, Aaji, Aai, and Baba laughing loudly below us.

I looked at Deepak. I could feel the carpet vibrating, just like when Aai and Aaji sang in the basement and I was upstairs.

"Geetanjali, come say hi," Aai called up. "Geetanjali! Ek . . . don . . ." Aai jokingly began to count in Marathi for me to get down before she reached 'three,' like I was a little kid.

I gasped. "I know what it means!" I shouted as quietly as I could. "Just a minute, Aai!" I called back. I wanted to be extra careful that Heena Mavshi couldn't hear us. I grabbed my comforter, stuffing it into the gap under the door to stop any sound from escaping.

"Why'd you do that?" whispered Penn.

Deepak pointed at the comforter. "To make sure Heena Auntie doesn't hear the vibrations of our words."

"Oh." Penn turned to me. "So, what are the teen dear things?"

"It was just about approaching it from a different way, something Aaji told me to do," I said softly. "See, it isn't teen with a hard *t* sound. It's the same letter that's in my name. The one I always mispronounce."

"Teen," Deepak said, pronouncing the *t* by putting his tongue behind his top front teeth. "Three."

I nodded, turning to Penn. "That means three in Hindi and Marathi. It is *three* dear things. Heena Mavshi needs three dear things and then her transformation into an evil ichchhad-hari naagin will be complete."

CHAPTER 38

As the grown-ups and Alaap sat at the kitchen table, I stood behind the counter with Penn and Deepak, my notebook and pencil in hand in case we needed to communicate in front of Heena Mavshi.

"It's a shame I might miss Geetanjali and Veena's last performance with Aai here," Baba said, talking about Aaji. "But that buyer sounded so anxious. I have to make sure she wants what's best for the property, so that's why I haven't booked my return ticket yet."

"I totally get it," Lata Auntie said, bouncing Alaap on her lap while making faces at him to make him giggle. "Besides, we'll be sure to record it and send it to you so you can see it in Konkan."

I watched Heena Mavshi sitting at the far end of the table by the patio door, sipping her chaha. The smell of lemongrass and ginger wafted through the kitchen. She didn't even look at me. Instead, she seemed to be fixated on the snakelike coils of steam coming out of her teacup.

Just then Alaap spit up all over Lata Auntie's cardigan.

"I'm so sorry," Aai apologized, taking Alaap and offering Lata some cotton napkins to wipe the mess off with.

"Oh, it's nothing," Lata Auntie replied as Heena Mavshi

looked on, disgusted. Lata Auntie took her cardigan off.

Aai frowned, picking up the lid on the glass container of milk on the floor behind Lata Auntie, in the patio door's sunbeam. "That's so strange, the dahi looked like it was going to set, but it's still so cold despite being in the sun."

"I hate when that happens," Lata Auntie said, about Aai's yogurt. She turned to us. "What book are you reading, dear?"

"Book?" I felt my stomach drop. Had everyone downstairs heard us reading from Aaji's book?

"Oh, it's just a notebook full of stories we write together," Penn said quickly. Technically he wasn't lying. We *had* written a story in it at the start of summer.

"Hopefully we can hear some of your stories soon," Aaji said, smiling at me.

I smiled back, but I felt that same discouraging distance between us that was there last night. Aaji didn't want to hear my stories. She didn't believe them, even when the proof was right before her eyes.

I turned the notebook to a clean page as the adults started talking about the Indian cricket team and wrote down: *What could be the three dear things?*

Penn shrugged as I turned back to our company. Was it Aai, Aaji, and Baba? No. Why would Alaap be left out? What else came in threes? The dead mice? No. If that were the case, Heena Mavshi would have been invincible already and we'd all be snakes.

Penn took the pencil from me. "Primary colors," he wrote.

"Musketeers," Deepak added.

"Bad news," Penn wrote down.

I looked at him.

"My mom always says bad news comes in threes," he whispered.

"What about you three?" Lata Auntie asked. "Are you going to join us, dears?"

You three. I shook my head, backing away, my pulse quickening. "We have . . . homework." I cringed, wishing I had said something more believable than homework in summer. I ran to the stairs and the boys rushed after me.

I think it's us, I mouthed, making sure Heena Mavshi didn't hear.

Deepak's eyebrows scrunched together as he tried to piece together what I was saying.

Lata Auntie always called kids "dear." We were dear. Heena Mavshi gave Deepak mithai. She gave me paintings. She gave Penn, well, I didn't know what she gave him other than maybe a friendly wave if she ever saw him outside. "It's the three of us!" I whispered, pointing to him and Penn.

CHAPTER 39

T hat doesn't make sense," Deepak said that night at Spark in the Park.

We had brought our lawn chairs to sit by the iron clock tower and white wooden gazebo, putting up with the mosquitoes, for an hour of watching the Deadwood fireworks as we scarfed down chocolates from the chocolate shop downtown.

Aai and Baba were back home, complaining about the booming fireworks and barking dogs that were stopping Alaap from sleeping. And Aaji was resting there too, her hip too sore to walk to the park with us.

"Why would we be the three dear things?" Deepak continued loudly, over the notes of the high school marching band that was playing the soundtrack for the show. "You probably are the closest to her out of all of us."

"I barely even know her," Penn added as the band stopped and Mayor Conovan made an announcement from the microphone at the gazebo.

"Hope you're all having a blast tonight, Deadwood!" she said to scattered applause. I did appreciate her wordplay, though. "Make sure you support our local businesses, and be sure to block your calendars for Accent Mark in the Park, July thirteenth!"

Deepak frowned. "I hate that name. It's so othering. Everyone has accents. That festival should have a better, more inclusive name."

"I agree," said the mayor from behind us.

"You do?" Deepak asked, craning his neck to make eye contact with the mayor.

"Definitely," she replied. "And I'm open to suggestions."

Penn turned to me. "Geetanjali's really good with words and multiple meanings."

I gave Penn a small, thankful smile.

"I remember," Mayor Conovan replied. "So Geetanjali, what do you have for us? What rhymes with park but is also inclusive and representative of that festival, celebrating our town's diversity?"

I squeezed the armrests of my chair and thought hard. It seemed like every possible rhyme was taken, with all the events and festivals celebrated in Deadwood. As a spiral of blue and white lit up the sky above us, I turned to Lark's mom.

"Maybe it doesn't have to rhyme," I said slowly. "Maybe it's time for a new approach. It should just say what it is. Our Voices in the Park."

"Huh." Mayor Conovan tilted her head for a second. "You know what? I like it."

Deepak grinned. "She likes it!"

The mayor nodded. "It's inclusive and it says what the day is all about, without any gimmicks. Straightforward and to the point. It's perfect. Thanks, Geetanjali."

I turned to the boys, who were beaming proudly at me, my insides bursting with joy, like the fireworks above us.

. . .

Back home, after the hour we were allowed to be at the park alone before it got too late, as the noise from Spark in the Park could still be heard in the distance, Penn, Deepak, and I stood in my backyard, trying to catch lightning bugs and put them in jars.

Deepak raised his arm and gently scooped one into his jar. "I hate to say this," he began. "But it's a stretch of the imagination to say the poem fits Heena Auntie. If she is an ichchhadhari naagin, she had to have been one since birth, like Geetanjali said. That means she would have been switching from cobra to human form as often as she wanted since you've known her. Why would she suddenly be acting strange? Why would a cobra have just been seen around town now and not earlier?"

My heart sank a little as I watched the firefly light up in his jar. I thought I finally had people who believed me. But they were just turning out to be doubters too. "I didn't imagine the mice. That's physical proof."

"It's physical proof of something," Deepak corrected, opening the jar so the bug could fly off with its friends. "We just don't know what. Just like all these strange things are proof of something. But are they proof that Heena Auntie is an ichchhadhari naagin? I'm not so sure. . . ."

"She's cold," I replied. "She's venomous."

"Not everything has multiple meanings," Deepak replied as Aaji opened the screen door and approached us with a bottle of her own.

"Are you catching fireflies with us?" Penn asked. "Or is that a jar of one of your pickles? Because I'd be fine either way," he added with a smile tinged with our chocolate from earlier.

Aaji laughed. "I'll make a bottle of watermelon rind pickle for you later this week. But for now, I'm here to help you catch these fireflies!"

Aaji swooped her jar around some blinking bug butts and caught four of them at once. Her eyes lit up as the bugs did too. "Look at that! I bet I'll get to one hundred in no time."

I ducked as an overly zealous lightning bug zipped toward my face. "Speaking of one hundred, Aaji, what does the 'shambhar' in the poem you translated in your book mean?"

Aaji paused her bug collecting. "It's one hundred years old. Legend says the ichchhadhari naag or naagin must get three dear things by their hundredth birthday."

I nodded. "Thank you. And if they succeed, they'll live forever and everyone around them will be turned into snakes?"

A loud banging from the sliding screen door of Heena Mavshi's patio interrupted us.

"Enjoying the show?" Aaji called out, in between the loud fireworks, as Heena Mavshi grabbed a chair that had fallen over on her patio and straightened it out.

"Such a racket!" Heena Mavshi grumbled.

"Oh, Heena," Aaji called out. "I've been meaning to tell you, we ran into Preeti and Subhash at the Commons the other day when we were taking Alaap for a walk." She was talking about the auntie and uncle therapist and psychologist who lived near Lark on the other side of the neighborhood. "They said if you ever wanted to talk, they're here."

"Thanks, but I don't need to talk to anyone," Heena Mavshi said. "What I do need, is some peace and quiet. Good night," she said, in what must have been the coldest "good night" anyone had ever wished another person.

Aaji waved and turned back to catch a firefly. As a blossom of red and blue lit up the muggy sky, Heena Mavshi turned to go back into her house, making a dramatic show out of covering her ears. The eerie crimson glow of some of the fireworks illuminated her left wrist. My chest tightened as I exchanged a worried look with Deepak and Penn.

Heena's wrist was covered in scales.

CHAPTER 40

"Y our advice worked," Penn said, taking his shoes off in the foyer by my front door Wednesday morning. "I told my mom I liked Indian music and she signed me up for your mom's class. She said it would be a good distraction for me while she and Dad work. Plus, it will be another chance for me to sing onstage at Our Voices in the Park."

I smiled at the new name that Mayor Conovan and the city council had approved just the other day. "That's great, Penn. I'm glad you're here," I said.

"I spent the morning at Reptile Rescue Center's library," Deepak added. "I have to admit, those did look like scales on Heena Auntie's wrist."

"Thank you," I said, relieved someone was finally on my side again, as more kids entered for class and rushed downstairs after kicking off their shoes.

"But I also asked Ashok Dada if he knew anything about ichchhadhari naagins. He told me there was nothing science based about it, but his family had shared lots of stories about them in his hometown in India. He said sometimes it was okay to believe in two things at once. And then ... he said to be really careful if I thought we were dealing with one. He said they're extremely dangerous."

Aai started playing the harmonium downstairs.

"Come on. We're going to be late." I led my friends downstairs, comforted by the fact that Deepak believed enough to research ichchhadhari naagins on his own, but still worried that my guess about the teen dear things was wrong and we were all going to be in trouble soon.

"Everyone welcome Penn to class," Aai said as we got to the bottom of the stairs and headed for our spots.

The kids all said hi to Penn, who flushed a deep pink as he waved back.

"Are you Indian?" Ami asked curiously.

"He's not," I said quickly. "He's a really good singer."

Penn looked at me gratefully as Aai played Raag Kedar up and down the harmonium and smiled.

"We have four songs to do today," Aai said, glancing at the teal clock. "Did everyone practice at home?"

The kids nodded.

"Good. And Penn, did you practice with the videos I sent you?"

"Yeah," Penn said, a little shyly.

"Perfect," Aai said. "I want you to have a relaxing summer, but I also want you to keep up this level of practice. Because we only have one more class before Accent Mark in the Park. Sorry, Our Voices in the Park, thanks to Deepak's activism and Geetanjali's great idea."

I was so nervous, I couldn't even smile at the rare compliment Aai was paying me. I fanned through the pages of raags in my binder, safe in their protective plastic sleeves so the anxious sweat on my hands wouldn't ruin them. I had to make sure I sang loudly and confidently at Our Voices in the Park when the last two times I'd gotten onstage, I couldn't even sing a complete song. And I had to save all my family and friends from getting turned into snakes, while also figuring out how to save Heena Mavshi from becoming an invincible evil cobra-person. *So much for a relaxing summer*, I thought, just as the doorbell rang.

My palms grew sweaty, and I exchanged a panicked look with Deepak and Penn. Everyone from class was downstairs.

"Ah, good. They're here," Aai said. "I thought it might be good practice for us to sing in front of an audience."

Please be Shilpa and Maya Auntie, I thought in my head as I heard Baba's footsteps head over to the front door above us. But a moment later Lata Auntie walked down the stairs instead.

"Hi, dears." She smiled.

And if Lata Auntie was there, I knew who would be right behind her.

I felt my voice lodge inside my throat as Heena Mavshi appeared, staring directly at me.

CHAPTER 41

Her wrist," I whispered to Penn and Deepak as I took in the sight just barely visible under Heena Mavshi's snake bangle. In the basement lighting, way brighter than the Fourth of July night, there was a row of coppery, shimmering circles that could only be described as . . . scales.

"Geetanjali," Aai said in a low voice. "Stop staring."

"What happened to your family picture?" Heena Mavshi asked, frowning at the collage as she and Lata Auntie made their way to the sheets laid out over the carpet.

"It's a collage Geetanjali and I made together," Aaji replied, keeping her eyes locked on Heena Mavshi's wrist. "Thought you'd appreciate the art."

"Yes, but your head . . . ," Lata Auntie said, turning back.

I looked at the collage. Aaji's head was dangling by a drop of glue. Her smile was upside down, looking big and eerie. The rest of us, in the collage, were still grinning and looking straight ahead, like nothing was wrong, kind of how everyone around me was still acting about Heena. I couldn't help but think of everything Aaji had been saying about her health, and her possibly not being well enough to come back here next summer, as I took in the unsettling sight of the collage. Was it a sign?

"That's ominous," Deepak whispered.

"No it's not," Penn said quickly. "Wait. What does 'ominous' mean?"

"Like a warning of something to come," I explained as Aaji walked by us to take a closer look.

"Oof," Aaji said. "That's disturbing. We'll fix it after class." She smiled at my mother, who was trying her best to act like the collage over our expensive family portrait wasn't making her really mad all over again. "Sometimes the paper is too thick for the glue to hold. It happens," my grandmother added, giving me a reassuring smile as she took her seat next to us and the harmonium.

"Well, I think it is beautiful," Lata Auntie said. "You have so much talent in you, Geetanjali. I wish I could sing like you and your family, let alone make art like this."

"All right, let's begin," Aai said, clearing her throat and cutting Lata Auntie off before she could praise the collage any longer.

I sat up straight, ready to get this song over with before Heena Mavshi decided to chomp on us. I took a sip of water from the stainless-steel cups Aai had placed out before us, preparing to belt out bravely and show Aaji I wasn't afraid to use my voice.

But then Aai put the microphone in front of me. Right in front of me.

"Ami." I waved. "Come sit in front of me. You're shorter."

"No," Aai said, touching Ami's shoulder. "I want her-age kids to be together. You big kids will be closer to the mics." Aai leaned toward me and lowered her voice. "And we'll be doing the songs over and over again until I hear you."

Heena Mavshi was smiling at my mother lecturing me in front of everyone, like she was taking pleasure out of my misery, something the old Heena Mavshi would never have done.

I clenched the side of my binder. "I'm not afraid," I said to Aai, hoping Heena Mavshi realized my response was intended for her.

Aaji squeezed my hand and Lata Auntie gave me a thumbs-up, and I suddenly felt the slightest bit better about everything. Everything except the fact that my neighbor could be turning into a snake-person, that is.

Aaji's fingers tapped across the harmonium keys. Aai was on tabla. At the right count of the sixteen beats, we began singing Raag Bhoopali's lakshan geet. I cringed as my tiny voice was projected on the speakers, thinking back to how awful I sounded at Gudhi Padwa.

I sounded like a baby then and now, and I hated it, like I was a scared little kid. Penn was sweating a lot more than usual and was redder than normal, but he and Deepak were singing with their mouths open wide, their backs straight, their voices loud, like they didn't even need the microphone.

"Voice" was in the first notebook I ever filled with definitions. It meant the sound you made with your mouth. It also meant an opinion. It could mean the range or pitch or tone that you sing in. And it meant to express yourself. Looks like I was failing at all definitions of it.

Aaji changed the tune to Ichak Dana, the riddle song. Ami and Apoorva were scream-singing their way through this one. I sang, voice still shaky, knowing there was no way I could be heard over them, and looked at Lata Auntie.

She was laughing and clapping, the naagmani on her necklace bounced across her chest, clanging against the blue teardrop gem on her ring.

Heena Mavshi was staring straight at us, without a smile, gently rocking back and forth to the music. Her copper snake bangle looked portentous, but her sleeveless salwar kurta was nice.

It was fluorescent orange with purple tulips and green vines crisscrossing across the tunic and pant legs. It had a neon-yellow odhni draped over her shoulder. But the moment I looked at her shoulder, I thought of her bloody birthmark. The little kids shouted the answer to the riddle, "Mor!"—a peacock—in unison and startled me, and I knocked the microphone down by Heena Mavshi's feet.

"Oops!" Lata Auntie said.

Heena Mavshi rolled her eyes and bent forward to pick it up with her scaly hand.

Her bright yellow odhni fell to the ground from her sudden movement, and I gasped louder than any sound I'd sung in music class lately.

That's because with the odhni no longer on, everyone got a clear view of Heena Mavshi's shoulder and upper back, what her sari blouses had been hiding. It wasn't a single, bloody circular birthmark. And it wasn't a bedbug bite.

It was two holes. Like a snakebite. Like the bites on the three mice.

Lata Auntie quickly draped her tan cardigan over Heena Mavshi and handed her the odhni. She then gently pulled the microphone and stand out of Heena Mavshi's hands and plopped it down in front of me.

My entire arm was coated in goose bumps, like an icy aura was coiling around me.

I had gotten it all wrong.

Heena Mavshi wasn't an evil ichchhadhari naagin.

Heena Mavshi was its victim.

CHAPTER 42

Penn, Deepak, and I sat at the kitchen table, notebook open as we scribbled notes to each other, shielded by our hands. Heena Mavshi and Lata Auntie had stayed back for chaha, and Lata Auntie was bouncing Alaap on her lap in the family room after she finished her tea.

I wrote vigorously, my pencil almost tearing the paper, *The bite is slowly turning her into a snake! That's why she's making art about them! Those are definitely scales! Her transition is starting!!!* I shook my hand as a cramp formed.

Penn took the pencil: *Why didn't she tell you this?*

He handed me the pencil. *She's not in control?* I wrote, taking a guess. *Whoever bit her is?*

She's like a snake zombie. Penn wrote.

Deepak frowned. The farther away we got from science, the less likely he was to be on board. I started writing: *We should tell Lata Auntie. She should know her bff from first grade has been bitten by a snake and it isn't bedbugs, and that Lata Auntie could be the next victim if we don't find the cobra that's slithering loose around our neighborhood!*

"Thank you again for being our test audience," Aai said from the family room next to us, getting the glass bottle of coconut oil from Alaap's changing table.

"It was our pleasure," Lata Auntie said in between making weird faces to try to make Alaap laugh. "And I'm glad I could stay after to play with this little dear. Do you want me to give him a tel maalish?"

Aai shook her head, tilting the bottle of clear liquid as she let Lata Auntie know Alaap didn't need an oil massage. "I just needed to put some in his curls."

Lata Auntie extended her hand. "I'll do it. Take some rest. Moms deserve some time off too, right?"

Alaap did not seem happy, but Aai gave in, handing the coconut oil over.

"Is your cousin going to be back later this summer? I'd love to meet them. They're so close to Deadwood," Aai said, warming up a little to Lata Auntie.

"Who?" Lata Auntie asked, rubbing the oil into my brother's hair. His eyes widened like he was going to cry in the strange auntie's hands.

I mouthed *poop* to him and he began to giggle.

"Your cousin?" Aai repeated. "In Plymouth? You told us at the airport that you booked your ticket but then she had to go out of town."

Lata Auntie nodded. "Yes, of course. No, my cousin won't be back for a long time, unfortunately." She smiled at Alaap, still holding the coconut oil bottle.

Deepak's eyes widened. *It's smurglegurble*, he scribbled in his sloppy handwriting.

Penn raised an eyebrow at Deepak as he took a spoonful of the watermelon rind pickle Aaji had packed for him last night. "Huh?" he whispered.

It's L-A-T-A A-U-N-T-I-E, Deepak scrawled back, taking the time to legibly write each letter as he stared right at her and the coconut oil massage she was giving my brother. *Coconut oil solidifies around 74 to 76 degrees Fahrenheit*, he added.

Why was he giving us coconut oil facts? *No way it's her*, I wrote, double underlining it for emphasis. Lata Auntie was the only one other than Aaji who got me. She knew what it was like to get cut down by Aai. She was so kind and caring. There was no way she was a snake-woman.

I watched Lata Auntie tenderly put the oil on Alaap's curls, like a thick, gluey paste. "I was telling Heena she could get a park bench named after Jatin at the Commons to honor him; perhaps it will also help her get some closure. She told me he liked to go over there and sit by the creek and feed the ducks."

"Well, he can't do that anymore now, can he?" Heena Mavshi snapped. "So what good is naming a bench after him?"

Baba and Aai exchanged a worried glance.

"Heena, have you tried talking to someone about what you're going through? Or what Jatin went through?" Baba asked softly. "Subhash and Preeti were saying—"

"I don't know why all of you can't mind your own business," Heena Mavshi said sharply.

"I think that sleep medicine has too many side effects, Heena," Lata Auntie said sweetly, like she was trying hard to make up for how angry Heena Mavshi sounded. "It gave her a rash on her hand and back and is probably giving her mood swings," she said to my parents and Aaji.

I chewed the insides of my cheeks. That wasn't what she'd told me when I'd fallen off my bike. She'd told me Heena

Mavshi had been bitten by bedbugs, and before that she'd said it was a birthmark. She also seemed to have forgotten about the cousin she had mentioned at the airport. Like it was all just a lie. And, come to think of it, why was that coconut oil a thick white in her hands as she rubbed it into my brother's hair instead of the thin, clear liquid it was when it was summer temperature? Is that what Deepak was talking about?

I looked at the boys. *But Lata Auntie wears a naagmani,* I wrote. *How can it be her?*

"You're going through a tough time," Aaji said to Heena. "I know what it's like to lose someone when you're young."

Lata Auntie nodded. "We both do. You should talk to us."

Heena Mavshi just glared. "We should go."

"Maybe I can stop by later to make you some of my raagi kheer that you like," Aaji said, talking about her sweet pudding made from finger millet and milk and spiced with cardamom powder.

"That would be lovely," Lata Auntie said.

Maybe it's fake? Penn wrote.

Just then Heena Mavshi walked by us, Lata Auntie behind her, her cardigan in her hand, on her way out. I snapped the notebook shut.

"Oops!" Lata Auntie said.

My stomach dropped. Had she seen anything?

"I was walking out the door with this!" she laughed, returning the bottle of oil to Aai.

The entire bottle of coconut oil was solid white, like it was in winter. Even though it was the middle of summer.

"See you later." Lata Auntie waved, her face shifting to an icy smile before she headed out the door.

CHAPTER 43

I can't believe I didn't put it together earlier," I said that weekend, from the Reptile Rescue Center mini theater as the end credits to the documentary about pythons in the Everglades rolled.

The boys and I had decided to watch the movie they had seen without me together, but none of us could really concentrate on the film with everything going on. "She entered the room when my dad was interviewing Aaji, and it was nothing but hissing when he went back to play it," I whispered, even though we were the only three people in the theater. "She pretended to be so nice and caring. But that's not who she is. She's a monster. A fictional monster come to life, no matter how strange that sounds," I added, looking at Deepak. "Was she just making up knowing Heena Mavshi from first grade as a way to find easy access to more victims to bite?"

I stood up and Penn and Deepak followed me out of the theater, into the lobby. "And who wears a fake naagmani?"

"Apparently, a cobra," Deepak answered, holding the doors open for me and Penn. "She's smart. Most snakes are. But the king cobra is considered most intelligent. I bet her cardigan keeps her warm. I always thought it was weird, wearing a cardigan when it was ninety degrees outside. Now it's all making sense." Deepak twisted his brows. "Sort of."

"No, it is," Penn said while we turned the corner. "If the poem is right, we probably need to know when her hundredth birthday is so we know how much time we have to fix everything."

I frowned. "She told my family she has a big birthday coming up on July fourteenth. The day after Our Voices in the Park."

Penn's face dropped. "What if it's her hundredth birthday?"

"That means we only have five more days before all of us turn into snakes if she gets her three dear things, and we still have no clue what they are," I concluded.

"We have to find out more about Lata Auntie," Deepak added.

"Ashok Ajoba!" I shouted, and stopped in the middle of the sidewalk, almost causing the boys to run into me. "Deepak, you said your uncle went to first grade with Heena Mavshi. Would his school stuff be at Ashok Ajoba's home? Remember how Ashok Ajoba said he was organizing old photos the night of the party at my house?"

Deepak beamed. "Let's go get some evidence."

CHAPTER 44

"H ere you go," Ashok Ajoba said, plopping down four red cardboard boxes with decorative green-and-yellow dotted paisleys from India onto his coffee table. "These are all of Dilip's school pictures," he explained, showing us his grown son's old pictures.

"Thanks, Ashok Dada," Deepak said as we crouched next to him on the plush carpet in his living room and began to gently take pictures out.

"We need to find first grade," Penn said.

"It will be called 'first standard.' That's the word for 'grade' in India," Deepak replied.

There were black-and-white pictures of Deepak's uncle playing cricket and petting a bunch of kittens. There were pictures from his high school classes, and at the bottom of the pile were faded black-and-white pictures of his grades in elementary school. We flipped through the grades. There was fifth, fourth, third, second, and, finally, I pulled out the picture of their first-grade class.

It was row after row of children, girls with their hair in two braids, looped on either side and tied up with a bow as part of their school uniform. They were wearing salwar kurtas. I scanned the kids and immediately spotted the one with the biggest grin. Her eyes seemed to be twinkling with joy. I recognized that look from before Jatin Kaka died.

"It's Heena Mavshi," I gasped.

The boys nodded. "What about Lata Auntie?" Penn asked, peering over my shoulder, doing his very best to pronounce the *t* in Lata.

"Her full name is Naaglata." I bent down closer to see the tiny font with the students' names.

"I see my uncle," Deepak said, pointing to Ashok Ajoba's son. "But I don't see anyone named Naaglata or Lata."

"Me neither," Penn said.

"Same," I gulped. My hands shook a little as I stared at the class picture. This was confirmation. Lata Auntie convinced Heena Mavshi on the plane that they'd known each other as children. If Lata Auntie was lying about that, what else was she lying about?

CHAPTER 45

"This is why our parents tell us not to talk to strangers," Penn said as we rode our bikes in nervous figure eights in Reptile Rescue Center's abandoned parking lot on Sunday.

"How could Heena Mavshi have just fallen for it?" I asked, zipping around the white parking-spot lines in front of me.

"Maybe she was thinking of other things, like Jatin Uncle, and just wanted to believe it because she needed a friend?" Deepak suggested, coming to a stop halfway on the sidewalk bordering the parking lot, almost hitting a man and woman walking by with a sleeping baby in a bright orange stroller.

"Sorry," Deepak said.

"Wrong country," the man muttered as they continued down the sidewalk.

"There's no place for your xenophobia here!" Deepak called after them as they crossed the street at the light. "Come to Our Voices in the Park! Get to know your neighbors and see what you have in common with them!"

"Deepak," I whisper-yelled. "Stop. What if he comes back to yell at you?"

Penn sat on his bike with his mouth open, like he was stunned any of this was happening. "How could they say that to you?"

"Ask them." Deepak shrugged. "It happens all the time." He turned to me. "We have to keep speaking up, Geetanjali. You can't let fear silence you. Now back to the snake problem. We have to confirm it's Lata Auntie."

"Shh!" I said, looking back at the center. It was empty of people, but it was still full of reptiles. "What if the snakes in there are her spies?"

Penn shook his head. "No way."

"How can you be so sure?"

"Because I know Gertrude was at that party to help us. Snakes don't like evil snake-people. They give them a bad rep. So we have to figure out how to protect our families and the good snakes. We need to enjoy the rest of our summer! Even if that means listening to Deepak studying that weird language."

"It's not a language. It's trigonometry. Although I guess it is rather poetic to refer to math as a language." Deepak beamed, probably dreaming up a math problem in his head.

Penn turned around on his bike. "And we may have less than a month together if you don't tell your mom how you really feel about robotics camp. Or even less than that if we get bit by an ichchhadhari naagin this week."

"Why do you think she bit Heena Mavshi?" I asked. "Could someone grieving be one of the three dear things? We don't have a lot of time to figure this out," I added as a nervous churning sensation filled my intestines.

"Maybe we start by proving she fits all the other lines of that poem and then that may give us a clue?" Deepak suggested.

"We've got the cold one proven," Penn said, counting on

his fingers. "And the bite being venomous; we see how mean Mrs. Karwande is now that she has been bitten."

"'Her anger is fiery, forked, un-guarded,'" Deepak recited, standing to pedal his bike. "How do we make her angry to see if she has a forked tongue?"

I watched the couple push the orange stroller in the distance, and thought about how Deepak fearlessly said something back to them. I needed my friends by my side to save the day. But like Aaji said, she might not always be here. Just like there would be times when Penn and Deepak wouldn't be by my side. I needed to learn to start standing up for the things and people I cared about without always depending on others.

"Maybe if you put antivenom everywhere in her house? That might make her mad," Penn said, talking about the purified antibodies against snake venom. Antivenom was used to treat poisonous snakebites. "But where would we even get it from? We can't break into Reptile Rescue."

"There has to be another way to make her mad," Deepak chimed in.

While the man and his family turned the corner, out of our sight, I squeezed my handlebars tightly and turned to my friends as something came to mind. "I know how."

CHAPTER 46

I rushed home to grab the book Aaji had made me. I threw it into my backpack, got on my bike again, and then cut across the path between my yard and Heena Mavshi's to follow it down to the playground at the Commons. I had told Deepak and Penn to meet me there. Even if we didn't know how far Lata Auntie could hear with her snake abilities or whatever powers she had as an ichchhadhari naagin, it just felt safer the farther away we were from her.

I zipped past the pig and big bad wolf, and looked around for Penn and Deepak. Maybe they hadn't gotten to the park yet. I paused to catch my breath and noticed Lark was almost at the top of the Wall of Doom, sweat dripping down her face. Rohan and his two friends were sitting on the swings nearby.

"What song are you singing for the park today?" Rohan taunted, his words full of venom.

I watched Lark's ears burn red. She was still looking like her usual super-confident self, but I bet she was scared of Rohan and his friends. I thought about how fearless Deepak had been at the reptile center when that couple was being racist. Or how brave Penn had been when he'd told me exactly what he was feeling after Bark in the Park. I was going to have to be super courageous in a few minutes with Lata Auntie, so now seemed like a good time to prove to myself I could be just that. But could I?

One of them turned her phone in my direction. "Hey. You're in our way," she snickered.

"Sor—" I stopped myself from apologizing. I hadn't done anything wrong. They were in the wrong.

I wiped my sweaty hands on the front of my shirt and grabbed one of the neon grips sticking out of the wall. I took a shaky step up, my insides dropping like I was on a turbulent plane. I wasn't going to let Lata Auntie hurt my family. I could do anything I set my mind to. Starting with this wall.

I pushed myself, reaching for one neon grip after the next, until I was by Lark, close enough to see that wasn't sweat on her face. It was a tear. I frowned at the older kids down below.

"She's really brave to sing in front of everyone, you know," I said loudly, almost shocking myself at the volume of my voice. It wasn't my talking-to-grown-ups voice this time. "And you're all being really mean. So you should stop."

Rohan rolled his eyes at me. He waved at his friends to get up and follow him.

They headed down the black path closest to the swings. "I mean it," I called after them. "Stop howling at people. Stop laughing at people. Just be nice!"

Rohan waved his arm back at me, not bothering to turn to face me. "Yeah, yeah," he said.

I wasn't sure I had stopped Rohan from ever being mean again. But maybe he'd do it less often now that both Deepak and I had stood up to him. I looked at Lark. "I'm sorry I didn't help you the last time they laughed at your song."

Lark turned to me, a small smile crossing her face. "That's okay. You helped me now. Thanks."

"Are you singing at Our Voices in the Park?" I asked her.

Lark shook her head. "I'm singing at Park in the Park in September."

I smiled back at her. That was Deadwood's classic car celebration. "I'll be there."

Lark beamed, and all the fear of being on top of the wall melted away. Just then Deepak shouted my name. I looked down to see the boys standing by the shelter, next to their bikes.

"I'll see you around," I said to Lark as I headed back down the wall and ran toward the shelter.

"I thought you were afraid of heights," Penn said. "You just climbed the Wall of Doom."

I shrugged. "I'm sick of being afraid."

"Good," Deepak said, and smiled. "Then let's do this."

I unzipped my backpack. "I looked over the lakshan geet. It isn't easy," I said, handing it to Deepak.

Penn cocked his head at the notes. "Whoa. That's really high. And really low." He squinted, reading what taal, or beat, it was in. "And really fast at one point?"

I nodded, reviewing the notes once more. I hadn't bothered reading the raag until now, when we needed to see what help the book could offer us. I turned the page. There, Aaji had written about how her ancestors had composed this raag centuries ago, when they sang in a raja's court in the palace.

Raag Naagshakti is one of the most powerful raags there is. It harnesses the power of cobras, making

the same vibrations as the earth. Many have tried
to sing the lakshan geet and failed. Many have
succeeded and had bad luck immediately after.
When I last sang this song, something terrible
happened in my house. Shortly after, your ajoba
passed away from a mysterious illness. Some say it
was a curse for singing this song. But I don't think
we should let fear silence us. Do you?

That's just what Deepak said. I held my head up high. I wasn't going to let fear silence me anymore. I was going to find out if Lata Auntie was the naagin. I cleared my throat, and I began to sing.

"You have to be louder than that," Penn said gently. "You have to show her who's boss."

"You have to make her think you're really going to sing it before you stop," Deepak added.

I nodded, starting over, preventing myself from dreaming up the worst that could happen. I sang loudly, despite the fact that some kids walking by were staring at me, despite the fact that Lark had turned from the wall to watch my performance.

Let them, I thought. *Let everyone hear me sing.*

CHAPTER 47

My whole body felt weak and jiggly, but I steadied myself as I rang the doorbell at Heena Mavshi's house. I looked back. Penn and Deepak were standing in Penn's yard, watching me, ready to help.

Lata Auntie opened the door and smiled warmly. She had tricked us all for so long, by pretending to care for people who were feeling isolated or sad, like me and Heena Mavshi. I felt my heart thumping in my chest but reminded myself I had been next to Lata Auntie many times before and survived. Besides, she didn't know I knew what she was.

Lata Auntie ushered me in. "Come to get your aaji?"

"Aaji?" I asked, confused. I paused to take my shoes off by the door and glanced to my left, at the living room, and gasped.

Because Heena Mavshi's beautiful, massive painting of a cobra and mongoose was covered in globs of dripping, blood-red paint, like someone had violently thrown a bucket of it all over. There were splatters drenching the wall and even on the sofa below it. I felt a queasy lump form in my throat and tried to swallow it down.

All this time, poor Heena Mavshi was trying to communicate what was really going on. That Lata Auntie was an ichchhadhari naagin. That Heena Mavshi had been bitten and was losing control as the venom took over. That we were all in danger. And instead of my immediately understanding, like she had trusted I would, my imagination thought the worst of Heena Mavshi instead.

"You didn't know your aaji was here?" Lata Auntie asked as she led me into the posh navy-blue-and-white kitchen by the sunroom.

Aaji was standing alongside an irritated-looking Heena Mavshi near the kitchen island and its collection of yellow vases and a bowl of sunny lemons.

"Heena, what is this rash all over your hand?" Aaji said.

Aaji's smile faded when she saw me. "What are you doing here, Geetu?"

"Hiss, hiss, it's all amiss. Soon we'll be in serpentine bliss," Heena Mavshi whispered.

Aaji dropped her hand, taking a step back as our eyes met.

I nodded at Aaji. I knew she heard what Heena Mavshi had said. There was no doubting it. I had one last thing to do, the proof I needed for Aai and everyone else. And with Aaji here, I felt safe, and strong, and unstoppable.

"I ... I wanted to sing that lakshan geet you've been asking for, Lata Auntie. Raag Naagshakti's," I said.

Aaji turned to Heena Mavshi's hand and then back toward me, a look of concern in her eyes, like she was piecing something together. "What are you doing, Geetanjali?"

I squeezed my naagmani necklace. "It's okay, Aaji." I looked down at my toes. I could feel everyone's eyes on me, and my ears were burning, but I had to do this. I took a deep breath and began the opening line of the lakshan geet. It was soft, it was shaky, but it was the lakshan geet. I was hitting every single note.

I took a quick glance up and saw Aaji shake her head, like she was trying to say no. Like she wanted me to stop. But I had to get this first line out. Besides, if Aaji finally believed that Heena Mavshi was the victim of an ichchhadhari naagin, we needed proof that Lata Auntie was the culprit so my parents would believe us too. We needed to see the forked tongue.

I peeked over to her side and saw the blue stone on Lata Auntie's ring glowing brighter and bigger with each note I sang until it almost looked like the flame of a birthday candle. Her pupils seemed to reflect that blue light, and her smile was growing wider by the second. It was now or never.

I shut my mouth.

"What happened?" Lata Auntie snapped, the blue glow disappearing from her eyes and the gemstone.

My knees shook like an earthquake. "A . . . A . . ."

Lata Auntie looked down in a panic at the gem on her ring, which had shrunk back down to its old size. "What?"

Aaji glanced at the stone and then at the bite that was peeking out of Heena Mavshi's back, by the collar of her salwar kurta, and the color drained from her face.

". . . April . . . Fools?" I said in my softest voice, breaking every rule we had about respecting our elders, since it clearly wasn't April.

"What did you say?" Lata Auntie asked, her eyebrows elevated; I wouldn't have been surprised if smoke started coming out of her ears. She pushed a yellow stool to the side, slamming it against the stainless-steel fridge, as she charged toward me.

I squinted, looking in her mouth for a hint of a forked tongue, but it was hard to see when she was jerking her head around in a temper tantrum.

"You dare pull this trick on me! Do you know what I can do, dear?!"

"No!" Aaji shouted, rushing in front of me. And before I could say anything, Aaji began to sing the lakshan geet from the beginning in a clear, strong, loud voice.

"Aaji!" I screamed.

But Lata Auntie backed down, her face calm and serene as she began to sway to the music.

I watched Aaji hit every single note with ease, her forehead beading a little. I could feel the ground vibrate ever so slightly with each new line Aaji sang. The music felt powerful. Her voice felt powerful. It was mesmerizing.

Lata Auntie's blue gemstone ring grew and glowed, burning bright, elongating, the flame from before reappearing. Her eyes seemed to have the same fire in them and she couldn't look away, as she finally got to hear the song she had been asking for, for weeks.

But Heena Mavshi's face wasn't enthralled. She still had the same irritated expression she had been wearing since the night she'd come home, since being bitten by a venomous snake. Except there was one change. A single tear was rolling down her cheek, like an alarm. Only, before it could say anything more, it plopped onto the hardwood, silenced.

CHAPTER 48

Aaji clenched my wrist and rushed me out of the house the moment her song ended.

"What's going on, Aaji?" I asked, my heart thumping in my throat as we got to our driveway and the boys ran to join us.

I didn't think Aaji could run this fast anymore. She had said she couldn't ride the pig at the park and yet here she was, making me out of breath just to keep up with her.

I turned to Penn and Deepak as we got to our porch. "I'll fill you in as soon as I know more."

Penn and Deepak nodded, hanging back as Aaji pulled our door open and ushered me toward the stairs, her voice dropping to a whisper. "I shouldn't have told you about ichchhadhari naagins."

She took one step up the stairs and closed her eyes.

"Are you going to faint?" I asked, grabbing her elbow to help support her.

But Aaji shook her head. "I'm suddenly very tired," she croaked, like she was losing her voice as well.

I helped Aaji up to the second floor. "Should I get Aai?"

Aaji shook her head again, crawling into her bed, her hand resting on her sore hip. Her eyelids seemed to be so heavy, she couldn't keep them open. She turned to her side and her head sank into the pillow. "Just . . . ," she whispered, falling asleep, ". . . stay away . . . from Raag Naagshakti. . . ."

Aaji's mouth remained open, but she slept in complete silence.

Like someone had stolen her song.

CHAPTER 49

We still don't have clear evidence that Lata Auntie is an ichchhadhari naagin," Deepak said the following morning in his room, scribbling some answers in a new workbook at his desk, which was covered in sketches of reptiles with facts written below them. "We never saw the forked tongue."

"I think it's pretty much confirmed," I said, eyeing the big encyclopedias on space, rocks, animals, and elements scattered around Deepak's messy room. "I mean, who else gets that mad about stopping a song about snakes?!"

"Maybe she's really into music," Penn suggested from the small space on Deepak's bed in between a bunch of pink and green stuffed bears, a hand-stitched brown baby doll that Deepak had probably sewed when he was two at some genius-baby sewing camp, and his week's wardrobe. "Just kidding. She's clearly the naagin, Deepak. I'm really into music and I wouldn't go into full attack mode if someone stopped a song I liked."

"And now Aaji's not feeling well. She warned me to stay away from Raag Naagshakti and has been super tired ever since we came home yesterday; she's barely said anything."

"Did you check if she had a bite mark?" Penn asked, taking a seat on Deepak's swivel chair and spinning around.

"None that I could see. Besides, Heena Mavshi wasn't sleepy and exhausted after she was bitten. She was just mean and making creepy cobra art."

Penn almost collided into one of the five bookshelves in Deepak's cluttered room. "Right. So something different is going on with your grandma."

"My mom said that sometimes Aaji gets really tired when she exerts herself too much or strains her vocal cords. But I am positive Lata Auntie did something to her. I'm not sure how or what. All I know is, this is a bad sign. Really bad," I said.

Deepak sighed. "You're right. I'm sorry for gaslighting you."

I raised an eyebrow at Penn. I knew what "gaslight" meant. I heard Maya Auntie saying it during the election last year, when they lived in Troy. It meant a type of lamp. But it also meant when you make someone question their own story.

"I wanted different forms of proof, but I shouldn't have kept doubting you when you noticed so many things we never saw," Deepak added.

I nodded. "Thanks. And it's okay. You believe me now, and we're going to save everyone from turning into a bunch of snakes."

"Why does she care so much about the lakshan geet?" Deepak asked, chewing his pencil. "It didn't attract any snakes. Did Gertrude look like she attempted to escape yesterday after Geetanjali sang?"

Penn shook his head. "Maybe it gives her power."

"Like she absorbs the powerful earth vibrations it supposedly recreates?" I guessed. I flipped through a book full of "Mathtastic Fun." "And I think Aaji finally knows something is wrong."

"I think your aaji finally believes you but doesn't want to," Deepak offered. "Because it's illogical and yet it really is happening. Like what Ashok Dada said to me about believing in science but also believing ichchhadhari naagins can exist."

"Maybe Aaji's energy really was sucked out by Lata," Penn suggested. "Like in *The Little Mermaid*."

I frowned. "She didn't bite her, though. I didn't see any marks on Aaji, remember?"

"But you said her ring started glowing as your grandma sang. Maybe it was draining your aaji's power."

"My grandmother isn't a superhero, Penn," I retorted. "No matter what Aaji said about your voice being powerful, it couldn't really have power in it that Lata Auntie sucked up in a gemstone like a Disney movie."

Deepak joined Penn in the pacing. "Clearly there's a connection we're missing."

I stared out the window, watching Maya Auntie and Shilpa chatting on lawn chairs under the pergola. Mother and daughter, laughing and connecting. "There was this story Aaji told me. A mom and her daughter were singing the raag when a cobra came up to them, attracted to the music. They tried to shoo it out of the way, but the dad accidentally killed the cobra."

Penn shot up off the chair. "What if Lata knows that cobra?"

"What?"

"This is revenge. Didn't you say they take revenge if their mate is killed? What if that cobra-man was the ichchhadhari naagin's husband, Lata's husband!"

I shut the math book. Could Penn be right? "If that's true, then it still doesn't explain why Lata Auntie wants to hear the song again. Why would you want to hear the song that was sung right before your husband died?"

"Maybe she wanted some kind of confirmation. Like we do," Deepak said.

"Confirmation about what?" I asked.

"That your grandmother and mom are the mom and daughter in question. That they were the ones singing that song all those years ago. Your grandma's book basically says that your grandpa died from a curse after she sang that song."

I felt my palms grow sweaty. I had assumed that story took place hundreds of years ago, in the time of Tansen and emperors and queens. But Aaji never said when it had happened. And Aai hated snakes and had torn the page on Raag Naagshakti out of her binder and refused to sing it. Like she wanted to forget it ever existed.

"My mom used to see a cobra every now and then; it would startle her and lunge at her or slither toward her. As weird as it was, she was positive it was the same snake every time. What if that snake was Lata Auntie?"

CHAPTER 50

After dinner I headed straight to Aaji's bedroom. Aai and Baba had helped her up the stairs to her bed, and I needed a moment alone with her to talk about what had happened at Heena Mavshi's house.

I turned the doorknob and the door opened with a loud squeak, but Aaji didn't even budge.

"What are you doing?"

I jumped in the dark room. From behind me, the hallway light fell onto my mom.

"I'm getting ready for bed," I said hesitantly, focusing on Aai's downturned eyebrows that said I was doing something wrong.

Aaji stirred in bed behind me, her bangles jingling. I turned to the sound and gasped. There on her wrist was a little bump that hadn't been there before.

"There's a scale on her hand!" I said to Aai, as softly as I could despite being terrified.

Aai led me out of the room. "She's not feeling well," she whispered. "Maya Auntie is coming over to check on her once she gets done at the hospital. Let her get a good night's sleep without you tossing and turning all over her."

"But I won't be able to sleep by myself!"

Aai closed Aaji's door. "You're going to have to try."

CHAPTER 51

P enn, Deepak, and I leaned against our bikes in my driveway, the evening before Our Voices in the Park.

"We're doomed," I said over the hum of a weed whacker in the distance. I was groggy, having slept with my light on all night, thanks to Aai's new no-sleeping-next-to-Aaji rule.

"My parents told me there's no such thing as a cobra-person," Penn said. "And then they shut their office door so Mom could run a virtual meeting for LawnBot."

Deepak's shoulders caved inward. "Shilpa didi told me creativity is good, but I could use the time I spent dreaming up this story to work on some geometry problems."

"You know how in the books we read at school, kids always save the day?" I asked. "I think there might be a reason they're called fiction."

Penn and Deepak looked down. I was about to slump my head too, when movement in the garage caught my attention.

I walked toward the tiny plastic purple house, heart racing. "It's garage mouse!" I gasped.

The boys and I stood at the park with a paper bag containing the mouse house. I had picked the location, far enough from the woods in our neighborhood that hopefully a certain cobra wouldn't try to make garage mouse another midnight snack.

All around us, crews of volunteers were setting up the stage for Our Voices in the Park. It was noisy and chaotic, but I couldn't help feeling a bit calm, too. Garage mouse had survived. A mouse had survived all the horrible things happening to mice on our street. It was like there was finally some much-needed hope.

"Okay, now we get the trap out of the bag," I said, my left hand shaking a little as I held the bag out to Penn.

"She's your garage mouse," Penn said with a slight shudder, backing away toward the iron clock tower.

I nodded, reached into the bag with my gloved right hand, and picked the trap up. The mouse inside was so scared it was unable to move.

Deepak put his face way closer to the mouse than I would have. "See this lever here? It opens this mechanism that lets the mouse out." He pointed.

"What if she jumps onto my hand when I do that?"

"She wants to get away from you," Deepak responded.

"Right," I replied. I could do this. Releasing a mouse was nothing compared to defeating an evil cobra-person.

I crouched down and pressed the lever. The purple door swung open and the mouse sprang into action, hopping out and running through the park.

"You did it!" Penn cheered.

"I knew you would," Deepak added, giving me a proud look.

"Make good choices!" I called out to the mouse, like Aai would normally say to me.

"Looks like kids can save the day," I declared triumphantly as I stood up and turned to leave with my friends.

I immediately came to an abrupt stop.

Straight ahead of us, across the street from the park, stood Lata Auntie.

She gave us a smile, wide and unfriendly all at once, as she continued walking down the hilly street until I couldn't see her anymore.

And all my hopeful thoughts, of being able to save my friends, family, and town, seemed to fade away into the distance with her.

CHAPTER 52

I t was the day before Lata Auntie's big birthday, the very last day we had before we were doomed to all become snake minions, and we weren't any closer to solving this mystery.

Aaji told us she wanted to rest, barely a whisper coming out of her mouth. So we headed to the airport to drop Baba off without her.

"Poor Aaji seemed so tired this morning," Baba said as Aai drove us down the freeway.

Alaap cooed and I gave him my finger to squeeze.

"She's not exhausted," I replied. "She might be turning into a snake, though. Just like Heena Mavshi."

Aai frowned at me through the rearview mirror. "She's old, Geetu. Maya Auntie had us make an appointment to get her checked out this afternoon and look into what that spot on her hand is. She told me Deepak has also been telling her stories about Lata being an ichchhadhari naagin."

"First Heena, now Lata. I get that it's fun to have a little summer adventure," Baba said, fiddling with the air-conditioning vents. "But you and your friends can't accuse neighbors of being made-up monsters."

"Even when the monster did something to Aaji?" I asked, gripping my shoulder belt tightly.

"I'm sure when I get back, Aaji will be back to normal," Baba replied.

I couldn't believe Baba was still going to India when there was another potential snake on our street, and this one just happened to be my grandmother.

"Why don't either of you believe anything I say?" I said, gritting my teeth.

"Geetanjali, please, I'm about to go on a really long trip. Can we just have some normal conversation?"

I slumped in my seat as much as I could with the belt holding me in place.

"Now, I put my number in India into Aai's phone. If it is ten forty-seven a.m. here, what time is it in India?"

I wasn't sure why Baba thought car rides were the perfect times for pop quizzes in math, but I guess I shouldn't have been surprised. I counted on my fingers. "Nine seventeen a.m."

"India is ahead of us, Geetanjali. That means it is night there when it is day here."

"Nine seventeen p.m.," I tried.

"You'd be right if it were winter. But it is summer right now, EDT, or Eastern Daylight Time, not EST, Eastern Standard Time," Baba said. "Remember when I showed you that map last year of all the places in the same time zone as us? Florida, eastern Mexico, the Bahamas . . . So you are nine and a half hours behind, not ten and a half. So it is eight seventeen p.m. Either way, please don't call me in the middle of the night to tell me more neighbors have become snakes."

I felt tears sting my eyes and began to blink quickly. I didn't know if Alaap noticed, but suddenly, instead of squeezing my finger, he was batting his little fist at me and cooing.

I sniffled and gave him my palm. He swung at it happily, gurgling. I didn't want to burst his happy little baby bubble and let him know he was in for a childhood full of impromptu math and not being believed just because you have a creative mind. And before I could stop myself, tears of frustration and sadness began to fall down my cheeks.

Aai glanced my way in her rearview mirror and shook her head. "I think we're being a little too hard on her."

Baba's face flushed pink. "I'm sorry, Geetu," he quickly said as I cried harder, my nose running. "Please don't cry. I'm not making fun of you."

"All you do is laugh at my imagination. At who I am," I sniffled.

Baba shook his head. "No, Geetanjali. I love who you are."

"You sprained your ankle because of who I am." I rubbed my eyes, starting to feel even worse about myself than I thought I could.

"I sprained my ankle because I ran into the bathroom and slipped on water. You're so creative. So smart. Look at all those word tricks you can do. I can't do them, even if I tried. I'm sorry if it feels like we pick on you sometimes." Baba paused. "I actually see a lot of myself in you."

I looked up, meeting Baba's eyes for a fleeting instant in the rearview mirror. "You do?"

Baba nodded, focusing back on the road. "I used to worry a lot when I was a kid. Remember when we watched that documentary that showed how Los Angeles and Mumbai were one of the few big cities that had large cats?"

"Yeah," I said softly, wiping my eyes, remembering how scared I felt to go to either city after seeing that documentary with Baba.

"Well, one day a black panther had left the jungle bordering the city. I was so scared after one had been spotted prowling near a playground, terrified someone was going to get eaten by it. I'd cry all night when I wasn't tossing and turning from nightmares. My aai was so fed up. She yelled at me, told me to stop being a scaredy-cat." Baba sighed. "I think I went too far in the opposite direction, making jokes instead of wondering about others' feelings, always pretending I wasn't scared or that I didn't care. But that's not right either. Because at the root of that fear and worry is a deep sense of caring. I worried about that panther because I cared so much about other people and animals getting hurt by it. That's a good thing. I'm glad you're that thoughtful."

I held on to the handle above the door as Aai switched lanes for our exit.

"But the part deep down inside that makes you too scared to make those changes? You must show that part who's in charge. Because the world needs you. You're brave and powerful and you're going to change things for the better."

"I'm trying to change it. I'm trying to save it, actually," I added. "But I can't if no one believes me."

"I believe you that something is up with Heena Mavshi. We are trying to be there for her and we will keep trying when I get back from India; we'll make sure she gets some help, okay?" Baba said.

"I'll keep an eye on her while Baba's gone, Geetanjali," Aai chimed in.

"And you can call me anytime," Baba said. "Don't worry about the time difference. Except for when you're doing math problems about it."

I rubbed Alaap's soft cheeks and wiped my eyes as Aai exited for the airport.

"You know why we named you Geetanjali?" Baba asked.

"Yeah," I mumbled. "Because of your radio program."

Baba shook his head. "Not at all. It's because of what the word means. 'An offering of songs.' We named you that because you fill our world with music, and we know you'll fill the rest of the world with your song one day."

CHAPTER 53

After we said bye to Baba, I spent the car ride home pretending I was napping so I wouldn't have to talk to Aai. I then sat quietly while we took Aaji to the doctor, and when Aaji got her blood drawn, they then told us to take her home to rest while they waited on the results. The doctor also said if Aaji felt up for it later, she could sing this afternoon, since it was something she did all the time and it wouldn't stress her out. But only one song with the group after her opening solo. So I'd get even less time creating another summer memory with her to cherish.

My parents thought I was going to fill the world with my song? I knew I could prove I was worthy of my name by taking on Lata Auntie, even without their help. I just had to figure out how.

Back home, I sat next to Aaji's bed as she lay sleeping, her back to me, a stark contrast to the pictures on the wall behind her of all her lively performances.

"Aaji?" I said softly, a summery gust from the open window blowing my bangs out of my eyes. "Are you okay?"

Aaji didn't answer.

"Did Lata Auntie do something to you?" I asked.

"How are you, Aai?" Aai asked Aaji, entering the room with Alaap.

"Just resting my voice for our show," she whispered.

Aai bent over the bed to feel Aaji's forehead. And then she sat next to me, putting Alaap in my lap. He began to swing his arm at me, grabbing my hair and tugging it back and forth.

"I didn't want to tell you this earlier," Aai whispered to me as Aaji began to snore. "I didn't want to worry you, but Aaji told me this has happened to her a bit over the past year. She gets tired a lot quicker, and sometimes she has to sleep it off for a few hours, or even a whole day."

I ran my fingers through Alaap's soft curls but couldn't stop the lump from forming in my throat.

"It's a natural part of aging. And the blood tests will let us know if there's anything to be concerned about. But until we hear more, don't worry, okay?" Aai added, examining my face. "The doctor's on it. And if Aaji feels good enough by this afternoon, she'll sing onstage with us at Our Voices in the Park, which, by the way, I never got to tell you, is an excellent name and a lasting contribution here in Deadwood. Your legacy."

I nodded. I knew Aai was trying to make me feel good, but I didn't.

"Let's make sure Aaji gets enough sleep to perform. You should go play with Penn and Deepak right now. Get your mind off things. And then you can meet us at the park in a few hours. We'll sing and then get some mattar paneer and garlic naan from Spices!" she added, mentioning my favorite restaurant in Bloomfield Hills. "Doesn't that sound great?"

I sighed. "Yeah. Sure." It was all feeling hopeless.

"Actually, scratch that," Aai said.

I frowned. Not only was our turning into snakes inevitable,

but now I was going to lose my last meal before it happened too?

"Not the park plans," Aai clarified. "Your current plans. Don't go play with Deepak and Penn right now. You have all evening to do that after we sing. Let's spend some quality time together. We rarely get to do that nowadays, right? Why don't I make a collage with you?" Aai said, grabbing the pile of invitations, scissors, and glue bottle from Aaji's dresser. "I think that collage in the basement needs to be fixed, doesn't it? That's something that's actually scary," she chuckled.

I had grabbed the collage from the basement without giving any of the house-settling noises down there a second thought. I had bigger things to worry about.

Back upstairs, I watched Aai prop the frame open, and I turned collage-Aaji's head the right way, putting more glue on the cutout to make sure it didn't fall again.

"Should we put Alaap in our family picture too?" I asked.

Aai's face brightened. "That's a great idea! Now, do I cut a small circle for Alaap's face?" she asked, sifting through a bunch of brown invitations. Singing was her form of art, and she looked a little awkward trying to figure out how to make collage art.

I nodded. "I'll use this pink card to make him a swaddle."

"He does love pink, don't you?" Aai asked, rubbing her nose on Alaap's as he giggled.

"I can't get the hair right," Aai said.

I took the blob shape she had cut out and clipped it a little on the sides. "There. A haircut."

Aai beamed at me. I drew the face on just like when Aaji and I had first made the collage.

"See, Aaji." I held the little paper baby up to my sleeping grandmother. "It's Alaap. This way he doesn't feel sad when he gets older and sees he isn't in the family picture his aaji made."

I felt a lump form in my throat as I quickly chased away the thought that maybe Aaji wouldn't be around when Alaap was older.

Aai gave me a small hug. "It will be a nice surprise for her this evening when she gets her energy back."

I glued paper Alaap into our family picture. "Aaji told me a story about a mother and a daughter who sang Raag Naagshakti and a cobra died. And that when this happens, the mate will forever seek revenge."

Aai raised an eyebrow. "Well, there's no such things as ichchhadhari naagins. That naag was all alone when he lunged at my father. We'd never intentionally kill a snake. It was just an accident. It's a sad story. Not a horror story."

"But then your dad did die. He was cursed because you sang the raag."

"Nonsense," Aai said brusquely, picking up the clippings. "He got sick and passed away. It was months later. Unrelated."

"If there is nothing to fear, then why did you tear Raag Naagshakti out of your binder?"

"Because it brings back bad memories."

"Then why was it in your binder in the first place?"

"Because I wanted to preserve it. It's part of our lineage. But something made me feel like it wasn't worth protecting a bad memory, so I got rid of it right after Lata Auntie mentioned it at the airport," Aai sputtered, trying to come up with a reason that made sense.

"So why does Lata Auntie keep asking for it? It's because she is attracted to its vibrations. Lata Auntie wants to turn us all into snakes on her big birthday, Aai. I just know it."

"Don't be silly. She keeps asking for us to sing it because there is such a big legend around it and Aaji and me in Pune. We were the only ones who could sing that lakshan geet perfectly. In fact, I bet you could sing it perfectly too. But we sang it before the internet existed. There were no cell-phone videos. The few times we performed it onstage, only the people in the audience were the ones who got to hear it. And we never sang it again after what happened at home."

Well, at least I had my answer about Lata Auntie targeting my family for her revenge, I thought, as I snapped the fasteners on the back of the glass frame back onto the cardboard.

"I love your stories, Geetanjali."

I locked eyes with my mother. *Then help me save our family from a story with a bad ending, Aai.*

"I do," Aai continued. "I love that you have this incredible imagination, and sometimes it is so amazing, you even scare yourself with it. Aaji is the same way. Somehow those creative genes skipped me."

"You can sing. That's creative," I replied.

"You can sing too. You just choose not to."

I looked down at my feet. "The day of Gudhi Padwa, some older kids laughed at Lark when she was singing at the Commons. I was too scared to stick up for her, imagining all the bad things that would happen if I did. But then, the other day, when some of them tried to do it again, I spoke up. I stopped them."

Aai's eyes grew a little teary. "You did?"

I nodded.

She gave me a kiss on the head, the kind she'd only been reserving for Alaap. "I'm proud of you. And I know it's just the start. Just stop worrying so much, okay?"

I gave Aai a small smile, leaning into her touch, and looked at our new and improved family picture.

It was hard not to worry, though. I could fix Aaji in the collage, but I wasn't sure I would be able to fix her in real life.

CHAPTER 54

As ominous gray clouds rolled over Deadwood, I helped a well-rested Aaji to her seat in the front row at the packed park festival, right next to Deepak, Shilpa, and their mom. Aai sat next to us, wearing Alaap, who, in turn, was wearing a neon-pink pair of earmuffs and an ill-fitting cloth diaper he was loosening from the sides each time he batted his hand against it. A group of neighbors were onstage already, playing the most beautiful instrumental Thai classical music piece.

"Are you sure you're okay to sing, Aaji?" I asked as the music ended and the audience began to applaud.

"Always," she whispered hoarsely. *Just resting my voice,* she mouthed, and then turned to stare at the stage, where the Flanagan family from down the street was setting up to perform Irish Celtic music.

"Where's Penn?" I asked Deepak as Aai fiddled with her harmonium bag. "He's singing with us, right?"

Deepak nodded. "He is, but Gertrude has gone missing."

My chest tightened a little. "Do you think Lata Auntie . . ." I trailed off.

To the side of the stage, where the craft tables and food tents were, Lata Auntie was standing in front of a table of canvases with Heena Mavshi.

I frowned, standing up.

"Geetanjali?" Aai asked, turning toward me. "What are you doing? We're on in four numbers."

"We'll be back in time for it," I reassured her. "Promise."

I gave Deepak a look, and he followed me down the aisles full of Deadwood residents and music fans.

"Where are we going?"

"To investigate. Lata Auntie's birthday is tomorrow. I think we're safe in front of so many people. She wouldn't dare bite us with all these witnesses. But we have to find out if she took Gertrude. And we need to find Penn."

Deepak nodded as we approached the craft tables, where instead of setting up a table to sell her own beautiful art, as she had in years past, Heena Mavshi was staring at a painting of kittens and gerbera daisies that an old man was selling.

"Trying to catch a snake again?" Lata Auntie asked, turning toward us.

Her blue ring was glowing in the last rays of sunlight. It was eighty degrees outside, but I started to shiver. Lata Auntie wasn't wearing her cardigan, which must have been what contained her cold aura, as Deepak suspected. She didn't have it on when the coconut oil hardened or when the yogurt didn't set.

"I saw Penn searching for his snake a few minutes ago by the gazebo." She bent down and touched my naagmani. "Good thing you have this."

I trembled from her cool breath as her beady eyes sized me up.

"It's a naagmani," I managed to eke out, more to convince me than her.

"Yes."

"It keeps snakes away. It protects you from them," I added.

Lata Auntie raised her eyebrow as a smirk crossed her lips. "Away?" She giggled. "No, not all of them. Not a naagin." Her voice dropped. "It attracts them."

I took a step back. She was trying to scare me, but I wasn't going to let her. She had taken Aaji's voice. She was trying to ruin my last chance to perform onstage with Aaji this summer. And if she had done something to Gertrude, she was hurting my friend, too.

"Did your dad leave for India?"

I tried to force my mouth into some semblance of a respectful smile as I nodded, knowing I had no one and nothing to protect me since the naagmani was useless.

"Oh, how nice. I hope he and his family members make a good deal for his land," she said. "I'm really excited to hear you perform today with your mom and Aaji. I have to tell you, I have been singing that dear song of theirs ever since you left my house. Well, singing it badly. I'm not as talented as you three."

My ears perked up at the word "three." My intestines felt like a boa constrictor had knotted its way around them. Only it wasn't a boa constrictor I had to fear. It was a cobra.

Lata Auntie eyed me coldly. "Anyway, can't wait to hear your performance. All three of you singing together. What a treat. History in the making."

"Hisstory," Heena Mavshi repeated, turning to look at us wide-eyed with terror as she hung on to the *s*.

I nodded quickly to Lata Auntie and began to back away. "We have to . . . We have to help Penn. . . ."

I grabbed Deepak's elbow and ran as fast as I could, my soles pounding the pavement.

We passed Rohan and his friends throwing cheddar popcorn at each other's faces and laughing. We passed Mayor Conovan talking to a group of constituents, and Lark, and Ashok Ajoba, who was walking toward the audience. We passed neighbor after neighbor, but I didn't stop to say hi.

"What's going on?" Deepak asked as we rounded a bunch of oak trees and headed down the path to the clock tower.

Penn was there, crawling by the rosebushes surrounding the gazebo. "Gertie?" he called out as the Celtic performers finished their song onstage behind us to thundering applause.

"Penn," I gasped, out of breath.

He turned to look at us, his eyes full of tears.

"I'm so sorry about Gertrude. We're going to find her," I added, putting my hand on his shoulder. "But right now . . . We're in danger."

"What do you mean?" Deepak asked, scanning the ground for any sign of the missing snake.

I struggled for air, my heart still thundering. "I mean, I know what they are . . ."

"What *what* are?" Deepak asked.

"The three dear things."

Deepak and Penn turned to me.

"It's the lakshan geet. Raag Naagshakti. The one that only my mom and Aaji and, apparently, I can sing so well." My knees felt wobbly as I heard myself say the words. "It's our song."

CHAPTER 55

We stood at the base of the clock tower, sizing Lata Auntie up from a safe distance, as the next act began performing a thrilling traditional Lebanese song.

"We're all going to become snakes, and then I'll never be able to find Gertie," Penn whimpered tearfully.

Deepak shook his head. "No. They aren't singing Raag Naagshakti."

I watched Aai stand up from her seat and head to the side of the stage with Aaji and her harmonium, where the rest of the kids from class were waiting. She turned and began to scan the crowd, probably looking for us.

Lata Auntie ran toward her and began saying something to her. Our view was obstructed and I couldn't see what Aai said back to her, but Lata Auntie was standing there for a good three minutes before hugging my mother and walking away.

"We're just singing songs from music class, remember?" Deepak added, frowning as he watched the interaction.

"He's right," I said shakily, seeing Aaji hold the railing of the stage steps for support. "We have to get through this performance. We have to show Lata Auntie we aren't scared of her or anything. And then, we have to take her down."

. . .

Rumbling thunder was heard in the distance, and Deadwood was looking gloomier than ever. Penn and I held on to Aaji's arms and helped her around the mess of boxes the volunteers had left in the grass by the stage, and up the five steps to the stage itself. Deepak and Aai were already on it, setting up the microphones and harmonium; the younger kids took their seats.

Aaji slowly sat down next to Aai, and Penn and I took our spots next to the rest of the class.

I glanced out at the audience, hoping the rain would hold off so we could get through this performance without getting drenched. There wasn't an empty seat in sight. This was a way bigger crowd than at Bark in the Park and at our basement singing party combined. My heart thumped in my chest when I shielded my eyes from the spotlight's glare and spotted Rohan and his friends sitting next to Lark and Mayor Conovan in the first row, next to Penn's parents, Shilpa, Maya Auntie, who was holding Alaap, and Ashok Ajoba. And my throat tightened when I saw Lata Auntie, ring glowing, and Heena Mavshi sitting right behind them.

"Good afternoon, everyone," Aai said into the microphone, a little softer than she normally would. "We are so excited to be here with all of these wonderful singers and musicians, celebrating our diverse voices coming together at the park. This is a very special performance for me because my mom, my daughter, and I will be singing together for the first time this summer."

Lata Auntie stood up and began whispering something to the people around her. I could sense her smirking, like she was waiting for me to fail. I glanced at Aaji, who feebly opened her mouth to sing her solo that started this song, as Aai played Raag Bhairav on the harmonium.

I could barely hear Aaji. I looked at her. She gave me a wide-eyed, worried glance back and I squeezed her frail hand. My heartbeat thumped in my throat, and my insides felt like I was on a Tilt-A-Whirl, but I forced myself to focus on the song. My grandmother was counting on me.

Besides, I wasn't the scared kid with stage fright that I was at the beginning of summer. I wasn't going to let my worries take over any longer. I'd come up with the perfect way to start the Reptile Rescue Center grant and thought of the new name for this inclusive festival. Plus, I had just solved a mystery, believed in myself. Sure, we weren't safe from Lata Auntie yet, but I was working on it. I took a deep breath, leaned into the microphone, and opened my mouth.

But nothing came out.

Aai neared her microphone to take over, like she had done onstage at Gudhi Padwa. But she stopped, turning to me with a whisper. "My voice feels . . . weak," she said, and she began to sing as softly as Aaji, just barely heard over the harmonium.

First Aaji. Now Aai. I couldn't fail. I couldn't let my family down. I couldn't lose this opportunity to sing onstage with Aaji.

A staticky shout came from the audience. "Go, Geetanjali!" It was Lark on her portable microphone. "You can do it!" she cheered.

I gave her a grateful smile and turned to Aaji. She was singing even quieter than before, every note taking more and more effort to get out.

It was now or never. I opened my mouth again. A clear and

strong sound filtered through the microphone. I sang with Aaji, our voices swirling together, merging, growing, connecting the dots as the line continued from her generation to mine.

"Wah!" I heard Ashok Ajoba exclaim from the audience. "Kya baat hai!"

Aaji turned to me as we wrapped up our solo, her eyes meeting mine, and although she was too tired to smile, I could see one in her eyes.

Deepak, Penn, Aai, and the rest of the class joined in. I beamed at Penn, who gave me a grin in between stanzas as he finally got his non-school stage performance. We finished the song and I gave Aaji's hand one last squeeze before releasing it, turning to the audience with a triumphant smile to receive their applause.

But it was silent. Eerily silent.

All except for Alaap's cries.

"What's going on?" I asked the boys, trying to see past the haze of the spotlights shining in our faces, when I noticed a spot on Penn's forehead that shimmered like copper whenever the light hit it.

"Penn," I gasped, my voice dropping to a whisper. "There's a scale on your forehead. A snake scale."

Penn swatted at it, almost hitting his microphone as Aai looked out into the audience, confused that no one clapped.

"Get it off me!" Penn whispered. But the scale wasn't a bug you could flick off.

My mouth dropped, looking at a small cluster of coppery scales on the back of Deepak's neck as he scooted over to help Penn. "You have some too, Deepak!"

Deepak felt his neck, and his eyes widened while looking at me. "So do you."

"On your right ear," Penn added.

My hand shot to my right ear, and I felt a few bumps. "How?" I asked, utterly perplexed. "We haven't been bitten."

"Maybe we don't need to. Your grandma wasn't," Penn said.

From behind us, the whispers began, "Hiss, hiss, it's all amiss. Soon we will be in serpentine bliss."

We turned.

Sachit, Apoorva, Trisha, Mona, Ami, Deepti, and Divya stood up, swaying side to side, all whispering the same phrase.

Before I could reply to Penn, Aaji collapsed from her seated position on the stage.

"Aaji!" I screamed, rushing to her side. "Aai, do something," I whimpered, checking Aaji's pulse. Her heart was still beating. She weakly opened her eyes and looked at me, eyebrows furrowing in sorrow. "Aai," I screamed again.

"I . . . I'm just so tired, Geetan—" Aai didn't even finish saying my name before she, too, fell to the stage floor.

I gasped, realizing what Lata Auntie had done before we got onstage. "Aai, did you . . . did you sing for Lata Auntie?" I asked.

Aai slowly opened her eyes and blinked, like she was replying yes.

"No . . ." My stomach sank.

Alaap's cries grew louder as a collective hissing sound came from the audience.

"Hiss, hiss, it's all amiss. Soon we'll be in serpentine bliss."

"Alaap!" I screamed. I turned to Deepak and Penn, the rest

of the class swaying behind them. "Where is he?"

Deepak rushed to a spotlight at the front of the stage and turned it to the audience.

Deepak's mom and Shilpa were chanting, swaying back and forth. By their sides, Lark, Mayor Conovan, Heena Mavshi, Rohan and his friends, Penn's parents, Ashok Ajoba, they were all doing it too. And Alaap was nowhere in sight.

Neither was Lata Auntie. My legs felt weak.

"Our parents," Penn said shakily.

"And Shilpa. And our friends. And the mayor . . . No . . . How is this happening?" Deepak trembled.

Penn gasped. "Lata must have entranced them." He moved the spotlight across the swaying crowd. "I saw her walking around while we were singing."

I suddenly felt short of breath. She wasn't whispering to our neighbors. She was putting them under her spell. In plain sight.

"Cobras are fast," Deepak mumbled, staring at his mom and sister.

In the distance, at the very back of the audience, a blue glow started to wash over the crowd. Our entranced neighbors and residents of Deadwood parted, making way for the source of the blue glow:

Lata Auntie's ring shone brightly from her hand, the disturbing blue light caressing my crying baby brother, nestled in Lata Auntie's arms.

CHAPTER 56

All I wanted to do was run away, but I was the only one who could save Alaap.

My stomach turned. The only thing she needed now was my unfinished song.

There was no time for fear. I took a step toward Lata Auntie, reminding myself of what Aaji had written on the cover of her book. *Geetanjali—Ek Shoor Mulgi.* Geetanjali the Brave.

"Let him go," I said, trying to steady my voice.

"Let him go? Why, I just got him, dear," Lata Auntie replied as she began climbing the stairs to the stage.

Alaap wailed louder, batting Lata Auntie's naagmani necklace.

"Hush, child. Yours isn't the voice I want to hear," Lata Auntie sneered through gritted teeth.

"Don't hurt him," Deepak chimed in, standing by my side.

"Yeah," Penn added, hiding behind me. "And leave all our families alone!"

"Such disrespect," Lata Auntie chided in a singsong voice. Before we could respond, the blue light from her teardrop gem rose from her ring to a full flame, floating by her side. Lata Auntie's eyes began to glow, reflecting the light. "I'm getting strong. Very strong. Soon you'll be the ones taking orders from me."

I clenched Deepak's and Penn's arms as Lata Auntie walked in a circle around my mom and grandmother. "Your mom sang such a beautiful song for me, it wore her out. New moms never get rest, hain na?" she asked in Hindi, tickling Alaap's neck.

My stomach turned. All she needed now was the song I hadn't finished.

"Can I . . . can I hold my brother?" I asked, afraid of what Lata Auntie's answer would be.

"Sure," she said, walking toward us.

We gasped as the blue flame rose to her side, flickering as it followed her around obediently.

"Just sing Naagshakti, make my flame a little stronger, and I'll give him back."

Alaap smiled when he saw me. His small fist had wrapped its way around Lata Auntie's necklace, and he continued batting his hand.

"What a little dear," Lata Auntie added. "I wouldn't want anything to happen to him, would you? I mean, he would make a good appetizer." She smiled, her dimples and fang-like canines showing.

"Moving from mice to humans," Deepak stated matter-of-factly as some more scales appeared on his skin and, now that I noticed, on mine and Penn's.

"And trying to make everyone think Gertrude was at fault!" Penn sputtered.

"Oh that. Yes." Lata Auntie circled us. "I needed to do something to stop that useless snake of yours from coming to my house all the time. That's before I realized the pathetic thing only ate eggs."

Penn's cheeks flushed. Lata Auntie knew what buttons to push. "Yeah, well, she knew a snake had moved into the neighborhood, so she was probably trying to welcome you because she's super sweet like that."

"Welcome me?" Lata Auntie laughed. "No, dear. She was trying to warn you. Just like she is now." Lata Auntie rolled her eyes. She then turned around and kicked the ground as hard as she could, sending Gertrude flying into the tower of boxes left on the grass, beside the stage.

CHAPTER 57

No!" Penn ran down the stairs, Deepak behind him.

My hands rushed to my mouth, stopping the sob that wanted to escape. I hadn't even noticed Gertrude onstage. She was trying to help us and now . . . now she was hurt, because we'd been unable to stop our naagin neighbor on our own.

"She's not moving," Deepak reported, frowning.

"What a shame. I'd hate to have any more deaths around here. Like your family members." She stuck her fingernail into her teeth, picking at them. "I think I still have a little piece of flesh stuck in my teeth. Oh well. That's what floss is for." She shrugged, flicking something off her nail that landed by Lark's feet in the front row.

Penn began to cry. Deepak put his arm around Penn's shoulder, leading him back up the few steps to the stage to face Lata Auntie. I was glad Penn had Deepak by his side because right now all I was feeling was mad: at seeing my friend hurt, my neighbors in trouble, and an innocent animal killed because of a monster.

"How could you do that to Gertrude?" I said, surprised by the volume of my own voice. It wasn't high-pitched any-more. It wasn't even the stronger voice I'd used to talk to the middle-school bullies. It was even more powerful. It was fierce.

"Oh, like this," Lata Auntie said, moving so quickly she was almost slithering as she rushed to Penn and Deepak and bit Penn's hand.

"No!" Deepak shouted, backing away as Penn slumped to the ground.

I stared in horror as Penn lay lifelessly, then stood up, and just like the others, swayed back and forth, chanting, "Hiss, hiss, it's all amiss. Soon we'll be in serpentine bliss."

I looked at Deepak. His lip was trembling, tears slipping down his face. This was bad. Really bad. There were just two of us left who could stop Lata Auntie and hopefully turn everyone back to normal. "Leave them alone," I sputtered. "Leave us all alone. You know what it's like to lose someone."

Lata Auntie raised an eyebrow. "Do I?"

"Your husband was listening to Aaji and Aai sing in Pune, and then when Ajoba tried to shoo him out, he attacked, and Ajoba accidentally killed him. And now you'll hurt anyone to avenge your husband."

"You really have been listening to too many of your aaji's stories, haven't you?" Lata Auntie ran her fingers through Alaap's curls, turning the coconut oil on them a solid white. "I sympathize. I had to listen to her yap my ear off on both flights. But, see, your tall tales get everything twisted. I'm not some pitiful woman doing something for a man. That snake wasn't my husband." Lata Auntie sneered, any sign of the kind auntie I had first met long gone. "She was my mother."

My shoulders slumped; the weight of Lata's words filling me with sadness. Lata Auntie had grown up without a mother because of my family. "I'm so sorry," I said softly.

"You should be," Lata Auntie snapped, her eyes growing beadier by the second. "And you should also understand it's only fair I take your voices forever as revenge."

Deepak blew his nose loudly in the corner with a Kleenex from his pocket, still staring in shock at swaying Penn.

"Ugh." Lata Auntie shuddered, turning back to me. "I should have just gotten your mother when she and her friends used to play in that abandoned fort. Saved me the trouble of having to deal with you and your irritating friends."

"All this time you tried to make me think Heena Mavshi was a snake." I gritted my teeth, annoyed at how she was able to trick so many of us for so long. "You made me think she bit the mice, you—"

"*Made* you think, dear?" Lata Auntie interrupted. "No, you and your wild imagination did that. I bit those mice out of habit when I was in my human form. Your Deadwood mice are a bit salty for my taste, but once I remembered to transform into a cobra, the next mice went down the hatch and I felt better."

"Transform into a snake right now," Deepak said, looking down at the tower of boxes in the corner.

"So you can try and fail at catching me? Silly kids. You can't outsmart me." She laughed louder, and somehow each cackle had a resounding hiss at the end of it. "Now listen. I sent your father away after he came over to check on Heena and was asking all these questions about my connection to Raag Naagshakti. I didn't want him getting your mother and Aaji suspicious when I needed their songs, and I couldn't just bite him. If he started acting just as bitter as Heena, he'd make everyone suspicious before I'd gotten even one song. Good thing I do a great impression of a rich hotelier interested in oh-so-precious ancestral land."

Lightning split the sky in the distance. Lata Auntie tricked Baba into flying away so there would just be the three of us to deal with?

"That was before I decided to use the Voices in the Park audience as blackmail to make sure I get what I want. Your aaji and aai are indisposed, and, well, it's my birthday tomorrow." She smiled. "Midnight baby. We're considered special. So, for my present, you're going to sing to me. I'm going to say this incantation"—she pointed to the tiny, inscribed words on the naagmani Alaap was clenching tightly—"and not one of you will interrupt. And then you and your family and friends and neighbors and all these people will become snakes, doing my bidding for eternity. Got it?"

"Why would I want to speed up your plan and sing?" I asked as Lark's eyes turned beady.

Lata Auntie glared, but before she could answer, the locket came loose in Alaap's hand.

"Give me that, you brat." Lata Auntie started to pry Alaap's fist open and he began to cry.

"Stop it!" I ran toward them. "You're hurting him!"

I tried to pull her ice-cold fingers off his little hand, but the naagmani slipped out instead and went rolling across the stage.

Lata Auntie turned for it just as Deepak dove forward, dumping his rock collection bag out.

"Ah-ha!" he said triumphantly, body flat on the stage as he searched for the stone. "Now try to find your rock!"

I smiled. Rock couldn't beat paper, but it definitely just beat ichchhadhari naagin.

CHAPTER 58

Lata Auntie just shook her head, bored. "Aren't you supposed to be the genius of the group? This is why you'll never outwit me. I've had this necklace since I was born. I've got the mantra memorized. I just didn't want this gross thing getting his germs all over my stuff," she added, pointing to Alaap, who started whimpering.

"There's no way out," she snapped, reaching down to scoop up the naagmani out of the cluster of rocks. She glanced at me. "So just sing and get it done with already."

From my spot in the center of the stage, I looked at Deepak for some ideas. He shook his head, and I could see more scales growing around his neck and Penn's forehead. I turned to Lata Auntie.

"They're turning into snakes because you got two of your dear things. So if I give you the third, they'll be totally transformed. And so will all our parents. And Alaap and Aaji. And everyone out in the audience and all the kids onstage. Including me."

I looked at the few audience members the turned spotlight was still shining on. Sure enough, scales were popping up all over their skin, and their eyes were turning beadier by the second, like Lark's were.

"And if you don't give me the song," she said, practically snarling, "I'll bite your brother. Who knows if he will survive it, being so young. And then I'll bite you next, after you watch him scream and cry."

My shoulders sank. "Okay," I said, trembling, knowing I was now stuck. I locked eyes with Alaap. I had messed up at Bollywood movie night and didn't protect him. I couldn't let that happen again.

I began the opening notes of the lakshan geet, just as I had practiced days earlier at the playground. Unlike in Heena Mavshi's kitchen, though, my voice wasn't shaking. I stared straight into Alaap's brown eyes, knowing I had to do this right.

The stage began to vibrate, but I stood still, determined. The dancing blue flame of the ring, which was hovering by Lata Auntie's face, began to grow brighter with each steady note. The stage and audience full of transforming humans was bathed in its icy glow, and I started to shiver. Still, I kept going, singing the high notes in the second line with ease, just like Aaji had. Maybe I did have more of her genes than I had thought.

The flame started to flicker as it descended near Lata Auntie's waist, slithering to the music, just like her. I watched the string of drool from Alaap fall onto his legs and drip down, barely missing the flame as it rocked back and forth.

And I knew what to do.

CHAPTER 59

Instead of singing the low Sa, the first note of the scale, like Do, for the third line, I clenched my teeth and made the loudest *ssss* noise I could, cueing my brother.

It worked. He did his business, and it leaked out of that loose-fitting cloth diaper, right onto the blue flame. It went out in a dying hiss.

"No flame of immortality. No immortality," I said, my voice strong and sure.

Deepak rushed to my side as the stage warmed up a little.

"You did it!" Deepak exclaimed.

Lata Auntie wiped her hands on her side, cringing. "This is really getting old."

Just like that, the flame popped back up; the park was once again illuminated by the freezing blue hue.

"The only thing that douses it is my death, and that's clearly not happening."

Rain began to drizzle down on us, not impacting the flame one bit. My knees felt unsteady. I was out of ideas.

"Step away from the kids!" shouted an unsteady voice from the back of the crowd.

I turned, stunned to see Baba standing there wielding the kersooni as our swaying neighbors began marching toward him, forcing him to the stage probably a little faster than he'd have liked. He ran up the stairs, shooing the neighbors away with the grass broom. Deepak and I ran toward him as Baba put his arms out, shielding us behind him.

"What is this, a family reunion?" Lata Auntie asked, letting out a bored sigh.

Aai and Aaji suddenly stood up.

"You're okay!" I exclaimed.

But they weren't. They were under her cobra spell. They stood up, scales on their rain-soaked skin, and began parading in a circle around us, with the kids from singing class and Penn. Every now and then one of them would bump into a speaker or a microphone stand, but they were completely unbothered, like they were drawn to the pulsing blue light by Lata Auntie and didn't care what happened to them as long as they were near it.

Lark, Shilpa, Maya Auntie, Ashok Ajoba, the mayor, and Penn's parents stomped up onto the rain-slicked stage to join them. Rohan and the rest of the audience moved toward the stage as well, spreading out on the grass until we were surrounded on every side. It was as crowded as one of our singing parties in the basement, but way scarier.

"I thought you were in India," I whispered, my eyes locked on Lata Auntie in case she made a move, while being acutely aware of the angry, now even more scaly, neighbors and Aaji and Aai closing in on us.

"I had to listen to my gut, to the caring side of myself, Geetu," Baba said. "I couldn't stop thinking about what you said. When they announced the flight was delayed, I knew I had to get back to you. Because if my daughter was this afraid of someone, I had to listen."

"Is your story about done?" Lata Auntie yawned.

"Give me my son." Baba shook the Indian broom in his hand at Lata Auntie. He shrugged at me. "It was the only thing I could find at home that I thought might help shoo a snake."

"Sure. Come and get him." Lata Auntie smiled, baring two fangs.

My stomach dropped at the sight, and I squeezed Baba's arm. "Baba. She's going to hurt him."

"I won't let her." Baba gritted his teeth and charged at Lata Auntie, but she was quicker and darted her head forward like a cobra, plunging her teeth into his neck.

Alaap began to sob as Baba dropped to the ground.

"Baba!" I shouted, but Deepak grabbed my arm before I could even attempt to break out of the circling neighbors to run to him.

Baba sat up suddenly, scales sprinkling his face like someone had thrown glitter on him, his eyes full of rage. And then he began to whisper, "Hiss, hiss, it's all amiss. Soon we will be in serpentine bliss."

"No . . ." I trembled as my brother continued to sob, still in Lata's arms.

As the rain grew stronger, drenching us, Baba pushed his way into the zombie circle. He, Penn, Aaji, Aai, and all the neighbors were saying the phrase at different times. There was no pause, no break from the haunting words. Just a repetitive, overlapping, inundating, unstoppable reminder that our situation was hopeless.

"There's no way to stop her," Deepak said softly, looking defeated.

Lata Auntie nodded. "Your friend's right. There is no way to defeat me. No way to save your brother. No way to save the day. So, you can keep wasting my time, or you can sing."

I opened my mouth, but no sound came out. I was too scared. Or a part of me knew giving her this song was wrong. Because the poem was wrong: it wasn't the cobra's song to have, it was my song.

"Stage fright? Again?" Lata Auntie scoffed, glancing at the clock tower by the gazebo. The little hand was on two and the big hand was nearing the six.

I glared at Lata Auntie, anger growing fiery inside of me.

"Take your time. Be scared," Lata Auntie taunted.

Sure, I was fearful when Lata Auntie first met me. Afraid of noises in the basement. Worried about sharks in the shower. Apprehensive about bridges. Bothered by circles. Fearful of Aaji getting old. Terrified of a snake-woman. But that was all in the past. This was now. And now I was going to use my voice to change the world.

"I've got all day," Lata Auntie said, exhaling, although I could tell from the annoyed way she was rocking Alaap, now fussing from the rain, that she was getting tired of waiting.

I squinted at the hands on the clock through the downpour. How many more hours did I have before losing my voice forever, or worse, something bad happening to Alaap? I was growing more anxious by the second when I suddenly thought about Baba's math problems. And just as quickly, I realized I wasn't a failure.

"Sing or your brother's gone," she yelled. "And don't try anything funny. You're no good at saving him from snakes." She winced, turning her sensitive ears from my baby brother's gaping mouth as he wailed.

"Were you born in Michigan?" I asked over the noise, watching the big hand inch closer to the six.

"What a foolish question," Lata Auntie snapped, holding Alaap a little tighter. "There are no wild cobras in Michigan. Start singing."

I nodded, looking at Aaji, Aai, and Baba as they hissed. "Okay." I opened my mouth to sing, but instead asked, "Florida, maybe?"

Lata Auntie let out an exasperated sigh. "There are no wild cobras in Florida. Not my kind, at least. Now sing."

"Sure thing." I paused, reminding myself I was brave. "Maybe in Panama?"

Lata Auntie's brow furrowed.

"What are you doing, Geetanjali?" Deepak asked, his face growing pale. "You're making her really mad."

"Boy-genius is right," Lata Auntie snarled. "Sing."

I cleared my throat, but I kept asking more questions, enjoying projecting my voice. "Eastern Mexico? The Bahamas?"

"You know I was born in India. You really are bad at remembering things. You must be as bad at school and math as your parents say you are. No wonder they're so embarrassed of you," Lata Auntie said, adding a little hiss at the end of her sentence as the minute hand hit the six. "No wonder they think you're pathetic," she sneered.

I shook my head. "They don't think that." I watched the red

second hand zip around the face of the clock, about to reach the twelve.

"Well, I do. Now quit stalling."

"Oh, I'm done stalling," I said, and smiled. "See, I was asking you all those questions to see if you were born on Eastern Time. Because if you weren't, if you were born on Indian Time like my fearless aaji . . ." I searched for additional adjectives for my family members to slow things down more. "Like my amazing aai, like my puts-his-foot-in-his-mouth-but-still-caring-baba . . ." I pointed to the clock tower. The red hand passed the twelve as the clock read 2:31 p.m. "It's twelve-oh-one a.m. in India. July fourteenth. Happy birthday. I'm sorry, but I won't be giving you my song," I said.

Lata Auntie's face drained of color as she looked at the clock. "No!" she gasped.

"Yay, math," I said happily.

"Happy birthday, snake murderer," Deepak glowered.

Lata Auntie wasn't celebrating, though. Her skin was slowly turning into scales. Her head began to mutate into a cobra hood. Her arms started to shrink down faster and faster as all the neighbors stopped circling us.

Deepak and I rushed past them to scoop Alaap out of what was left of Lata Auntie's limbs.

"Look at that. I did save my brother," I said, squeezing him protectively as the whites in Lata Auntie's eyes began to fade along with the cold blue light, a blue beam from it swirling toward Aaji and Aai, like their song was being returned to them.

The scales began to disappear from my hand. I brushed my

soaked bangs out of my eyes and watched the scales start to fade from my family members and neighbors as pale-blue light leaked from their bodies, rose into the air, and disappeared.

We backed away as Lata Auntie's long fangs emerged from her mouth. She dropped to the ground, and in the downpour, Lata Auntie's permanent transformation to a snake was complete.

"Run!" I shouted as the cobra charged at us. I backed into the neighbors as Deepak cut through the crowd and rushed up with a spilling stack of boxes. He threw half the pile at me, and we began chucking all sorts of boxes at the cobra.

Deepak grabbed a cardboard box just as the cobra lunged at him, and dropped the box down, trapping the snake. "I did it! I caught a snake like the Crocodile Hunter!"

There was a sudden, warm, peaceful sound—the incessant hissing had once and for all gone away—as Penn, Aaji, Aai, Baba and all our neighbors were now back to normal. The spell was broken; the blue light, floating just above the box, was now half the size of when it had been a gem on Lata Auntie's ring.

"Geetanjali! Alaap!" Aai said, looking around the packed stage frantically.

I ran into her arms and she held on to me, like she never wanted to let go.

"You're okay!" Aaji exclaimed, her normal energy returned as she put her arms around us. Baba, Heena Mavshi, Deepak, Penn's parents, Lark and Shilpa and Ashok Ajoba came around us too, apparently venom free, all scale-less and back to their old selves.

"Oh, thank God you're all okay, shona," Heena Mavshi

cried, pinching my cheeks, back to her old self, as Penn's parents hugged him and Deepak's mom and sister hugged Deepak too. "I can't believe I fell for her lies," she lamented, looking at the box to our side.

A forked tongue briefly slid out from under the box, and Aai shuddered.

"There's the forked tongue." Deepak pointed, from within Maya Auntie's arms.

"Yeah, I think we had confirmation on that in other ways a while ago," Penn said as his mom brushed his hair with her hand.

"But thanks, Deepak," I added, sitting on the box with an exhausted plop.

Ashok Ajoba shook his head at Aaji. "An ichchhadhari naagin in Michigan. Now I've seen everything," he said, out of breath, his voice shaking from adrenaline.

The neighbors began to stare at each other, utterly perplexed at what had just happened to them.

"The missing cobra has at last been caught!" Mayor Conovan declared, taking a break from scratching her head in confusion as she tried to calm down the equally perplexed crowd.

A few people began to clap, and Baba hugged me, tears from his eyes spilling onto my already drenched shoulders. "Thank you, Geetu."

"It's okay, Baba," I said, feeling like I might start sobbing too, if I saw my dad cry any longer.

Baba shook his head. "No. It's not okay. I'm so glad you cared enough, and believed in yourself enough, to know you were right to be worried when you noticed what was going on around us. And in the end it was your words that saved the day. Just like those words you fill your notebooks up with."

I wiped my dad's tears. "I used a little math, too."

He let out a small laugh. "You saved us. You saved us all."

I gave him a tired smile. "Deepak and Penn and I did. Together."

Baba nodded and Aai dropped down to her knees beside me. "We should have believed you. You were so brave, trying to warn us of what Lata really was, and we all just ignored you." Her eyes grew shiny.

Alaap in my hands, I gave her a hug and Aaji and Baba joined in, tears of relief hitting my shoulders.

Aaji squeezed my arm. "I knew you'd find that brave girl inside of you."

"I found her," I replied. "And she's not going anywhere. I don't want you to be disappointed in me ever again."

Aaji shook her head. "I could never be disappointed in you, my shoor mulgi."

I beamed at Aaji from my spot in Aai's and Baba's arms. "Can someone get me a phone please," I said, my heart still beating like I had run a marathon.

"Who are you calling?" Penn asked.

I looked at Aaji and Aai, safe and sound, and at my friends, who had stood by me and helped me do the hardest thing I had ever done. I smiled. "The only place that can handle our problem."

EPILOGUE

Three Weeks Later

I looked at Gertrude slithering around a big tank at the Reptile Rescue Center, the August sunlight pouring in through a small corner of her space from the nearby window.

"Gah?" asked Penn.

She was moving slower than normal, but she was alive, thanks to the healing hands at the rescue group.

I shrugged in my sleeveless blue-and-green salwar kurta, trying not to shiver from her scales. "Just half a gah. She's not so bad."

"She's adorable," Lark added as she pressed her hands in a heart shape against the glass.

"Yup." Penn beamed. He tapped on the glass. "Just a few more days to heal and then I'll take you home, okay, Gertie-pooh?"

Gertrude flicked her tongue and coiled herself into a ball to rest.

"Did you get the new terrarium set up for when she goes home?" I asked, giving Gertrude a little wave goodbye.

Penn nodded. "My parents went all out with it. They said it's the least we could do to thank her for trying to save us."

"Yay! That will make her so happy," I replied. Almost

everyone else in Deadwood who had been entranced at Our Voices in the Park had only remembered that a vicious cobra had been on the loose and tried to attack everyone onstage that night. Gertrude, Penn, Deepak, and I had been lauded as heroes for capturing the snake and saving lives. Mayor Conovan even gave us all Hometown Hero medals.

"And I'm so glad Reptile Rescue Center won the community grant and got the money to take care of all the animals who needed help," Lark added.

Penn nodded. "Even the unfriendly ones."

I laughed. "Speaking of, want to check on our neighbor? We have a few minutes before we get picked up."

Penn sighed. "Sure."

We walked down the orange hallway, turning into a dimly lit room with a sign that said: NEW FRIENDS.

Dozens of heat lamps glowed in their terrariums. But only one of them was blue. Inside that tank, a female Indian king cobra slithered back and forth, herhood out, like she was ready for a fight, next to a barely lit flame of immortality, now resting on the bottom of the tank.

The cobra saw me and Penn and began to hiss loudly, banging at the glass as the lamp seemed to get duller and duller by the second. But I didn't flinch. I knew I was safe.

"The vet said she's really old and doesn't have much time left," a voice said from behind us.

We turned. Deepak was standing there in a bright-green Reptile Rescue Center shirt that said VOLUNTEER, a tote bag in his hand.

"But she'll have a safe home here, until the end."

I grinned. "How's the new gig?"

"I'm learning a ton. Ashok dada said I'm a natural."

"And you don't have to go to Boston for camp! So we have way more time to hang out before school!" Penn said, jumping up and down with his arm around me, Deepak, and Lark.

"Save the voice for the concert, Penn," I laughed.

"You're right. Did I tell you my parents are coming?" he asked excitedly. "I promised them there wouldn't be anyone there who could turn them into snakes this time."

"Just about a hundred times." I grinned. "And I'm glad."

"Me too," Deepak said.

"I'm guessing there's some backstory here that I don't know," Lark chimed in. "But it doesn't matter. I'm glad your parents will be there, too, and pretty thrilled no one will try to turn us into snakes again."

Penn grinned. "We'll fill you in on the drive. My mom even had her assistant put special time with me in her work calendar, so she'll make sure to do that every day. And she and Dad canceled the rest of their retreats for the year so we can all be together instead."

"That's amazing," I said as Mrs. Charters peeked her head in.

"Hi, Deepak," she said before turning to me and Penn. "Is one of you named 'Gee-tan-jelly'?" she asked, mispronouncing my name.

"It's actually 'Geetanjali,'" I replied, smiling at Deepak.

"You make the *t* sound by putting your tongue behind your teeth," Penn added, pointing to his mouth.

"Sorry about that," Mrs. Charters said. "I hate getting

names wrong. Geetanjali," she tried again, "your family is waiting at the front desk."

I thanked her and headed out of the room with Penn and
Deepak.

"I'm kinda nervous," Penn said as we headed for Aai and
Aaji, who were decked out in shiny, matching blue-and-green
saris and gold jewelry. "It's my first time performing since Our
Voices in the Park."

"Don't be nervous. You've got this," I said, eyeing the tanks
around us.

Lark skipped ahead. "Plus, it's my first time getting to sing
with all of you."

"Everyone's excited for it," I said. "And we're going to raise
so much money to help the animals at Deadwood Dog Rescue." I had reached out to them after seeing how much we had
been able to help Reptile Rescue Center and wanting to do the
same for the rescue dogs who needed homes. I was hoping we'd
raise even more money at this concert than the one Aaji and I
had put on a few summers earlier.

"Geetanjali wrote the best speech ever about it," Deepak
said as we turned the corner for the lobby.

Penn nodded. "It's how I learned dogs mean unlikable
people, mechanical devices, names for feet, a verb for bugging
someone or tracking someone . . ."

"But the kind of dog we're most interested in today are
the dogs at Deadwood Dog Rescue who need good homes," I
continued from my memorized speech.

"Doggone it. You're good." Penn grinned, and we all laughed.

Aai was leaning into a vertical tank at the front of the

center, full of colorful snakes rescued from the exotic animal trade. Heena Mavshi was standing next to her. "They're kind of cute, I guess?" she asked, showing them to Alaap, who gave a laughing gurgle in response. She turned, spotting our reflection in the glass.

"My heroes." Heena Mavshi beamed.

"All set?" Aai asked.

"Yup!" I said as we headed out of the center. "I hope you like all the songs, Heena Mavshi."

"Your aai told me it was your idea to sing all of Jatin's favorites today."

I nodded, feeling a little lump in my throat at the thought of Jatin Kaka not being at the fundraiser to appreciate them. "Oh, and I wrote something for you." I reached into my pocket, pulling out a small note card, like the kind Heena Mavshi would give me mini paintings on.

Heena Mavshi's brow furrowed as she read my words out loud. "'How did the singers call each other? With a micro*phone.*'"

She gave me a confused smile.

"I thought you might be missing some of Jatin Kaka's cheesy jokes. It's no Natural Hisstory Museum punchline, but it's close."

A tear slipped from Heena Mavshi's eyes as she began to laugh. "It's perfect, shona."

Aai put her arm around me, pulling me closer to her heart as we walked toward our minivan in the parking lot. I watched Heena Mavshi wipe more tears from her eyes, knowing the stages of grief could go back and forth, making progress, having setbacks, until she finally got to the acceptance phase.

Baba and Aaji stood by the car. "Everything okay, Heena?" Baba asked, concerned.

"It will be," she said softly. "It won't be the same. But I'll be okay."

A loud cawing caught our attention. I glanced at Penn and Deepak, and we all followed the sound with our eyes. There, behind the minivan, sitting on a bright-pink beech tree, the crow with the feathers missing on its side held a shiny copper bangle in its beak. I squinted in the sun and took another look.

"That's your snake bangle!" I pointed, looking at Heena Mavshi.

"It's the crow's now," Heena Mavshi said with a little chuckle. "I want no reminders of Lata in the house."

Baba opened the door for us. "Ready to perform?" he asked. "Channel Twelve is already setting up."

"Good," I said. "I'm ready." After defeating a snake-person at Our Voices in the Park, I wasn't scared of anything about today's performance.

"I know," Baba said. "I'm proud of you, Geetu."

"We all are," Aai said, tucking my hair behind my ear as we walked across the parking lot.

Aaji beamed. "I don't have to worry about you anymore. My brave Geetanjali."

She squeezed my hand and I rested my head on her shoulder, taking in a deep inhale of her sandalwood and rose soap, wishing I could bottle it up and take it out anytime I missed her. I blinked back some tears and looked up at her. "You'll come back next summer, though, right?"

Aaji's eyes grew shiny. "I'm certainly going to try. And I think I might need one last go on the big bad wolf at the Commons this summer. If you're up for it."

"I thought it was too dangerous for you now?" I asked.

Aaji shook her head. "I thought of a new approach. I'll go slowly. It will be a good change. Maybe it will be even more fun this way."

"It will last longer," I said, wishing I could make this summer last longer. Wishing I could make Aaji stay. Wishing I wouldn't have to say bye to her in a few weeks and she'd be by my side in Michigan forever.

The crow began to caw loudly as it flew over us, Heena Mavshi's bangle glistening in the sun in his beak.

I watched him fly into the distance, like he was saying goodbye. "Maybe we should fill your aai's trunk with some new stories," I said to Aaji. "Stories we make during the rest of our summer?"

"I'd love that." Aaji smiled, hugging me tighter.

"Why don't we practice our songs?" Aai suggested, turning the engine on as we all climbed inside. "We go on in a few minutes." She hummed to find her Sa and began the raag.

I lowered the window, singing over the whoosh of the wind outside, watching our song dance out into the world.

I wasn't hiding anymore. I was proud of my voice. My voice had saved us from Lata Auntie.

It started with a song. And it was going to end with a song. A song I'd be singing loudly, clearly, and fearlessly.

Nothing would stifle my voice ever again.

ACKNOWLEDGMENTS

When I was fourteen, I went to India. My last trip there was three years earlier, and during that time period, thanks to racist bullying in middle school and high school, I ended up feeling really shy and unimportant. When I went to the city of Pune, Ashok Mama, my maternal uncle, played a raag on the keyboard, and tried to get me to sing along. He knew I had taken almost a decade of Hindustani classical singing lessons at that point. I knew I could sing the raag. But I froze. I felt awkward and embarrassed of my own voice, terrified my song wouldn't be good enough, certain it wasn't important enough. So I just stood there in silence, shaking my head, too self-conscious and scared to sing.

Ashok Mama passed away when I was writing *The Cobra's Song*. We shared a love for books, libraries, and music. I miss him a lot, and he's the first person I have to thank because he showed me the importance of your song and making sure the world heard your voice, in whatever shape it takes.

To my brilliant editor, Krista Vitola, thank you for your wisdom, guidance, and insight, for solving this mystery with me, helping me figure out the heart of this story, and for making this book what it is today. It has been such a joy getting to work with you to help Geetanjali's song go out into the world.

To the wonderful team at Simon & Schuster Books for Young Readers, including Chava Wolin, Morgan York, Cassandra Fernandez, Samantha McVeigh, Michelle Leo, Nicole Benevento, Amy Beaudoin, Christina Pecorale, Victor

Iannoe, Emily Hutton, Anne Zafian, Lucy Ruth Cummins, Alyza Liu, Hilary Zarycky, Jen Strada, Kendra Levin, and Justin Chanda, this book would not be possible without all of you! I'm so lucky to get to work with you. And thank you to cover artist Dana SanMar and designer Lucy Ruth Cummins for bringing Geetanjali and the power of her voice to life in the absolutely stunning cover.

To my amazing agent, Kathleen Rushall, I am so grateful for your friendship, your kindness, and your strength. Thank you for always being in my corner and for believing in my stories and in me. You've made so many dreams come true and I can't thank you enough for that.

Thank you to author Ali Standish for reading so many early drafts of this story and helping it get better each time.

To Zuey, Leykh, and Arjun for reading all the drafts of this book and for your helpful feedback. You are fearless advocates and allies, and you inspire me daily with how you use your voices to make our world better.

To Brynn for being my first reader. To Katelyn and Elle for all the help so I could write this book. To Sachit, Andrea, Dave, and Jim Burnstein. To Deepa for answering my Pune bird questions. And thank you to my parents, for the help with the Marathi and cultural details. Any mistakes are mine alone.

Thank you to the kidlit community, my brilliant author and illustrator friends for their support during the writing of this book, including Raakhee Mirchandani, Karina Yan Glaser, Jarrett Lerner, Kristin L. Gray, Ali Standish, Simran Jeet Singh, and James Ponti, to name just a few. What an uplifting, inclusive community the kidlit community is. It's one I'll always be honored to be a part of.

To the wonderful principals (Hi, Devon Caudill!), educators, librarians, and booksellers. Thank you for helping readers find my books, connect with my stories, feel seen, and for all that you do every single day. I'm in awe of you and proud to call so many of you my friends.

The Cobra's Song was written over the course of several years that were incredibly tough for people around the world. I'm grateful to the amazing teachers in my children's lives who helped make such a difficult time better. Thank you, Sharon Trumpy, Pushpa Lohithaswa, Rose McDougall, Cori Charboneau, Markus Hartnett, and Blake Vertrees. You are heroes. You're changing the world through your work, and my family and I are so lucky that our paths crossed.

When I was growing up, I only got to see my three living grandparents once every couple years when we would go to India, or they'd come here. Doing namaskar to them when we would leave India with a lump in my throat, blinking back tears, not knowing if it was the last time I'd ever see them, was one of the hardest things I had to do as a kid. And eventually those farewell namaskars really were my last in-person goodbye to them. Although it has been decades since they passed away, a piece of each of them lives on in me and in this story, and I'm grateful for everything they taught me in our short time together.

To Limca, who sat by my side for years as I wrote this book and others. Thanks for always being there when things got tough. You were the very best and I will miss you forever.

To the rest of my family and to all my friends, I know I would not be where I am today without your love and support. Thanks for cheering on all the various forms of my "song."

A special thanks to Aai for all the stories, especially the snake ones. And to Dad, for filling our world with music on Geetanjali and beyond. You are both instrumental in my love for sharing my story, for sharing *our* story.

Finally, to you, dear reader. Thank you for reading my books. I hope *The Cobra's Song* inspires you to share your song with the world. I can't wait to hear it.

ABOUT THE AUTHOR

Born and raised in the Midwest, Supriya Kelkar learned Hindi as a child by watching three Hindi movies a week. She is a screenwriter who has worked on the writing teams for several Hindi films and one Hollywood feature. Supriya's books include *Strong as Fire, Fierce as Flame; Brown Is Beautiful; American as Paneer Pie;* and *That Thing about Bollywood,* among others. Visit her online at SupriyaKelkar.com.